My Cradle, Your Grave

The Haunted Past Series Book 1

By Sharon Jackson

Can they work out the riddle,
And discover the rhyme.
Follow the clues,
To solve it in time.

Prologue	8
Chapter One	13
Chapter Two	23
Chapter Three	33
Chapter Four	43
Chapter Five	56
Chapter Six	66
Chapter Seven	68
Chapter Eight	75
Chapter Nine	85
Chapter Ten	94
Chapter Eleven	106
Chapter Twelve	121
Chapter Thirteen	123
Chapter Fourteen	132
Chapter Fifteen	140
Chapter Sixteen	149
Chapter Seventeen	151
Chapter Eighteen	161
Chapter Nineteen	170
Chapter Twenty	180
Chapter Twenty-One	183
Chapter Twenty-Two	192
Chapter Twenty-Three	201
Chapter Twenty-Four	204
Chapter Twenty-Five	213
Chapter Twenty-Six	222
Chapter Twenty-Seven	224
Chapter Twenty-Eight	233
Chapter Twenty-Nine	240
Chapter Thirty	243
Chapter Thirty-One	252
Chapter Thirty-Two	254
Chapter Thirty-Three	266
Chapter Thirty-Four	275

Copyright©copyrighthouse2023 the moral rights of the author have been asserted. Written by: Sharon Jackson

All rights reserved. By payment of the required fees, you have been granted the non-exclusive, non-transferable right to access and read the text of this book. No part of this text may be reproduced, transmitted, downloaded, decompiled, reverse engineered, or stored in or introduced into any information storage and retrieval system in any form, by any means, whether electronic and mechanical, now known or herein invented without the express written permission of Sharon Jackson

Acknowledgements

I would like to thank my family "the Jackson clan" for always being there for me. We are a wolf pack in human form. I also would like to thank my colleagues for their encouragement and help with my Schrodinger's cat problem.

I would also like to thank my avid and motivational reader of each draft, Jean. I may not have got to the end, without your constant interest in the next chapter (I'm laughing as I type this.) Also Tammy and my sister for their encouragement. Of course, Open Eye Editing for their work on the editing and for humouring me when I get over excited about ideas. Also a shout out to my Arc readers for being awesome.

And lastly, a shout out to Moreno's café for allowing me use of their business name as the café my characters use. Also Creative Paramita for the fabulous book cover.

                    Thank you all.

*Dedicated to Philip Raymond and
Doreen Bernadette Edwards
A lifetime together, a short while apart
Together once more and never to part.*

Disclaimer

This is a work of fiction. Names of characters, places, and incidents either are a product of the author's imagination or are used fictitiously. Any resemblance to actual persons dead or alive, events or locales is entirely coincidental.

Content warning

This is a crime thriller story about a detective dealing with the past that includes violence and abuse. As such, the content contains triggering content, including graphic or explicit violence/deaths on a page, Sexual violence or threats of sexual violence, abuse, graphic medical descriptions, or bodily fluids (especially blood or internal body parts described on the page) harm and abuse to children, reference to abortion due to ectopic pregnancy, removal of body parts, drug abuse, stalking, flashbacks to sexual violence, domestic violence, kidnapping, torture, and other criminal activities.
If any part of this list disturbs you in any way, then it is probably best to read no further. Otherwise, enjoy the book!

Prologue

February 9th, 1990

It was dark, so very dark and that set his nerves on edge, clouds had gathered over what little light had been cast by the partial blood moon. He shivered as he recalled the sight, it was almost a foreboding prophecy of the night to come.

He nearly hadn't come, and wouldn't have if he had known it wouldn't be enough to spare him, they wouldn't be satisfied with his family's death, only his own. By the acknowledgment of that truth alone, maybe he could at least save his son from the fate of his family. Maybe he at least would get to live. They'd told him, by giving them what was owed, they both could walk free. He had many flaws but even he had limits to his own stupidity. He hadn't considered they might go so far, as taking his wife and children.

By the time he'd returned from trying to gather the funds, he had missed the first warning and knew his wife had already collected the debt and paid with her life. His daughter by all accounts was gone now too, by death or worse he couldn't even contemplate. However, his son lived still, or so he was led to believe. It was much more possible, in reality, that this was yet another punishment and he was walking, not blindly yet acceptingly, to his own end. He had all but concluded his son was also lost to him, but when all was said and done, he couldn't take the chance and not try. His end would follow regardless of this, he was certain, so running would only delay and most assuredly only further provoke them. Better instead to meet it, his son's fate may still be altered from this evil path even if his own could not.

Walking along the street, he crossed paths with a drunk who knocked into him as he stumbled to and fro. "Watch where ya goin' thessa nuff room for both of us ya know" the drunk slurred.

"Apologies," he muttered. He didn't have time to deal with a drunk. He had somewhere to be.

He finally reached his destination and wondered again at such a strange choice. It was true, it would be very much deserted even if the hour hadn't been so late, but he was still confused by it, there were much more obscure places that could've been better served for this exchange than the present location.

As he made his approach his skin crawled in anticipation. Sweat began to bead on his brow and he held his breath. Rain began to fall and made the already cold night bitter, the droplets landing on his skin like ice, sharp needles stabbing at his skin. His body shook uncontrollably, whether in expectation or from the ever-growing frequency of the rain as it now poured from the sky relentlessly, he couldn't decide. He couldn't see the figure in the shadows watching him, studying him with a detached delight. Nor did he witness the gleam of calculating insanity, glinting in his eyes.

Lightning split the sky, the small flash of light startling him as it lit the pitch-dark night. Using it he studied the entrance, both surprised and a little wary to find it open on his arrival. He nervously looked around for any sign he had company and frowned when he found none.

"H...Hello? Is anybody here?" He called out, but received no answer.

He walked cautiously into the large storage facility, the rain now drumming on the roof he couldn't see, as he marvelled at how huge the area was. There were miles of it. He spent some of his precious time studying his surroundings; wandering aimlessly trying to see where the lights could be turned on with no joy. That was when he saw him, lit by another flash of lightning from outside. The small silhouette of what he assumed to be his child, resting hunched over on the platform of a carousel. It must be stored here for the winter, it was large, and he was surprised to find it fully assembled. He could only conclude that perhaps it had needed a maintenance check in preparation for the fayres that would likely commence for the Easter celebrations.

"Hello. I've brought the money... Anyone?" He called again.

When there was still no reply, he stumbled half blind to the roundabout. In other circumstances, it would be a universal picture of joy and fun, but not on this night. No, tonight it became a sinister setting. The painted horses' eyes were wide and ghoulish, they almost seemed to follow him, their menacing mechanical mouths with toothy smirks mocked him with a frightening promise as he carefully made his way onto the platform.

Suddenly thunder boomed and rattled outside in the night, followed by a kaleidoscope of light so blinding, that he staggered back, stumbling onto the now moving platform. He lost his balance, falling to his back as a new darkness towered over him. Despite his foreseeing of this very occurrence, he tried to shuffle away but the shadow loomed closer. Something sharp pierced his chest and wrenched down, in a tearing of flesh and sinew, and he gasped as hands quickly dug in the newly forged chasm in his chest. Lightning struck again outside but he didn't see it, as a scream pulled from his mouth and the last sound he heard was not the crack from the force of the storm raging outside, but the crack from his ribs as they were forced apart to the cheery tune of the merry-go-round melody.

"I do love that sound," the crazed man said to himself.

The assailant smiled down as the consciousness left his target. A man had to make a living, after all. Although he supposed it didn't have to be so much fun as he dug inside his mark's chest and found what he sought before ripping it free. Grinning in satisfaction, he looked down at it—still warm from its resting place—he took the heart and placed it to one side, then stood, shouldering off his tool bag and drawing from it a meat cleaver.

"Ah, yes, this will do," the assailant uttered to himself with a grin of delight, and approached the now lifeless body's head. He moved it to a more convenient angle and set about his task. As he hacked and slashed in a frenzy, he finally managed to detach it. Lifting it, he tilted his head to admire his work. His boss would be pleased. He retrieved the storage container, placing the trophies inside. Then as he turned, he stopped for a moment and a slow grin spread across his face, as he contemplated a new notion.

Picking up the bag with the money his victim owed and placing it with the container, he then proceeded to drag what remained of the body to the middle of the carousel and propped it into a sitting position. A whimpering sound came from his left and his eyes fell upon the boy. The drugs he'd been dosed with must be losing effect, he wouldn't remember anything, they'd seen to that, and he had been instructed to leave him alive.

"You're quite a wee lad, 'tis a shame you had to have such a shite for a Da," he said to him conversationally, though he knew he couldn't hear him, nor would he answer.

The small boy's head lolled slightly, the face covering he wore probably not all that comfortable. He strode over to the restrained bundle lifting him and carrying him easily, he deposited him into his now dead fathers arms, wrapping them around him and ensuring they would stay fast. His own face was concealed so he shrugged to himself, deciding to remove the sack from over the boy's small head, but leaving the duct tape still firmly in place over his mouth. He paused to reflect on the picture of death he had created. Satisfied with his macabre masterpiece, he collected his spoils and headed on his way, leaving the boy in the embrace of the headless, heartless corpse.

Chapter One

June 19th, 2014: London
24 years later

  DI Devlin Doyle sat in the local bar that was frequently used by the officers of his police station, brooding over his drink and replaying the findings of the internal investigation. He still didn't know how he felt about it, he was just numb. His team and himself had painstakingly gathered the intel. Months and months of work putting the case together and all it had taken was the corrupt information of one C.I. to have the whole thing come crashing down around them, leaving them picking over the ashes of the mess and mourning the loss of several officers and an innocent girl, in the process. He'd been so sure, some declared arrogant, that he had forged ahead never anticipating that his haste would cost them all so much. He swirled his drink unconsciously, the bitter aftertaste from the previous mouthful lacing his tongue and sitting heavily in his gut, doing nothing to assuage the feelings he had resting uncomfortably there.
  As the time ticked by slowly, he nursed the drink mindlessly, sifting through the months trying to see how they hadn't seen it coming.

  The team were all in position and waiting for a go signal. Dev was watching from his spot paired with DC Tracey as the net closed in. Watching with close attention, he waited for the exchange of the ransom. He waited with bated breath as a young girl was dragged by her hair from the back of a van. As she was put down in front of the lead suspect he pointed his gun to her temple. A bag was thrown at his feet, and it was almost time.

"Did you want another?" The bar man asked him, interrupting his thoughts. Dev declined, shaking his head taking another long pull from the drink he was nursing.

He'd caught a brief glimpse of somebody in his periphery, but it all happened so fast. Suddenly there were shots being fired. The loud sounds of a firefight roared around him and before he could do anything to stop it, he watched as the gun pointing at the girl went off and as if in slow motion her small frame crumpled limply to the ground. Officers sprung from various positions, Dev calling urgently for them to take action. He ran into the fray and as he began to take control of the situation, he felt himself being shoved to the side, as DC Tracey stiffened above him and made a jerky descent to the concrete, blood spraying from a gash in her throat. All other thoughts forgotten he clamped his hands over it attempting to stem the bleeding, but blood gushed through his fingers, and he caught spurts of it with his face. He ripped off the sleeve of his shirt and desperately wrapped it to the wound, holding it there firmly before another sound caught his attention, a shout of alarm ahead of them had him raising his head and his eyes widened in shock as he saw another member of the team run for them, instinct making him less conscious of the looming danger, until it was too late.

A loud smash sounded in the bar as a waitress dropped a tray of glasses and Dev startled as the patrons hooted and cajoled her as she rushed to clear away the broken shards.

Another shot rang out and a cascade of blood and debris exploded like pink mist, through the front of his fellow officer's forehead, onto the floor and his body dropped like a dead weight. Dev used one hand to hold the neck wound he was attending to, then reached out quickly for his two-way radio, shouting into it in desperation. Amongst the carnage of fallen officers he couldn't see who was still in play, but the sound of gunfire slowly receded. He knelt frozen, holding pressure on Tracy's neck and praying it had finally stopped. Voices called around him, but they didn't register any more than a dull humming… muffled and incoherent. He felt somebody take his shoulders roughly and shake it, as he returned from his semi-aware trance and his gaze became focused once more.

"Are you okay, Sir?" A waitress asked him, looking at him like she wasn't sure. Dev nodded absent-mindedly. "If you're sure Sir," she said unconvinced but continued with her work.

"Sir? Sir, are you hit?" DS Morgan asked briskly trying to keep his voice steady.
"I…I don't know…" Dev said disjointedly.
"Just hold on. Help is coming" he urged, standing to wave through the ambulance. An explosion of movement around him made him dizzy and he could hear a voice telling him to let go now. 'Let go of what,' he thought, confused. He felt firm fingers tugging on his grip around the shirt sleeve as he clumsily shuffled to the side and stood on shaky legs. He was usually so

composed he didn't know why he was so disorientated. His gaze settled on a familiar face. Not from his team, but the face of the C.I. that had given them their intel. Understanding dawned on him as he replayed the events now that he could concentrate. It was a set up. As one of the suspects was led away he struggled and stumbled in front of Dev. Officers rushed to apprehend him but before they could, he spoke angrily.

"We have your number, Doyle...They're coming for you. They won't let this slide, you hear, they're coming." As he was pulled away and put into a vehicle, Dev swayed on his feet and a paramedic addressed him with concern.

"Sir? Is any of that blood yours?"

Dev patted himself down before pain shot through him. The world tilted on an axis, and he had passed out before he hit the ground.

In hindsight, it seemed almost obvious, he sighed heavily and registered the approach of DS Alec Morgan but chose not to acknowledge him in the hope he would get the hint. He didn't.

"So, this is where you've been hiding," he began gently.

Dev raised his glass in a mock salute but remained otherwise in position. His tie loosened haphazardly around his neck, his clothes rumpled from wear of the exceptionally long day as it dragged almost painfully to its close. His dark, slightly too long hair hung in disarray around his face, almost concealing the dark frown he wore there. He sat silently waiting for him to say whatever he had come to say so he could continue his pity party in peace.

"We waited for you. After you left, we waited for you to come and talk about how it went…but as time went by, I told them to get on home." He continued before pausing and waiting for his answer. When it didn't come he pushed further, "Are you going to talk to me?"

"What would you have me say?" Dev replied wearily. "It went about how you'd expect when the decisions I made cost people their lives."

"The decisions *we made,* Dev. This was a team effort, we all had a part to play in this. Even those who aren't here to speak for themselves. They knew what they signed up for, they were as much a part of this as any of us. They wouldn't want you taking all the blame on your shoulders for this going south, don't disrespect their memory that way." He scolded quietly.

"But the buck stops with me. That's what I told them then and it's what I stand by now." Dev stated dismissively.

"So, what now?" Alec asked.

"The verdict is in, the future is bleak, and the consequences are being decided. I will return tomorrow to find out what those will be," he trailed off taking another swig from the lukewarm liquid in his glass. It burned on its way down but offered no solace. Alec's shoulders slumped in resignation, and he summoned the barman over with his hand.

The barman approached and Alec ordered a drink. Once a glass was placed in front of him, he raised it and said with a forced smile, "It matters not if the glass is half empty or half full, all that matters is there is room for more."

Dev's lip curled up into a barely there smile at his friend and tipped his drink in acquiescence before draining the remains of the foul-tasting liquor from his glass and standing.

"Where are you going, we just got started?" Alec asked.

"No, my friend, you just got started. I have a meeting to attend in the morning." Dev called behind him on his way out of the door. As he took his leave into the cold night the chilly evening breeze swirled around him, and he pulled his phone from his work jacket and called for a taxi. He'd left his car in the station lot, but he could pick it up tomorrow. He waited patiently for his ride home, letting the cool night air breathe some sobriety back into him. When the car pulled up he nodded to the driver, opened the car door, and headed home to sleep off the day.

Dev woke up the next morning with a start and a hangover, his head pounded, and his mouth felt drier than a camel's foreskin. He smacked his lips together several times and shook his head with disgust. He sat up cautiously and wiped at his tired eyes, before swinging heavy legs to the side of his bed and looking to his bedside table for the time. Glaring at the painful neon on the face of his electric alarm clock he saw it was 6.30am. Groaning loudly he dragged his ass from the warmth and headed into the ensuite bathroom in the adjacent room.

There he relieved himself before turning to look at himself in the mirror above the sink's basin. At 6ft 2 Dev was not a small man, with a lean yet muscular frame, he took up most of the small space in the bathroom. He studied his reflection and found his skin was slightly clammy, giving him an almost sickly pallor. His deep green eyes looked bloodshot and squinted as the light invaded them, making him wince.

His hair hung limply in a sweaty mess and clung to his skin almost suffocatingly, he looked every one of his thirty-two years, if not older. Grimacing, he turned away to turn on the shower and let it run to heat up while he brushed away the foul taste lingering in his mouth. Once this was done he stepped into the spray, leaning one hand on the wall to steady himself and let the water wash away the night's sins.

When Dev finally walked into the station, he looked almost presentable; he no longer had the fogginess clouding his head, the only sign he had been in any way ruffled by the previous day, was the remaining scruff of stubble adorning his face, which only added to his edgy appearance in a roguishly handsome way. Being of Irish descent, he could pull this look off without anyone passing comment. Whilst he looked completely in control and confident, he was on edge about the meeting he was due to attend with Superintendent Andrew Panderman a.k.a. Andy Pandy when he wasn't within hearing range. Dev often wondered why he hadn't chosen to change his name by deed poll, there wasn't a snowball's chance in hell he had made it through school and not heard that before. He either chose to ignore it or never bothered to check the reference, Dev wasn't sure if he admired that about him or found it concerning.

He walked through the building heading first to make himself a coffee that was strong enough to wake the dead. He took a sip and felt it had just the right measure of "Fuck me, I'm awake already!"

He took one more slug before entering into the room his team resided in. The mood was dour, you could feel the grim spectre of apprehension and sadness hovering in the air, and it took a moment for them to notice his entrance. Slowly there were nudges of elbows and nods in his direction and the team straightened and met his hawk-like scan of the room.

"Morning Sir," floated from their mouths and with a chastising tone he addressed them.

"Well? Are you gonna laze around all day or do you have work you could be doing?" he prompted. The small team moved in a fluster of arms and legs and the moment was lost in a flurry of activity. All but Alec, who raised a questioning eyebrow. Dev shot him a look and headed to his office, leaving the door ajar for his friend, who he suspected would follow behind in his usual, unrepentantly nosey way. He wasn't wrong.

"Now there's the grump we all know and love" he cajoled from the doorway. Letting himself in and sitting in a chair without invitation he leaned back casually and asked. "So what time is the meeting?"

Dev looked at the clock on the wall and answered curtly, "About 20 minutes, I was just hoping for a moment of quiet with a caffeine hit before I face the firing squad."

"They can't actually fire you, you followed the procedures, you did all the work, you made decisions based off of the intel you were given, surely they can't be too hard on you?" Alec reasoned.

"That may all be true, but somebody has to be held accountable and the forecast is saying that someone is me." Dev countered dryly.

Alec nodded slowly and rose from the chair, walking steadily towards him, and offering him a commiseratory shoulder pat, before murmuring, "May the force be with you," and leaving the office.

Thirty minutes later, Dev was summoned to the Superintendent's office. He strode stiffly into the room, shoulders back and braced for what he knew was coming.

"Take a seat Doyle." The Super said, indicating a chair across from his desk. He waited as Devlin sat and then began. "The board has discussed this case at length and while they believe you have acted with the utmost dedication within your role here, mistakes have been made. I have no wish to drag this on any longer with preamble or blow smoke up your ass to make you feel better. Your record is immaculate, and you are held in high regard by your peers. However, the concern is more for your safety; threats have been made and while they could be lenient for the errors, your personal safety is of paramount importance. With that in mind we will be transferring you from this area for a temporary reassignment." Dev opened his mouth to speak but the Super gave him a laser stare and continued, "You will be supervised initially in your role in the MCU unit of this new area until you have found your feet. There will be no alternative option to this, but keep your head on straight, knuckle down and after this period is over you can either choose to stay with their team or return to your position here. We will be asking DS Morgan to oversee your current cases in your absence since he is already familiar with the progress. The decision is non-negotiable, Devlin" he finished quietly.

"OK" Dev managed to grind out, hanging his head slightly in defeat, "I hear you, but this is wrong, you know that, right?"

"I know, believe me, I fought this hard, unfortunately the powers that be have tied my hands and the decision is final. Final but temporary; keep your head down, work hard and wait it out, then come back to us, son." The Super said with sincerity.

Dev let the news sink in and eventually nodded his acceptance. He allowed a few moments of silence to hang in the air before he swept his gaze to meet the Super's grey eyes with his sharp, green ones. Taking a breath, he asked. "So, where am I going?"

Chapter Two

June 26th, 2014,
Welwyn Garden City, Police headquarters

  DI Serenity "Wren" Jones, left the meeting in a rage. She had just been assigned "babysitting" duty of a DI from London's metropolitan police force and was to take a "supervisory" role for the immediate future. The very last thing she had time for was to run around chasing some arrogant prick from London with a superiority complex, who thought he was all that and a bag of chips with the misconception that the rules didn't apply to him. She was so irate she wanted to punch something. I know, get the "little woman" to take care of him, although at 5ft 9 she was hardly considered little. This was bullshit. She barrelled out of the building and kept a punishing pace to get to her vehicle. She'd been told she was free to return home so she could be fresh to meet her new "ward" tomorrow. Irritation boiled inside her and she wanted to scream with sheer frustration. She got inside her car, closed the door and swore profusely, slamming her closed fists down on the steering wheel, displaying a temper tantrum a five-year-old would be proud of and language her mother most certainly wouldn't be. Taking a long, deep breath, her anger eased slightly, and she sat for a few moments gathering her equilibrium.

  Her given name, Serenity, unfortunately did not match her fierce personality. Despite her very logical and analytical mind, others told her she had what some may perceive as an argumentative nature. Only in moments where the situation would be considered highly volatile did she live up to her name. In those situations, it was as though she were watching events unfold through the eyes of a third party and she went into autopilot, becoming the voice of reason, while exuding a peaceful and soothing calmness that seemed somewhat contrary to her usual character. Personally, Wren didn't think they knew what they were talking about, she thought she was a fucking delight.

She slowly regained control of herself as she noticed Matt approaching her car and wound down the window, so they could talk.

"You going somewhere? It's the middle of the day?" He asked in confusion.

"The Don has sent me home, we have a new detective joining us tomorrow and she wants me to show him the ropes," she answered through gritted teeth.

"What about your food?" He asked.

"Sorry, I'm not really hungry anymore. You have it," she offered.

"Won't say no to an offer like that," he said grinning, "See you tomorrow then, Wren."

Waiting for him to move away, before starting the engine, Wren found herself grateful for the usually grating drive through the city, as it provided her much needed time to go over all that had been discussed in a more detached and composed manner. By the time she pulled up at her home, she found herself still quietly fuming but in a much more manageable and contained way. With a sigh, Wren pushed herself from the car and fumbled through her handbag for her house-keys, finally finding them as she reached the front door. Entering her quiet home, she walked on autopilot down the hall, towards the small kitchen and dining room, before discarding her bag onto the large dining table. Heading to the kitchen, she switched on the kettle for a much needed cup of tea. She tried to only drink coffee first thing to get herself going and switched to tea after throughout the day. Sleep eluded her at the best of times, add in the crazy hours and it was almost a myth some days, therefore she tried to help it along by tapering down on the caffeine where she could, and tea was the slightly better option but not by much. As she cradled the mug in her hands, allowing it to cool a little, she studied her home with a critical gaze.

Wren had been here a while now, coming up on two years and there was still much to do, but with such long and unpredictable hours, she found she had procrastinated somewhat. Home improvements had never really been her area of expertise in the previous chapter of her life, the one that had led her here, that unfortunate role had fallen to her ex-husband. They'd met while she was still in college. At first she'd thought he was going to be like the boys from school; just another who wanted to tease and torment the tall, gangly girl with albinism. Wren had spent more time scrapping in the schoolyard than playing thanks to snarky girls and insulting boys. So when he'd first approached her she'd been immediately dismissive, even though she'd finally filled out her tall frame. However as he continued to pursue her, she'd softened towards him and hesitantly agreed to a date.

Over time they'd become quite the pair and after several years together he'd proposed. They'd been happy at first but after they were married it began to take a turn for the worse. She'd attended university, while he'd built up a construction business. But towards the end of her final year, her close friend had been brutally raped and disfigured, the attack had such an impact on Wren that it set her path on a new course and she had decided to join the police. This course created a gaping chasm the size of the Grand Canyon between her and her then husband.

Over time the hostility and resentment between them became so great and the arguments so volatile and frequent, that it was a surprise she hadn't become a victim in the case files dispatched to the MCU, instead of a detective working in it. It wasn't until she'd been sent to a domestic violence call, that she began to accept that her marriage was reaching its end.

It had fallen to Wren, on account of her being female, to talk to the woman at the hospital, when she'd finally regained consciousness and the doctors allowed the police to get her account of the incident. Listening to her making excuses, explaining all the small nuances that had developed over the course of her relationship, she'd seen the similarities. Studying and documenting her injuries, she'd noted in her head the occasions she had started to sport some herself.

Although it hadn't nearly come to this level of abuse, she had been glazing over it. Hearing the battered woman describe how it had slowly descended into this hell she was now living, Wren had found her words echoing excuses she had used herself, when thinking about her own troubled home life.

However, its conclusion came a little over six months later, when the next call came, and their paths crossed for a second time. This time there would be no other time, by the time she had reached the hospital in the ambulance she had drawn her final breath. Wren had resolved right then and there to leave her own husband and her life veered in a new direction. The Major Crimes Unit became her new horizon and she'd forged determinedly toward it and finally transferred in two years prior.

Alone again and divorced by age thirty, she was disillusioned and far more cynical than she had once been. She'd started fresh, carving out a new reputation for herself. Gone was the Serenity of old; the naive, hopeful newbie wanting to change the world and help people, have a happy married life and a devoted husband, maybe a few children. In her place was Wren, the avenging angel who kicked asses and took names. Whether you loved or hated her it didn't matter, because either way, you damn well respected her. Wandering into the living room she sat down in a large plush armchair and drank some of the tea she'd been clutching while she thought back to her meeting with the Super.

Superintendent Jan Wright was one tough bitch, who could make grown men flinch with one penetrating, icy glare or with sharp, cutting words from her equally sharp tongue. Her quick mind and shrewd assessment of people made it feel as though she could see right through to your soul and made her talented when it came to delegation. She knew the strengths and weaknesses of her entire workforce and had a gift for figuring out how to fit their strengths to tasks for maximum efficiency. Around the unit she was affectionately dubbed "The Don" in reference to the fact that she treated you like family but if you decided to play hardball with her she would "make you an offer you couldn't refuse." You crossed her to your own detriment, and you chose to underestimate her at your own peril.

She was a force of nature with a nature of force, yet in contrast had a sense of humour that made her popular amongst staff, a sunny disposition and a surprising warmth that seemed out of place with her other characteristics. Which is how, Wren mused, she had somehow been roped into this supervisory gig. She was the proverbial "iron fist in a velvet glove." A paradox if ever she met one.

"Could I see you in my office for a moment, Wren?" the Super asked as she breezed through the unit.
"Yeah, I'm just finishing up this report and I'll head in-" Wren began to reply, her focus on the screen in front of her, frowning at the tedious task.
"I apologise, DI Jones. I made it sound like there was a choice, but it was actually a directive. It won't take long, finish it up in the morning." She laughed before whisking passed in the direction of her office.
"Yes Ma'am," Wren muttered wryly. Saving her progress, she swiftly followed the path the Super had swept through before arriving at her door. She knocked hesitantly, unsure if she should just enter or wait for an invitation.
"Come in Wren! Let us not wait for the grass to grow." She called from the desk and continued as Wren entered, "It really is just a quick chat, I have a special assignment in need of supervision, and you are just the person for the task." She smiled warmly.
"Me Ma'am?" Wren asked in surprise, her curiosity piqued.
"I don't know if you remember the incident in London, a month back..." She trailed off giving Wren time to filter through and come up empty, before elaborating, "sting gone south, some tough losses amongst the team." Wren's expression turned sombre as she caught on to the thread. The Super continued again, "I see you

do. Following this unfortunate outcome I have been asked to delegate an officer of my choosing to oversee the arrival of a DI who will be joining us here for a time. Just while the dust settles. Of course, when I deliberated on who I felt would be best to give this responsibility to, I found myself thinking of you." She let the words hang there and waited.

"Woah hold on one minute Ma'am, no disrespect-" Wren began, her pale face filled with heat, her unusual eyes flashing sparks as a fiery protest lit them.

"Are you saying I've misjudged your capabilities, Wren?" She cut in, a brow raised in challenge, shooting her a stern, expectant look.

"No Ma'am... I mean... Well..." Wren spluttered and then closed her mouth deciding it was better to hold her tongue.

"I see we are in agreement then," she declared, clapping her hands together and grinning victoriously, as she continued, *"It's settled, pack up for the day, your new assignment will begin tomorrow. Go home and come back here fresh in the morning."* She concluded by waving Wren off.

"Ma'am?" Wren said, as the Super began rustling papers on her desk, she stopped and lifted her gaze impatiently nodding as though to hurry her along.

"Erm.. well.. You didn't say who I will be supervising? Wren questioned hesitantly.

"Oh" she chuckled, *"I didn't, did I? You will be meeting with DI Devlin Doyle. He should be arriving here at 9.00am. I will obviously be having an introductory meeting with him then, when I have finished, I'll bring him to you and you can make the necessary introductions. Now move along, I have things to do,"* she shooed.

"Ma'am" Wren replied sullenly before marching to the door.

Wren was pulled from her thoughts by the shrill sound of her phone ringing. She glanced down and Jen's name flashed on it with the phone icon waiting for a decision. Sliding her finger along it to the green phone icon she answered.
"Hey Jen." Wren answered, smiling a little.
"Don't you hey me! Where'd you slip off to?" Jen scolded. "You pulling half shifts now? One minute you were at the monitor, and I was dutifully slaving away in the canteen making the best brew of your life…" Jen embellished dramatically, "next, I arrived with said nectar of the gods, to find you had been abducted. So after hours of sending out alerts and scouring for your scared ass only to be told you are not, in fact, not in fear for your very life but you've done a bunk and buggered off home for an afternoon delight, I decided it warranted a phone call." She closed her tirade and Wren rolled her eyes.
"You done?" Wren asked in exasperation.
"Am I done?.. AM I DONE?! Oh, you little wench! I swear-" Jen began but Wren cut her short before she could begin a new more colourful tirade.
"I was summoned by The Don. We had a chat and she told me to go straight to jail, to not pass go and not collect £300."
"£300? You, Missy, are in the wrong line of work, you monopoly thief. It's £200… it's like I don't even know you anymore. You lie, you steal, you cheat, and you take half days. I think this relationship is over… You don't love me anymore." Jen teased.

Wren chuckled at her friend, while she was the prickly pear, DC Jen Cartright was everyone's friend. Wren couldn't think of a single person who didn't like her; easy going, a bit of a piss-take with some clown-like amateur dramatics, she was impossible not to like. If Wren was the straight man Jen was the funny man. Quick to laugh and personable, when they'd met she'd been the first to dub her "Wren" and made it a point to note that they rhymed and therefore she was stuck with her, apparently it was "se-Wren-dipity."

"So?" Jen asked emphatically. Wren had been so lost in thought she had completely forgotten the conversation.

"So, what?" she threw back confused.

"What did The Don want?" She bit out in an aggrieved tone.

"She wanted to invite me to the babysitter's club." Wren snarked, some of her anger returning. Before Jen could get more annoyed with her evasive answers, she hurriedly explained.

"Ok I'm hearing the anger but I'm struggling to see the source. Chance to look good to the boss…check. New gossip fodder…check. Hot new guy that has to be your bitch…Ding! Ding! Ding!... we have a winner!" Wren pictured her friend pulling up fingers as she noted the positives. Such a "Jen" thing to do, then doubled back on the last point.

"Wait a minute…Who said anything about him being hot?" Wren sneered.

Jen scoffed loudly down the line. "Obviously you know the scoop on the take down gone awry, but didn't you see his picture online?"

"No Jen, that's your area of expertise. I can barely type with two fingers. I hate being online." Wren reminded her.

"Well Girl.. You missed out, he is H.O.T.T. hot! What girl doesn't have a little thing for a tall drink of water with an Irish lilt and glorious green eyes. A little rough around the edges, some scruff, and an air of danger," Jen sighed.

"Have you been reading those romance novels again? They'll rot your brain, you know." Wren needled light-heartedly.

"Sweetness, I have a few to spare," Jen retorted, and she wasn't wrong. Jen was our resident information expert, what she couldn't dig up on a computer wasn't worth finding.

"Jen it's always awesome to talk to you but I'm going to have to go. I have a newbie to beat into shape in the morning." Wren excused and listened as Jen said her goodbyes. Wren got up from her chair, her tea long cold, and walked slowly to the kitchen sink, tipping it away resignedly. *Tomorrow was going to be a long day,* she thought and headed upstairs.

Chapter Three

June 26th, 2014

Dev felt like he hadn't slept in a month. After the Super had spoken to him and given him the news, he'd had to pack up his life and organise it to accommodate his swift departure from London. Luckily, with the career he'd chosen and the solitary life he'd led thus far his apartment had been sparse to say the least.

He had no family photos to speak of, no memory of his life at all before the age of eight. His first memory was of waking up in an intensive care unit, in pain and sleepy. At eight he had no real understanding of what had happened to him, but on reaching eighteen he had read through his case notes and found there was not much clue as to where he had appeared from. He had been hit by a car in a hit and run incident and was lucky to be alive. His injuries had been severe, there were also documented notes of older injuries which they'd estimated occurred at approximately one month prior to the hit and run itself. Nobody had reported him missing. Nobody knew who he had been for the first eight years of his existence and then he was somebody new.

He'd been entered into a temporary foster home upon his release from hospital and the couple hadn't wanted to call him John Doe. Due to his frequent nightmares in the night, the lady had dubbed him Devlin. When he'd asked why, she had replied sadly, *"At night the devil is inside you,"* but she hadn't explained beyond that. Reports from that time described him as quiet, watchful, and anti-social with violent night terrors. He'd never figured out what had tormented him when he was young and part of him was glad that whatever horror had haunted him had remained forgotten and had never been remembered. At first, the police had made regular check-ins in case his memory came back, as sometimes happens when the body has recovered. Unfortunately his amnesia had never faded. As an adult he was just grateful he had lost it so young, who really remembered their early life anyway, it would've been far worse if it had happened later in life when he might've lost many more years from his mind. He imagined that would be much more frustrating.

So, he had been given the name Devlin officially. His last name had been more random, he'd had a slight Irish lilt when he had spoken, and they'd decided to place him with Irish foster parents that they'd had in the system. Their last name had been Doyle and when he'd be sent there he had been given their surname in hope it would better help him settle there. He'd lived there for a time quite contentedly but had never really connected with them, though they'd tried many times he'd been instinctively suspicious and wary of adults, like his mind knew he had just cause not to trust them but couldn't quite tell him why. They had been an older couple and had both long since passed. While he didn't mourn them like parents, he was saddened by the news.

There were several other foster children there over the time he had lived with the Doyles and whilst he hadn't really considered them family he had considered one or two friends. Before moving to London he'd stayed in touch, however with distance and lack of free time due to his work, the contact had dwindled over the years, and they rarely spoke now. He had never really belonged anywhere and while sometimes he had longed to, for the most part he was content with his own company. He couldn't really miss something he'd never really had. He had chosen to serve in the police force as a result of his childhood, with his mysterious beginning he found he had a fondness for puzzles and a fascination for finding answers, where he had none of his own. He had an aptitude and relentlessness that had served him well in his career, up until the incident that had landed himself in his current position, he supposed.

With his meagre possessions packed and the arrangements all made, Dev had set off for his new assigned position at Welwyn Garden City. He was driving down the A1(M) and was approaching Hatfield Tunnel, otherwise known as "the sabre." when a small nagging voice piped up in the back of his head, although he couldn't recall ever being in this neck of the woods, while under his breath he whispered to himself, "You have to hold your breath while you're in there, if you breathe before the end, you'll die."

Shaking his head ruefully at the nonsensical thought, he entered it and found himself ridiculously holding his breath. Exiting the tunnel, air whooshed from his mouth and he shook his head at himself. What was he, five? He had no idea where that thought had even come from. Focusing back on the road he continued his journey, he had a lot to do today, before checking in for his new assignment bright and early in the morning.

****

Dev had taken a break, sitting on a chair that was placed haphazardly in the centre of his new apartment as he stared morosely at the remaining pile of boxes. He'd been at this for hours and the place still looked like he was having a garage sale. He glanced at his watch and groaned at the time he found there. Drinking the remainder of coffee from the flask he'd made up this morning, he sighed when he found it tepid. He had packed up all the kitchen boxes and had yet to unpack it. He stood now and shuffled through the remaining boxes giving a small shout of victory when he found the one labelled kitchen in big bold ink. He emptied the box and began storing things before setting the kettle in its place on the countertop. Tomorrow was going to be hard enough without having to start the day without a well needed caffeine boost. He took one final look around his apartment, sighing before heading down the hall to his bedroom, the rest could wait.

****

June 27th 9am

"I have made myself acquainted with your file Devlin, Can I call you Devlin?" The Superintendent asked before continuing, "I try not to get too stuck on formalities in private, it's a little too stuffy and stand-offish using ranks and surnames in an office when there are only the two of us present. I consider us a tight knit unit and while a certain amount of propriety is expected, I prefer to make the work environment one that puts people at ease, so they are free to communicate effectively and work together harmoniously."

"Dev's fine Ma'am." He replied.

"Now where was I? Oh yes, your file." The Super leaned forwards looking at him directly and proceeding. "I'll be frank, it's a very impressive read. I am always keen to acquire any resources that will improve the efficiency of my unit. Beyond the one incident, you have a good record of service, and I would bite a hand off to snap up a good officer. That being said, we do not need any lone rangers here, we are a team and a pretty effective one if I do say so myself. Do you catch my drift?" She narrowed her eyes at him and scanned his expression, as though she were a facial recognition machine, trying to catch the small clues she needed to get the answers she was looking for.

"I shan't be acting the maggot if that's what you're asking Ma'am." Dev assured her.

The Super looked bemused then nodded, leaning back away she made to stand and Dev following her lead stood with her.

"In that case, Devlin, welcome to Welwyn, let's go and get you to the officer in charge of your supervision."

She set a brisk pace out of her office, and he easily fell in line behind. He noticed that his new Super nodded and smiled at people as she passed but didn't stop until they reached a doorway, where she leaned in slightly and called, "Wren, can I borrow you for a moment?" before backing away from the doorframe and moving a little down the corridor to allow room for people to use the entrance. Dev followed suit and waited with curiosity to see who would appear.

He took a sharp intake of breath, his eyes widening with disbelief and muttered, "Holy Mary, Mother of God!" as a striking woman headed in their direction. Dev stared dumbfounded at what he could only describe as the image of what an actual angel might look like, not in a "she's so sweet" kind of way either, more like a celestial entity had come down and was here to show you the error of your ways.

Her face was almost ghostly pale, which made her full lips look darker in contrast, deep pink and glossy, they looked soft and inviting. Her long wavy hair, which was tied in a low ponytail, fell like a sheet of snow, stopping midway down her back. As she tilted her face upward, a few errant strands, curled loosely to frame her face and if she hadn't held her head in an upward tilt, to lock eyes with him in a moody glower, they would have likely hidden the most bewildering eyes Dev had ever seen. Her eyes were a stunning shade of violet adorned with white lashes. They looked surreal and enchanting, like they belonged to a mythical creature from a fairytale rather than a mere human. When you added the lithe but firm curves on a statuesque frame, it completed the look and Dev itched to turn her around and search for the wings. The glower turned to a scowl, and she pointedly turned her back to him dismissively and addressed the Super.

"You wanted to see me, Ma'am?" She asked abruptly.

"I did," the Super replied amusement lacing her tone. "I'd like you to meet our new DI; Devlin Doyle, this is DI Serenity Jones. She will be your new tour guide for the duration of your stay." She joked light-heartedly.

"A pleasure, to be sure," Dev said, tilting his head in a slight bow, his brogue a little thicker because of the sudden dryness in his mouth, as he held out his hand to the ethereal beauty before him.

"The pleasure is all yours then," she replied stonily and ignored his hand, which he retracted with a half-grin, his green eyes twinkling with a merriment he hadn't anticipated, considering the circumstances surrounding his placement.

"Now, now Wren," the Super admonished, "Play nice. I wouldn't want our new detective to feel unwelcome."

Wren looked down and flushed with guilt. "I'm sorry, that was uncalled for," she said with a little more warmth, "Why don't I take you to meet the team. Then I'll show you around."

She stepped back into the room she had come from leading Dev into a large busy area; desks and monitors were placed throughout and a handful of people looked up as they walked in, gazing at them with interest in their eyes. Wren opened her mouth to speak but words came from somewhere to the side of her before she could get a word out.

"Ahh, the fresh meat has arrived!" A cheery looking woman with a mischievous grin and short, dark curls, got up to approach them. She gave Wren a friendly smirk, "Are you going to introduce us or what?" she asked, giving Dev a wink, her brown eyes twinkling.

Wren tutted impatiently, "I was about to before you butted in," she remarked. "Everyone, this is DI Doyle, he will be joining us. The eager beaver in front of you is DC Jen Cartwright, over to the left—"she indicated to a tall, stocky guy with greying dark hair, "—is DS Matt Ainsworth," the guy gave him a nod and a smile before Wren moved on. "And these two guys just here are DC Ashley Carter and DS Dominic Watson. Watson is from one of the other teams. The DCI is currently on annual leave." The first sandy blonde one was wiry and lean, he gave a chin lift and the other tilted his head to him.

"How-a-ya," Dev greeted in return stoically.

"I'm a little disappointed. I was expecting you to say top of the morning," Dom teased cheekily. His dark features mocking as he studied Dev from his chair.

"Surprisingly, not used as often as they would have you believe on TV." Dev replied with a wry grin, making him look every bit like a charming, Irish Rogue.

"Ok, that's enough of that, you lot crack on, Doyle, let's show you around." Wren left the team to resume their posts and led him off.

After about an hour and a half of walking through a sea of strange faces and being shown the layout of the building, Dev was more than happy to be led to a canteen off to the side of the office area they had started in. Wren was giving him a run down on the temperamental coffee machine and fixing up two mugs on the counter as she spoke. When the machine finished, she handed him one and began dunking a tea bag in the other, while Dev sank into a comfy looking chair and mindlessly watched as she added milk and sugar. She finally sank into a chair next to him and they sat drinking quietly for a few minutes.

"I'm a bit sick of the sound of my own voice right now." Wren stated out of the blue. Dev's lip curled up, but he remained quiet. "Not much of a talker are you?"

"Not much," Dev confirmed.

"Is that a nervous thing or a personality trait?" She asked conversationally.

"Little of one, some of t'other." He replied with a small shrug.

"Well alright then..." she dwindled off lamely, and began to shift uncomfortably in her seat. She got quite anxious when she had nothing to occupy herself with and started lightly tapping one foot in a staccato rhythm. They drank the rest of their drinks in awkward silence. When they finished, she stood and without anything more to say, led the way back to the unit.

Once back in the unit, Wren found herself relaxing as they went over the cases currently being investigated. The rest of the day flew by as the team joined in with updates and worked to put information together. By the time they had decided to wrap up for the evening, Wren felt mentally drained. The new DI had quietly regarded the activity going on around him with an observant scrutiny, asking questions in the relevant places and seemed to absorb the information with interest. When someone spoke to him, his sharp eyes fixed them with a penetrating gaze, and you could almost see the cogs turning in his head when he was mulling over what they had said. Wren found herself thinking he wasn't at all what she had expected. She bid the team goodnight and, giving her arms a stretch, she allowed herself to switch off and head home.

Dev watched as one by one the team headed out. He paid particular attention to Angel as she worked her shoulders loose and ambled to her car. He found himself strangely fascinated by her but couldn't quite put his finger on why. He'd spent the afternoon studying the dynamics of the team as they worked through their cases and tried to catalogue as much information as he could. He wasn't particularly fond of being the newbie. He felt much more comfortable when he had his finger on the pulse of everything going on around him. He liked to be in control, probably something to do with his childhood and not having the basic details of his life at a young age. Whatever the reason, he found it somewhat unsettling to be playing catch up instead of leading the charge.

However, if he had to play second fiddle, he was glad it was Wren leading it. She seemed to have a dedication to the work he hadn't seen much of in recent years and a passion for seeing justice dealt to those who chose not to adhere to the law. She was a breath of fresh air, one he sorely needed after recent events had left him feeling somewhat jaded. Maybe, he thought, this wasn't such a bad thing after all.

Chapter Four

July 31st, 2014

Over the next few weeks, Dev spent his time getting acquainted with how his new team ran. The DCI had returned from his annual leave and was delegating the workload as it arose. He oversaw the cases and came and went for regular updates. On the DCI's first morning back, Wren had pulled Dev to one side to warn him.

"Just a heads up the boss is back and will be expecting a meet and greet, it will be a general discussion about what you will be assigned to and what he expects etc. I warn you that he has a somewhat…unfortunate name and it would be wise if you glazed over it without comment. He is a little touchy about it and he can hold a grudge, just so you are aware." She said in a low, hushed voice so as not to draw attention.

"Seriously? How bad can it be? Dev asked curiously.
"It's pretty bad." Wren chuckled.
"Are you going to keep me in suspense or clue me in?" Dev queried, intrigued by her evasiveness.
"It's DCI Head." She began, looking to her feet.
Dev tilted his head in confusion. *"I don't follow. Why's that so bad?"*
Wren's lips pursed tightly, and she inhaled through her nose. Opening them again she released a quiet wobbly breath, and her shoulders shook slightly. Dev watched in puzzlement but then slowly realised what was happening.
"Are you laughing?" He enquired with surprise.
"Ok! Ok! His first name is Richard…" she sputtered and suppressed a giggle.

"No. Really?" Dev asked in disbelief and at her nod, repeated, "Nooo…dickhead? Nooo. You're having me on, away with you."
"Unfortunately, I'm afraid, I'm not." Wren said.
"Aye, right you are, most unfortunate."

He gave a full grin and dimples appeared, startling Wren a little and without thinking she exclaimed.
"Woah now! Where have you been hiding those?"
Dev once again appeared baffled and looked at her in question.
"Never mind" She muttered uncomfortably, her demeanour changing, as she excused herself and went off to get some tea. Dev wasn't entirely sure what had happened, but he gave a mental shrug and went off to see what the others were doing.

Dev was pulled out of his thoughts by DS Dominic Watson.
"Morning Dev, Jen just called. She's up by Moreno's Cafe with Ash and she's going to do a coffee run, maybe some breakfast rolls or something. Do you want anything?" He asked cheerily.
"Marvellous! Tell her she's a star, a black coffee and a roll would be grand." As though in answer, his stomach growled hungrily. Dom walked off talking into his phone, nearly bumping into Wren as he went, he paused and held his phone slightly away and looked at her. "Jen's doing a coffee run, do you want your usual?"

Wren gave him a grateful look and nodded her ascent, then wandered over to Dev. Putting her hands on the desk he was sitting at, she leaned over and said, "Boss wants us all in the incident room in thirty minutes, he's got a case for us."

Twenty-five minutes later, they were filing into the major incident room with personnel from the investigating teams, representatives from the administrative teams and of course one or two from the scientific team. Jen was handing out food and drinks while everyone took up various seats around the room. The room was large, with long desks lined up facing towards the far end of the room, each sporting rows of computer monitors. Several large maps and several whiteboards adorned the long wall at the front. The DCI stood there with his "bagman" in a seat to his side, waiting for everyone to settle so he could begin. The room was alive with a sea of voices talking amongst themselves, before the DCI finally addressed the room.

"Good morning everyone, if I could have your attention." He paused as silence fell and everyone fixed their eyes to the Detective before them. "Good. Let's get started. As you are aware there has been a spate of sexual assaults in the area. A woman was taken to New Queen Elizabeth hospital and admitted after a particularly nasty assault in the early hours of this morning. DS Ainsworth and DC Carter attended the scene. We are still waiting for the crime scene officers to give us a preliminary report, however the officers spoke to the victim and she has given them her statement."

The bagman rushed over to hand him some papers before the DCI continued.

"Based on her description and CCTV footage in the area, we have identified the suspect as Vincent Walker, who also answers to Vinnie. At this time, we are unsure if this assault connects to the others, however it is looking promising. With this information in mind, I would like to assign tasks for each of you and see if we can nab this bastard. DC Cartwright, if you could do a thorough search for us? Gather as much information as you can, places he is known to frequent, any places he might be staying, the usual. DS Ainsworth has assigned officers to remain with the victim at the hospital. She will be remaining there for the immediate future, but a liaison officer has been assigned.

"The victim was leaving her boyfriend's residence and had walked to where she had parked her car further along the street when the assault took place. These are copies of the information we have so far." He handed a different set of papers to his bagman, and the man dutifully stepped up and distributed them. The DCI paused again to allow them to have a read through, before he continued. "I would like officers to do a door to door of the area where the assault took place, DC Carter; if you can arrange that. DI Jones, while DC Cartright digs up dirt for us on the HOLMES database, I'd like you and Doyle to go to his last known residence, speak to his ex-wife to see if she has any ideas on his current location…"

The DCI continued assigning tasks, his sidekick writing the important details which pertained to the case on the whiteboard, while people started to disperse. Wren stayed put, scanning through the information she'd been given again. Dev waited for her to finish so they could head out, impatient to get to work. She eventually lifted her head seemingly satisfied she had taken in the little information currently available and stood nodding to Jen who was already at a computer monitor, her fingers flying across the keyboard at breakneck speed. Jen, immersed in her task, merely lifted her hand and continued, her eyes never leaving the screen.

They walked outside and Wren got into the driver's side, with her knowledge of the area more superior, it seemed like a wise choice, so Dev took the passenger side and they headed out to speak to Vinnie's ex. According to the brief her name was Alma Hadley, beyond this there wasn't anything to really give Dev any clues as to what they may be dealing with. He cleared his throat and Wren glanced at him briefly but continued driving, lost in thought. Dev considered leaving her to them, however curiosity got the better of him.

"So, what is the crack with this Alma woman?" He asked.

"What do you mean?" Wren said, flicking a quick look in his direction.

"Do we know anything besides her name, address and who her ex-husband is? Any previous dealings with her? Anything I should know before we get there? If he's a suspected rapist, it's not too far of a leap to think that maybe they had some callouts to her while she was married. Any previous arrests, unexplained hospital admissions that triggered red flags suggesting abuse? Is there anything untoward I should know about going in?" He probed inquisitively.

"You're talkative now, huh?" Wren jested with amusement, "Personally I've only had dealings with her on one call out; back before I was major crimes I attended a domestic. It was called in by a neighbour who reported shouting and smashing sounds, some suspicious cries that made her suspect some abusive behaviour, but Alma wasn't very forthcoming. We did persuade her to allow us entry, although I suspect she only agreed so she could hurry us along before he returned."

"And were there signs of abuse?" Dev interrupted.

"There was some property damage that she insisted was nothing involving abuse. She said that he'd had a rare show of temper about something that had happened due to a falling out with one of his friends, which had led to the raised voices as he reiterated to her what had him so upset, but was most eager to impress that it wasn't directly aimed at her. We did press her when I noted a large, red mark on her arm consistent with a developing bruise, but she explained it away. Alma told us that Vinnie had thrown a cup at the wall in frustration as he recounted his story and in her surprise she'd stumbled back hitting her arm on the door handle which had been left ajar behind her. A simple case of not paying attention to her surroundings."

"So based on the assumption he has a history of violence to women, he could fit the profile," Dev muttered to himself. "What was the falling out about?"

"We questioned her further about his falling out, but she claimed that he hadn't gone into any details which had made any sense to her. He'd just been raving randomly, no real context she could use to comprehend his anger. I left her a contact number to call should she need our assistance further or want to adjust her statement. I also left a card for someone who could help her should she need help with any abuse in the future. She took it reluctantly at my insistence, but I doubt she kept it. That is all I know directly, however the drugs unit could probably give us more. They've had several interactions with her and her ex over the course of the years, although not much has come of it to my knowledge. We'll know more once Jen has finished her search." She concluded.

Dev had, for the most part, remained quiet during her summation and was now contemplating quietly. Wren returned her focus to the road, and they travelled the last five minutes in silence, before Wren pulled up to the curb and parked her car. They'd had to park a fair way up the street from Alma's address, due to the limited spaces available, which gave Dev time to search the surrounding area—an automatic practice when in unfamiliar locales—as they walked back.

When they got to the door, Wren knocked, and they waited. They waited so long they'd almost decided to give up, when the door opened a crack and a female face appeared, peering out cautiously to see who was on the other side and the owner of it hissed quietly.
"What do you want?"
Wren being closest to the gap was the only person visible to her, so she replied politely. "We're just here for a quick chat Miss Hadley, could we come inside? I'm DI Jones, do you remember me?"
The door opened wider and a handsome woman in her late forties appeared before them, her body stiff and her arms wrapped, defensively around herself. Still blocking the entrance way, she seemed undecided on whether to allow them in or not. Then her gaze fell to Dev, and she assessed him curiously.
"I remember. You, though, you're new. Who are you?"
Dev transformed before Wren's eyes, and they widened in disbelief. His stance softened from stoic and intimidating, to a more casual posture. His head dipped, allowing his slightly long hair to fall over his face as met her gaze in an earnest, almost humble way. His green eyes warmed, losing their normally sharp, assessing appearance and his mouth widened in a broad

inviting smile, letting those dimples appear. The whole look gave him an almost innocent boyish aspect that would make mothers everywhere feel the need to sweep him up in a hug. In short, he had Alma almost transfixed. Then he spoke in a soothing voice.

"Top of the mornin' to ya Ma'am. I'm DI Doyle but you can call me Devlin." He said, his grin becoming mischievous, "A pleasure, to be sure." He finished, his Irish lilt slightly more exaggerated than usual.

Alma's posture relaxed, her arms uncrossing, her eyes creasing at the edges and a small smile curling her mouth. Her lashes lowered and a slight pink flush spread over her face and she seemed to be immediately more at ease, gazing up at him with adoring eyes. She cleared her throat before replying coyly.

"Well, aren't you a charmer? Come in, I'll put the kettle on and make us a brew, I have some biscuits, the nice chocolate ones. We can have a spot of tea and you can tell me what this is all about."

Wren watched with surprise at the exchange, as Alma turned and led them down the hall, settling them into the living room, before she went off and busied herself in the kitchen. Dev's eyes connected with hers and she raised an eyebrow in question.

"What?" Dev asked, a picture of innocence.

"Top of the morning? Thought that 'wasn't as popular as you might think,' wasn't that what you said to Dom?" She taunted with dry sarcasm.

"Aye," he agreed, "It isn't but it's what's expected isn't it?" He countered good-humouredly. "Not much is friendlier than a charming Irishman, don't cha know." He laughed, giving Wren a cheeky wink. She rolled her eyes in mock disdain and tutted, about to give him a stinging reply, when Alma returned with a tray and a smile. Setting it down on a large coffee table, she placed some mugs in front of them both and took one for herself, almost completely different from the woman Wren had previously met with.

"There now, help yourself to a biscuit. A growing lad like you needs his energy." She admonished, giving Dev a shameless once-over with a familiarity contrary to the length of time they'd been briefly acquainted. "You too, dear" she added in Wren's direction as an afterthought, her eyes not leaving Dev, "Get started and then you can move along with your questions." She chattered amiably before asking, "Did you want sugar, Dimples?" She flirted, fluttering her eyes at him.

"No thanks ma'am, I'm sweet enough," he bantered with amusement, his green eyes twinkling in merriment. Wren shook her head with incredulity muttering "Seriously?" under her breath so only Dev could hear, and he chuckled quietly in return, while Alma moved to a chair just in front of Dev. She sat down in a large armchair and took a sip of her tea. They drank together, Wren sitting quietly allowing Dev to charm her while they exchanged pleasantries, he asked her about herself and complimented her home, in return her face became animated as she answered, genuinely enjoying his attentiveness. Eventually, they finished their drinks and Dev's face took on a more serious expression. Alma, noting this change, sat back in her chair.

"So, Dimples, what brings you to my door?" Alma enquired cutting straight to the point.

"Well ma'am, we've come because we are in need of your assistance, we are trying to locate your ex-husband, and this was his last known residence. From what I understand that is no longer the case, however we were hoping you might have some idea on his current whereabouts so we might catch up with him. Can you help us?" he asked, looking at her beseechingly.

Alma did not look surprised by his question, her face scowling at the reference to her ex. Her words fell out in a tumultuous tirade. "That no good, two-bit son-of-a… He's been gone six months now, the best damn day of my life was when he crawled back to whatever hole he crawled out of. Lying, cheating, narcissistic snake that he is. I prayed to the Lord for him to go, every day since the day I became tied to that man. If it weren't for the fact he was a mean son-of-a...gun I'd have left him years ago, tried a few times…" she stopped here, trailing off as her arms wrapped tightly around herself again, the slight tremor in her shoulders saying more than words ever could.

"He hurt you?" Dev pushed gently. Alma nodded so slightly it was almost imperceptible. "I know this is a lot to ask of you, you're obviously scared but if you help us find him, we will do our best to give you the justice you deserve."

"He came here a few days ago…"Alma whispered in a small voice. "I saw him from the window, I hoped he hadn't seen me, and hid. He knocked but I waited him out. He knocked for a good while, called through the letterbox saying he needed me, but I stayed where I was, couldn't have moved if I wanted to, I haven't left the house since. I don't know where he is and honestly I don't want to know."

"Any place you can think of where he might lay-low? Any place at all?" Dev coaxed carefully.

Alma thought for a moment, shifting uncomfortably then said. "He does hang out at a bar, a friend of his owns it, can't remember the name though...maybe he's laying low there? His friend Tommy, Tommy Morris. He and his four brothers share ownership." She concluded, nodding to herself.

Dev rose from his seat and crouched in front of her, looking down at her hands that were clasped and wringing slightly with her distress. Dev gave them a reassuring squeeze.

"Thank you, Alma, you did good, real good," he murmured to her comfortingly, "Take care of yourself and if he shows up here you call me, do you hear?" Taking his hand from hers, Dev reached into his jacket pocket and grabbed a notebook he spied nearby and pen. Then quickly writing something he tore the page off, before folding it and gently prying her fingers apart to place the paper inside her right palm, and closing her fingers around it. "I mean that Alma, call me and I will come." He reiterated with sincerity, then released her hand and stood. "Now ma'am, if you don't mind, DI Jones and I have a rat to catch. You've been a delight." He ended light-heartedly, lifting the seriousness of the moment, and a small smile returned to Alma's face.

Following his cue, she waved him off affectionately, "Get along then, Dimples, I've kept you here long enough."

Wren stood with an approving nod to Dev, as Alma guided them back to the front door and opened it, dismissing them blithely.

"Come along, Dimples, we have work to do." Wren teased as they left.

The two of them walked from the residence and made their way to the vehicle parked a way down the street. Wren touched his arm and he turned to give her his attention.

"You're good at that," she stated begrudgingly.

Dev started to smile at her praise, when movement to his right grabbed his attention and the smile froze on his face. His eyes widened, and the colour drained from his face, as his smile fell. Wren whirled to her left and found Vinnie also frozen. The two men's eyes locked in a peculiar stare down for a couple of moments, before Vinnie broke it, drawing a gun from his pocket and lifting it. Suddenly Dev snapped from his fugue state, and without thinking launched himself at Wren, shielding her as they fell to the ground as a gunshot split the quiet morning apart. Dazed, with Dev's heavy body covering hers, Wren met his green eyes briefly, as he pushed himself up taking some of his weight off her. He broke their gaze first, sweeping a glance around them to find Vinnie gone. Clearing his throat gruffly, he awkwardly ran a hand through his hair, "Howaya?" he asked huskily.

Ignoring his question, Wren pushed at his shoulders roughly, in a gesture for Dev to remove himself, he complied and as they returned to their feet cautiously, brushing themselves down Wren looked around her eyes bouncing from one area to another, almost maniacally, trying to locate their suspect. "Do you see him?"

Dev wrapped his big hand around her arms firmly to get her attention. "No, he's gone. Now answer the question, are you hurt?" he urged persistently.

"I'm fine, quit fussing and do your job. Where did he go?" Wren spat with frustration.

"I don't know, we should call it in." he said, reaching for his two-way radio and proceeding to speak into it and report the shooting. As he did, Wren spotted Alma running in their direction, concern for them clear on her face, before she could make it all the way, Wren shouted across in a tone that brooked no argument.

"Alma! Go back inside and lock the door! Stay there until backup arrives, you understand?" Alma halted in her tracks then nodded her head, and moved swiftly back to the safety of her residence. Wren looked back to Dev as he finished the call and the two of them waited for the cavalry to arrive.

Chapter Five

Keri McNamara made her way quietly into her parents' home, letting herself in with the key she'd kept after moving out some years back. Her family hadn't agreed with her decision, despite her being twenty-four at the time, they believed because of "their business," it wasn't safe for her to be anywhere but residing with them. For the entire first year after leaving home, they had men following her ensuring her safe keeping. It wasn't until she had embarked on a relationship with one of them and he moved in with her, their affection for each other eventually developing over their forced proximity, that they had finally deemed her well-being to be in safe hands and let her move freely without supervision.

She wondered how many other parents would consider a crime minion to be safe hands? But what did she know, she was just a *doctor*.

Her fiancé, Cameron, was one of her father's most trusted employees; the loyal son of a family friend. The two fathers had big plans for him. Someday, when they got too old to continue, he would take over with Keri by his side. He was everything her father revered in a man, confident, violent when required but respectful of his superiors and his daughter. Cameron was ambitious and hungry to reach the top, but not to the degree that he overstepped his position and questioned their decisions.

At least not to their faces at any rate, within their own home however, he insinuated his desire to be more involved in overseeing the business. This was one of the things Keri actually liked about him. With her own rebellious streak, she enjoyed that he had his eyes on the "throne" and wasn't quite as obedient as he would have them believe. He was cunning, calculated and treated her with a reverence she loved. He was every ounce a villain and they were perfect for each other. She was, after all, the daughter of Jack and Mary McNamara and they'd taught her well. With her father's ruthlessness and ambition coupled with her mother's deviousness and manipulative nature, she was both heartless and brutal. The only small weakness was her fondness for her fiancé. However, together they were a force to be reckoned with, a force so evil they could be likened to the embodiment of the devil himself, if there were two of him, that is.

As she wandered through the house, nodding to various men who regarded her warily, she caught the sound of raised voices drifting into the hallway. Curious, she slowed outside her father's office and discreetly eavesdropped on the heated exchange within.

"I'm telling you, Boss, it was him," the slimy voice insisted.

"It can't be him." Her father declared impatiently, and another voice agreed that it couldn't.

"I'm not lying, it was him, Keir! As I live and breathe, it was him."

"If it is, then someone is about to pay dearly," her father promised menacingly.

Keri froze and the cogs in her mind whirred, thoughts raced erratically through her head until suddenly everything became clear. She left, slipping out without anyone noticing, and heading back to her car. She needed to get home, needed to speak to her fiancé, this was a game-changer and time was of the essence.

****

Wren was frustrated. She'd had the suspect in her sights and then he'd vanished. He'd been right there, then he was gone, it was maddening. Police had attended the scene en masse, the street had been cordoned off and a perimeter set up. The entry and exit had been established and a log was in place, to make a record of any officers attending the scene with any details needed. The SOCO team had begun scouring the area for evidence, a bullet had been removed from a vehicle near where they'd been on the roadside and had been bagged and tagged, the first thing to begin the collection stored away for analysis later.

She and Dev were giving their account of events outside the perimeter, whilst the DCI stood off to another side, dividing officers and PCSOs between door-to-door calls, looking for witness accounts and searching the area for the suspect. A helicopter had taken to the sky for an aerial view to scope out the streets beyond, in hopes of locating our man, and the heavy police presence was drawing onlookers. They gathered with interest, attempting to get a glimpse of the restricted area and trying to figure out what had happened. Talking amongst themselves with an excitement that belied the severity of the situation. Minutes turned into hours, as the officers fanned out and the scene became less congested. The onlookers grew tired of the dull proceedings and eventually filtered off.

Appointed CID officers stood at the perimeter guarding the scene, while SOCO continued their work, methodically going over the location with a fine-tooth comb. Unable to be part of the tasks at hand, she and Dev had returned to the station for a debrief. A couple more hours slipped by, and they finally entered the incident room, where Jen was waiting to pounce on them.

"Oh my God! Are you guys ok?" She raced over hugging Wren.

"We're fine," Wren assured her impatiently as she tried to shake her off, before giving in and patting her awkwardly on the back, unsure of what else to do, until she let go.

"Well in that case, come over to my lair and let me show you my etchings." She cooed eerily.

"Little bit creepy, Jen love," Wren returned hesitantly, smoothing her clothes down after Jen's over-enthusiastic embrace. She caught Dev quietly observing the two of them with a smirk and snapped, "You can shut up too, Dimples."

Dev erupted in laughter, holding his hands up in surrender and they moved towards a large desk. Jen gave him an elbow and Dev looked at her in surprise, "Nice save, looking out for our girl," she whispered loud enough for Wren to hear, and an answering growl of warning came from the DI. As they approached the desk, Wren noted the chaotic disarray, papers askew and no order that she could discern. DS Matt Ainsworth joined their collective and Jen motioned for them to sit so she could give them the run down. Matt, having not long been back from the hospital getting an update, pulled up a chair and addressed Jen first.

"So, what have you got for us, Jen."

"Well let's start with his rap sheet and let me tell you it's quite the compilation. Our man is forty-eight and originally from Hemel Hempstead. He's been arrested multiple times for an assortment of offences and suspected of various others. The list goes as follows;

theft, burglary, public indecency, drunk and disorderly, aggravated assault, he's pretty mean with a knife F.Y.I, stalking, sexual harassment, and drug possession. NCA has him loosely linked to the McNamara's but no firm ties. He's friends with the four brothers who run the Rose and Crown, who are pretty thick with the family, so Vinnie's affiliation with them is sketchy at best." Jen powered through the profile at her usual rapid rate.

"Wait. Who are the McNamaras?" Dev interrupted with interest.

"Been in the area for decades, they've been the subject of many a stake-out, but nothing ever seems to stick." Matt chimed in. "Jack McNamara came over from Ireland, he's in his fifties now, there's speculation his father had some connections to the IRA but there was never anything solid enough to hold him to account. Settled over here after meeting his wife Mary, been here ever since."

"NCA have been trying to nail him and his partner, Connor O'Reilly for years," Wren added, "It's like they're invincible, no one can seem to touch them."

"Organised Crime has also had a crack at them on more than one occasion, same story there too," Matt agreed.

"Excuse me, I'm Jen, remember me? Don't know if you recall but I was kind in the middle of something," she sulked.

"Oh, behave yourself," Matt chastised, "We'll get back to your guy, although can't say as I'd see a fine-tuned racket like they have going on, having much interest in a bottom-feeder like Vincent."

"Judging by the information I have, he's more likely a glory-hound looking for a chance to get into the big leagues." Jen concurred continuing, "Which leads me to my next tidbit. It would seem our guy Vinnie has a new piece."

"A gun?" Dev chuckled derisively, "Aye, we are aware of that."

"No. Well yes, that too but nothing traceable that I've found in that department. I meant he has a new girlfriend. I found out just before you walked in," Jen replied smugly.

Wren leaned forward her full attention on Jen and gave a broad grin that hinted she smelled blood and was ready for the hunt. "Is that so?"

"Oh yeah…" Jen announced gloating "Give me a few hours and I'll get you the address."

****

Vinnie was a man with a lot on his mind, worry creased his forehead as he looked fearfully through the window, only half dressed behind the curtain. He should probably be moving on, it didn't pay to stay in one location too long, he had to keep on the move.

"Come back to bed, Vinnie." His new girlfriend Charlene whined. They'd had a bit of a barney a couple of nights ago and in a drunken stupor he'd regrettably left to visit his ex, Alma. When he'd had no joy there he'd had a bit of sport with a woman he happened upon not far away. He'd enjoyed giving the bitch what she had coming to her, what they all had coming to them. Having vented the worst of his anger he'd merrily gone about his business, leaving her where she belonged, in the gutter with all the other whores. He smiled to himself as he recalled the feel of his knife pressing into her pretty little neck, as he pounded unforgivingly into her. He got hard again just thinking about it. The smile slipped when the memory turned sour, and he remembered his return visit to Alma's. When he'd realised the heat was on, he'd decided to remind her why it would be wise that she kept her mouth shut. He hadn't expected them. He was about to step back when something caught his attention. His phone dinged with a message, and as he opened it, his heart stopped.

THEY'RE COMING.

That's all it said but he knew what that meant. He threw himself into motion, volleying down the stairs, bare chested and barefoot, he threw open the back door and hot footed it away. He must've made it a good mile away before he slowed, gasping for breath. Bent over he was unaware of his audience and before he could even regain his ragged breaths, there was a flicker of pain, and the world went black.

****

   Dev was alone. The DCI had returned to the incident room shortly after Jen's revelation and insisted that we take a few hours to go home and get freshened up. As soon as Jen had what she was looking for they could return and get the ball rolling. Unable to rest knowing they were closing in, once he'd got home he'd made a few calls of his own. It had been a long shot but "more hands make for lighter work" and all that. After an hour he'd dropped it, his head had been pounding. That had been two hours ago he realised, waking up still sitting in his chair. The headache was gone again leaving him a little fuzzy and cloudy, he'd felt like this before, when he hadn't been sleeping enough or when he'd been young, after a spate of nightmares.

This case was getting to him, and he wasn't sure why but something about Vinnie made him go cold. When he'd seen him on the street a strange sense of familiarity had stopped him dead. Somewhere he'd come across him before, but he just couldn't put his finger on it. A previous case he'd worked on but couldn't quite remember. Whatever it was, it was bugging the hell out of him. A cold case maybe? He let the thought go and sighed, wiping his hand down over his tired face. His phone rang beside him, and he sprung for it and accepted the call.

"Hello!" He bit off sharply.

"Hello to you too, old friend, good to hear you didn't become the life and soul of the party in your new station." Alec's voice came through the speaker and Dev's excitement petered out in disappointment.

"I'm sorry, Alec, I'm waiting for an update. Got a case on the go. Speaking of cases… I've got one playing on my mind. Do you recall the name Vincent Walker? Goes by Vinnie. He's our suspect and I have this gut feeling I just can't seem to shake." Dev explained, hoping that since it wasn't an update, at the least he might get to the bottom of that. The line went quiet, and Dev waited, giving Alec a chance to consider his question. It seemed however, a trail of disappointments were coming, thick and fast today.

"No mate, I don't think I do. I could look into it though if you like. Maybe it was before my time," Alec replied.

"If you get a chance, that would be helpful, although hopefully by then we'll have the bastard anyway." He went silent for a moment and started again, "I'm sorry,

I forgot to ask why you called." He chuckled, mentally berating himself.

"I just thought I'd see how you were settling in, how's it going your way?" Alec asked. Dev pondered on that for a moment.

"When they told me I wasn't particularly thrilled, but it was better than expected, ya know?" Dev's thoughts went to Angel and the others, "The team here is good though, they're smart and funny, before this I couldn't remember how long it had been since I'd laughed, not a little chuckle like, I'm talking full on belly laugh. I smile more too, they have some real characters, you'd like 'em. I also wasn't happy about being "supervised" but Angel. She's special, quick to anger but also to say when you're doing something well. She has a thirst for seeing justice done too. She's sharp and direct but also kind, bit of a live wire ya know? I'm not overly fond of authority, it's usually a necessary evil but if I had to choose to be beneath someone it would be her-"

"Oh, I bet you would." Alec cut in with a roar of laughter.

"Feck off, I wasn't talking about that! Ya dirty wee bastard." Dev snapped, irritated by his friend's crude joke.

"Tsk,tsk, Dev, my friend, hold your temper. Can you hear yourself? Angel's sweet and kind and funny and pwetty and smart- " Alec began, mocking him in a girly baby voice, but before he could finish Dev had hung up.

"Fecking eejit" he muttered to himself. The phone's ringtone shrilled again, and he yanked it up answered and raved into it, "If you carry on playing the maggot, I'll hang up again, Angel is stunning, Aye, it's true and

I won't lie she fascinates me, but I haven't—" he ranted.

"Who's Angel?" Wren's voice rang in his ear. Dev was mortified. A blush ran swiftly up over his face, and he'd never been so glad a person couldn't see him.

"Never mind. Does she have it?" He said changing the subject before he could further embarrass himself.

"She does." Dev could hear her satisfied smugness over the line, and it didn't help his equilibrium that was still shot from his unfortunate mishap.

"Then let's do this." He stood, phone still in hand.

"We've got to wait until morning." He heard her tone go sour with this last statement.

"What? Why?" Dev cried in frustrated outrage.

"The DCI says he wants this done properly. He wants to go over how we proceed first, cross the i's dot the t's, no wait scratch that, reverse it," she said disjointedly before going on, "some shit about 'thinking before you act and then acting decisively' or whatever. He wants us back at the station though, we may be waiting until morning, but he wants to discuss how this is going to go down." She told him.

"Ok, I'll see you shortly." Dev replied begrudgingly and ended the call.

Chapter Six

January 20th, 1990

  The voices of the men could be heard beyond. Whilst the scared family sat in the room unable to do anything but listen.
  "Your information was sound, Vincent, he was skimming money off the top. My men have picked up his family, they're in the back. Thought we'd give them a wee vacation while he comes up with the money." A voice stated coldly.
  "So, I did good?" Vinnie, presumably, asked.
  "Aye, I'll see you get rewarded." The other voice assured.
  "You know what I want…" Vinnie trailed off.
  "Aye, you're right, I do. You've been creeping on her since the day you met." The voice replied with distaste, "Very well, knock your wee socks off." He finished dismissively.
  The family shuffled back and huddled together in the corner of the room as they heard footsteps approaching. Fear permeated the air, and a man entered the room. The children cowered, the mother put herself in front of them while pushing them further back behind her, she was scared but bravely jutted her chin up in defiance.
  "Well, hello again, Mrs Whelan. Or can I call you Chastity? Such a sweet little thing, always so sweet. How about we see just how chaste you are?" He smirked with malevolent intent as he approached and undid his belt, zipping down the fly of his worn-out jeans almost simultaneously. He went to grab her arm, making her recoil and in the process she forgot to

guard her children. The man lunged for them, and on instinct the boy put himself protectively in front of his sister. Vincent grabbed him, dragging him from behind Chastity. He pulled him up roughly and a blade appeared in his hand. He pressed it into the boy's throat, a small rivulet of blood trickled down as he nicked him and the boy gave a yelp.

"Now Chastity, don't make me do something you'll regret," he chuckled icily, "I swear to you, I'll skin him alive if I have to. Just be a good little girl and do as you're told, then we can skip that unpleasantness, what do you say?"

Chastity's colour drained but she stood on shaky legs, and her voice hissed, "Let him go."

"I don't think I will." Vinnie said matter of factly, " How about instead, you come over here and get on your knees." He demanded in a slimy drawl.

Chastity locked eyes with her son and spoke. "Close your eyes, Keir. And whatever you do, don't open them, not for anything, no matter what you hear, you keep them shut. Do as I say, understand."

"But ma..." the boy began to protest but she cut a stern look at him.

"Do as you're told boyo." She commanded, "You too, baby girl," she threw behind her. The girl nodded and obeyed. The boy hesitated but finally he shut his eyes too and she took a breath. Dread spread in her chest, and she refused to look at the man as a single tear slipped down her face, shame filling her when she dropped to her knees before him.

Chapter Seven

August 1st, 2014
Present day

   Wren was gearing herself up ready to get into the action. She was really hoping that the extra few hours hadn't delayed them so much that they didn't get to him in time. She'd had enough of just missing this guy. Dev was quiet behind her, an intense look on his face, and she wondered what he was thinking about. The DCI had left to go and meet with the forensic team, and they were walking through the building to take their leave and get this scumbag. Wren had a pretty strong sense of justice, but rape cases especially, got her blood boiling. Her thoughts briefly flickered to her friend from university, and she decided when this was over she really should catch up with her.

"WREN! DEV!" A shout echoed down the long corridor, and she turned in alarm at the urgency she heard. DS Matt Ainsworth was running towards them and when he stopped before them he said in a rush of words. "Change of plans, they have your guy." He said between breaths.

"What?" Wren said, shooting a look at Dev for confirmation that she'd heard correctly.

"They've found Vincent…?" Dev asked for clarity.

"Yeah, but it isn't looking like he's coming in for questioning." Matt began to explain, "In fact he's coming in a body bag."

"What?" Wren repeated again, feeling like a moron but she wasn't following, what the hell was happening?

"He's dead." Matt confirmed, "You just won yourselves a trip to the crime scene, the DCI can't be reached, the Super is on her way but she's a way out yet. She told me to send you to get the ball rolling and for you to take Dev to keep you company."

"Well fuck!" Wren blurted. "Where are we going?"

"Not all that far." Matt replied enigmatically.

"Oh, for the love of God! Get to the bloody point!" Wren snapped at him. She didn't have time to play games, they had a scene to get to.

"Sorry, it's over at Stanborough park." Matt said, looking contrite.

"Best we all get a wiggle on then." Wren threw back sharply, not quite ready to let him off the hook.

A muffled laugh came from the side, and she swung her ire-filled gaze to Dev. "Are you fucking serious right now?!" She fumed. "Are you fucking *laughing at me*?" and fury flashed in her eyes.

Dev tried to contain it but when he covered his mouth to smother it, a snort of laughter came from his nose. Wren closed her eyes and counted to ten *really* slowly before taking a breath and speaking through clenched teeth. "Have a word with yourself."

Dev managed to contain his mirth to say, "I'm sorry but, get a wiggle on?" he sputtered again, a second wave of laughter hitting him. With a tear escaping one eye, he tried again. "You were so angry and then said get a wiggle on." *Nope, just nope,* he thought, erupting with another suppressed laugh, before once again pulling himself together enough to finish. "It was just so absurd it hit my funny bone." Dev finally spat out wiping at his eyes.

"I'll hit your damn bone, all right!" she seethed looking at him as if he'd grown a second head and he chuckled again. Wren rolled her eyes and stomped off furiously to the vehicle muttering to herself about men and their childish behaviour. Meanwhile Dev followed along behind her from a safe distance and regained his composure, thinking that probably wasn't the best way to endear himself to her.

By the time she'd reached the car, Wren was decidedly less annoyed and had begun to see the funny side. She opened the door and got in as Dev caught up and entered the vehicle. Sensing that she had calmed down somewhat, he quietly addressed her with a remorseful tone.

"Am I forgiven?" He asked, giving her a playful nudge that made her look over at him. He was looking at her with sad, puppy dog eyes that were so ridiculously exaggerated, she swatted him.

"Fine. I may have overreacted, just a teensy smidge," she conceded begrudgingly.

"No, it was inappropriate, given the circumstances," he admitted, "it was disrespectful and I'm sorry. Just caught me unawares. Are we good?" Giving her a less exaggerated, more sincere puppy dog look.

"Quit it with the eyes already, I said we're fine." she berated with an exasperated smile. "Now let's see about this crime scene." With that they buckled in, and she started the engine.

When they arrived at Stanborough park Wren pulled up to the parking area to find it had been closed off, two officers standing patiently, guarding it from the public. Wren noted that it was a lot quieter in the area without free public access and then groaned aloud.

"What?" Dev asked, with concern.

"Fucking fair is set up, we are going to have a hell of a time with people coming to visit the fair. Never mind all the shit lying around to sift through. The SOCO team is going to have a shit fit." She replied with discomfort.

"Feck!" Dev swore with realisation, dragging his hand through his hair unconsciously and pushing it back from his face.

One of the officers approached the vehicle, so she wound down the window and leaned out a little so they could talk. After showing her I.D. and informing them of the Super's instruction, he walked back and waved them through. After exiting the vehicle, Ash approached.

"You made it then. No dickhead?" he asked.

"Not yet," Wren confirmed, bemused by his use of the DCI's nickname. "Though probably best if you use his actual name on the crime scene. He's bound to be here sharpish when they manage to get hold of him. The Super's on the way though. Has the coroner's office been informed?" she enquired.

"Yeah, just under an hour ago. They're sending out the Divisional Surgeon. The photographer and the pathologist are also en route." Ash informed her, nodding back the way he'd come, "I'll take you over to the scene site."

They walked through to the park itself and Wren observed the tent erected just on the edge of where the fair was situated. A few officers were stationed around the area, ensuring that it wasn't disturbed so as not to incur the wrath of the SOCO team on arrival. As they reached the periphery, Dev asked the question Wren had been dying to ask yet hadn't gotten around to.

"How bad is it?"

"Well, it isn't pretty, that's for sure. A strange one no question," he said, screwing his face up in distaste.

"We're here!" A flustered voice came from behind them, turning towards it Wren saw the group approaching. She'd met both Katarina and Jodie before and was glad they were in attendance, both were efficient and adept, the third person she hadn't met. He was a short, stout man and with the camera he was clutching she assumed he was the photographer. They were all geared up and ready to go, as both Wren and Dev began pulling on protective footwear and gloves, preparing themselves for the scene. With Katarina, and the Divisional Surgeon in tow, they entered the tent. The detectives allowed Katarina to approach first while they surveyed the scene uncomfortably.

"Bejesus Christ!" Dev exclaimed, and Wren could get on board with that assessment.

"Oh, he is *definitely* dead. One hundred percent dead. No question." Katarina confirmed, getting up and exiting the tent while Dev and Wren stared at Vinnie. He was laid out with no shirt and barefoot but still wearing trousers. From the waist up to his neck, he appeared to be black with white matter scattered over the top. His arms were similarly decorated as far down as his wrists anyway, where his hands appeared to be untouched, except for the tips of his fingers, which appeared to be missing. His face also seemed mostly untouched, but his eyes were covered with what looked like money and the piece-de-resistance was the bullet hole smack dab in the centre of his forehead. There appeared to be no blood to speak of which was odd in itself.

The photographer entered and took his time photographing the scene as they watched on, careful not to disturb anything. As he began to finish up he looked up and nodded in greeting to the pathologist entering behind them.

"Well, that is something."

Wren started as Jodie Malone spoke. The pathologist looked to Dev and said matter of factly. "I don't believe we've met. I'm Doctor Jodie Malone, I'm the pathologist assigned today."

"DI Devlin Doyle." He responded with a nod.

"Ahh nice to meet you, Triple D." Jodie replied and headed to the body.

Wren pulled a face and snarked, "Triple D? What's with you and the weird ass nicknames. Should I tell her about your dimples, we can round them off and just call you 4D after your big square head," she mocked.

"Big square head? Bit harsh, Angel." Dev retorted without thinking.

"What did you call me?" Wren said, raising her eyes in surprise.

"Forget about it," he muttered and addressed Jodie. "So, the white shite...is that rice?"

"Looks like," she agreed, "but I can't confirm it right now." She went back to assessing the body taking samples.

"One other thing," Dev continued "Why's his top half black? Is he burnt? He doesn't smell burnt."

"It appears to be a sticky substance, could be tar but that usually goes hard. Mind you it is warm. I'll have to get back to you on that when I know more. Though if they were going for a "tar and feather" thing, have they never seen a feather before?" she joked. "Although they do appear to have had better luck identifying a gun." She plucked the coins from his eyes and let out a gasp and muttered, "Didn't see that coming. Get over here Carl. I need pictures."

"What didn't you see coming dear?" The voice of the Super called, once again startling the two DI's.

"Doesn't anybody knock anymore," Dev jested as she entered the tent.

The Super subjected him to a cool glance and asked for an update. Wren proceeded to give her an overview of the situation while Jodie and the photographer co-ordinated themselves, in the background. As Wren drew to a close and the Super had all she needed, she dismissed them from the scene instructing them on their new tasks, before they left the tent and went on their way.

Chapter Eight

Keri walked into her home and dropped the keys into a bowl on a table along the entrance way. Her fiancé, Cameron, sauntered in her direction. Picking her up and playfully swinging her around before setting her back on her feet. He leaned down to give her a quick kiss on the cheek and she greeted him with her news.

"Did you hear? She asked.

"Hear about what, my Keri-blossom? He returned, wrapping his arms closed around her and kissing her neck, clearly in a particularly good mood today.

"Enough of that," she snapped reproachfully, playfully swatting him about the head, "This is serious, Jack's called for a meeting." she told him, referring to her father. Cameron straightened at that, his eyes going sharp and predatorial.

"Oh, he did, did he? He began, "Is this about our poor dear friend, Vinnie?" He queried, sarcasm enunciating the word "friend" in his sentence.

"It would seem he met with a most unfortunate accident." She replied feigning a sob, before breaking out into a gleeful chuckle when she couldn't keep up the act.

"Never did like that guy, he gave me the fucking creeps. Won't lie, I'm glad he's dead now." Cameron added. "So, what's the meeting for? He's not upset that he's dead, is he?"

At this Keri laughed out loud. "Oh no, my heart, far from it, he never liked that weasel from day dot. He had these delusions of grandeur that Jack just couldn't stand, Vinnie really thought he was hot shit. No, he's more concerned about the way things are unfolding. He's even considering bringing in "The Executioner."

He's called for your father so that they can discuss the idea." Keri informed him,

"Well, isn't that going to be a barrel of laughs, that guy is about as mad as a march hare." Cameron commented.

"Oh, he's far more dangerous than that, my heart. He's crafty and unscrupulous. You are fortunate indeed if you come into his crosshairs and live to talk about it." she said, as Cameron paused to consider this new development.

"Will he get in the way?" He asked, frowning.

"Only if we allow him to." She said, smiling deviously.

"And are we allowing him to?" Cameron mused and chuckled.

"Let's wait and see how it unfolds before we decide." She answered.

With that settled, she permitted him to sweep her up and kiss her passionately as he carried her up the stairs to the bedroom.

****

It had been a long forty-eight hours with little sleep and a lot going on. After leaving the tent, Dev took a moment and realised the pathologist had never actually told them what she hadn't seen coming. Wren was currently speaking to Ash, getting information on the pedestrian who had been unlucky enough to stumble upon Vinnie's body.

The rest of the crime scene team, otherwise known as the SOCO team, had arrived, some groaning over the location and how long it was all going to take to process. They were getting started on the area surrounding the tent until the pathologist had finished dealing with the body.

Dev, left to his own devices, had taken a moment to consider the things he knew. He'd already ascertained that they had at least got a time frame for them to work with for the murder. They had seen Vinnie themselves just yesterday, not quite twenty-four hours ago. So that narrowed down the time in which the death could have occurred. He took out his notebook as he also realised that had Vinnie been holed up at the girlfriend's house as they'd formally suspected, they could likely narrow that timeline down even further, maybe gauge where he'd been taken from. It was clear that he had been taken, this location couldn't be where the actual crime had been committed. He was no pathologist but even he could see the lack of blood in what had likely been a blood bath. Also, the rice was curious. And despite what the pathologist had said about there being no definite, until it was confirmed, Dev suspected there wasn't much you could mistake for rice. Also, what was the tar-like substance about? It didn't matter how much he thought about it he couldn't explain it. If they tarred him, why only the top half? And he was bare chested, was barefoot...then why were his trousers still on? Not that Dev was complaining mind you.

Wren returned from talking to Ash and hitched a shoulder off to the side, indicating where a short, grey-haired woman sat on a wall just outside the perimeter. Her eyes were red and puffy but any distress she'd initially displayed before their arrival had waned, however the fear remained in her gaze. "That's our pedestrian," Wren said unnecessarily.

They walked over to her and the officers with her nodded and moved away to make room so they could speak to her.

"Good morning," Wren began, "Miss Thompson is it?" And the woman nodded. "Well Miss Thompson, I'm DI Jones and this is DI Doyle, we're here to take a statement from you."

"Oh, I thought the nice young man I spoke to earlier had done that already." She said, confused.

"He did speak to you, to get a preliminary report, but it's our job to go through your statement in greater detail so we can get a clearer picture of this morning's events." Wren explained, kindly. Her face had gone soft which had a calming effect on the woman.

For the next forty minutes or so, the woman gave her account of her morning leading up to the discovery of the body. Unfortunately, from the statement given they weren't really any closer to having any idea how Vincent had ended up at the park dead or who had committed the crime. There were of course some suspects with cause to want him dead, but to Dev's mind the two they currently had knowledge of were either in hospital or seemed unlikely to be able to not only overpower Vinnie but also to move his body either with him conscious or unconscious.

CID were now left to take over the crime scene and with this part of their job done they left for the station to check in with the incident room. Having been gone for the best part of the day they hadn't yet been in to see what information, if any, had been found throughout the day that they had yet to be updated on. With the Super in attendance at the scene, the DCI had taken charge back at the station; gathering all the computer information they could, checking out any footage they'd managed to find, and adding anything of interest noted in the area from nearby homes and witness accounts taken from anyone who could be found, besides the person who'd found the body. We had that part for all the good it would do. There would eventually be the preliminary report from the crime scene and the actual report would follow, but with SOCO still combing the crime scene and the body not long being taken from the tent, it would be some hours before that particular update would be ready.

With that in mind the only thing they could achieve now was to see what suspects Jen had dredged up, ranging from people who had dealings with Vincent, to people who had reported him through a crime he'd committed. The person from the aggravated assault charge might be worth a look and there were of course the many assaults on women they'd been investigating him for when this had all gone down. The women might be less likely, with the chances of them actually being able to move the body being harder for them to achieve, it seemed more plausible there may be some significant others out there who would take their partners being assaulted as a just cause for violence.

DC Matt Ainsworth was currently en route to have a chat with Charlene Dalton ordered by the DCI after Dev had rung him from the scene to suggest it. Having an accurate timeline of Vinnie's movements would help with narrowing down the suspects some. The remaining part of the afternoon consisted of various notes being added to the whiteboard and digging up as much information as possible. So far they had at least five victims of assault that may or may not have been perpetrated by Vinnie, however with his DNA now being processed, confirmation of this with any DNA taken from the rape kits some of the victims had agreed to, meant they would at the very least know if they'd had the right man for those crimes. Even if the man was currently on the slab in a pathologists lab. It didn't exactly make for what you could call a successful way to wrap up the case but from the victims' perspectives at least they would finally find some peace of mind, knowing the guy who'd taken so much from them was now permanently unable to continue ruining the lives of others.

There was also the chance that there were other victims who hadn't come forward. In cases of rape, many victims didn't want to report it for various reasons, none of which he could blame them for. It came with many stigmas and a brutal process of finding evidence that could be contested in most cases if the perpetrator claimed it was consensual. If the attack itself hadn't caused enough trauma then the process of prosecution and the subsequent defamation of their character in courts often meant a less than satisfactory conclusion for the victims who made it that far. Many more were dropped without ever making it as far as court simply due to lack of evidence or the victim themselves letting it drop. It was a part of his job that Dev found particularly hard. He wanted to help, put in as much groundwork as he could and at the end, more times than not, the results did not work out in their favour.

The few other suspects lining the board consisted of Alma, though having met her he wasn't inclined to believe that to be the case. Not because he liked her, though he did but because she had endured years of what he could imagine to be mass amounts of abuse and had finally managed to get free from his clutches.

While he could see that she had the motive, she'd still seemed pretty afraid of him, and he just couldn't see her as the person committing this crime.

Of course, Charlene too had made the suspect list. It seemed there had been some disagreement between them earlier in the week about a barmaid Vinnie had been giving too much attention to. He'd also visited his ex, which would be quite the slap to the face if she had found out. All in all, she did look good for it on paper. Most times, murder was usually committed by a person the victim knew, though he was loath to use the word victim in the same sentence as Vinnie. There was also the victim of the aggravated assault. A man who'd been in the Rose and Crown only a year prior, he'd had a less than subtle dig at Vinnie and when his back was turned had been on the receiving end of the knife Vinnie seemed to favour.

Overall, Dev found it unlikely that any of the women on the board could have murdered Vinnie alone. Been a party to it, now that was possible, but with the change of locations and disposal of the body, it would've taken quite some strength. They may not have had this issue getting him if they'd lured him somehow, but they certainly would have had some issues once he was dead. With the body being a deadweight.

The DCI headed back into the room, he'd left briefly for the preliminary report from the pathologist. While the analysis part would take longer the initial overview of findings would give them a place to start. He addressed the room, and everyone stopped what they were doing to give him their full attention.

"The preliminary report is in and there are a few things to note from what Dr Malone has divulged without the need of analysis. The first thing she noted was her estimation of time of death. The short version is between 4-6 hours prior to the bodies discovery, so pretty fresh which we knew. A few things we didn't know though. She believes the official cause of death is likely to be the bullet to the head, however there were other severe wounds found that may have ultimately caused his death if not for the bullet. While taking a sample of the tar-like substance on the top half of his body, Malone discovered that beneath it, the skin that should've been there was not."

"The skin was missing?" Wren interrupted, seemingly unclear on exactly what he was getting at. Dev too had questions, so he waited for the DCI to answer.

"It seems the entire top half spanning from the neck down the back, front and arms was removed with what she believes to be a knife." He clarified. Wren opened her mouth to say more but the DCI continued. "Before you ask, let me tell you, this assessment was based on the fact that the knife was discovered during the examination. She believes it to be a fit for the markings left during the skinning process but will confirm once further analysis has been done. Furthermore, it appears that the knife may have belonged to the victim. She found an engraving with the victim's initials carved into the handle."

"Where was the knife found on the body, when I was at the scene I don't recall seeing it?" Dev couldn't help but ask.

"A very astute question, DI Doyle, it was discovered after his trousers and briefs were removed lodged into the opening of his rectum. After removing said knife, Dr Malone found extensive damage to the cavity and signs of a significant amount of rectal bleeding." He replied and the room seemed to give a collective wince at the answer.

"So, do I have this straight," Matt pitched in. "He was skinned and fucked with his own knife?"

"The short answer to that very direct and crudely descriptive question, is yes." The DCI said coldly. "Other things she noted were the two penny pieces found on each eye. They themselves were not an usual thing to find at a murder scene but what she discovered upon removing them, she found to be surprising. On examination it would appear the eyelids had been sewn shut, and when she unstitched them his eyes were gone."

"We'll just add that to the list of fucked up things that happened to this guy." Ash muttered.

"The substances that were taken from the body have left for analysis and she will try to get it back at the earliest opportunity. With luck, something useful will come from those. Also, the DNA samples have been sent for analysis in conjunction with other DNA collected from existing cases believed to have been perpetrated by our victim. Now with all that said, I believe we should wrap it up for the night and begin fresh again in the morning. Some, if not all of you have been going on this for longer than expected and a good night's rest will see you able to focus all the better on this in the morning. Have a good evening." The DCI said before sweeping out of the incident room, leaving his sidekick to get busy updating an ever-growing mountain of information on the whiteboards.

The room began to empty, and Dev started walking to his car. Outside Wren had been accosted by some press lingering by the entrance. The only good thing about being new was that nobody knew his face here, so he sidled around without much notice being paid to him, listening as Wren made several "no comments" before she managed to get to her own vehicle. He'd just sat in his seat and began closing the door when he heard her voice from across the lot. "See you in the morning 4D." Dev found himself smiling as made his way home.

Chapter Nine

Jack McNamara waited impatiently for his partner to arrive, he'd called a meeting to discuss recent events and to plan their next moves in order to get ahead of the game. He'd only gathered the inner circle together, it wasn't necessary for everyone to be involved. A lot of them would have no knowledge of the events which had transpired twenty-four years prior, so having them present wouldn't add anything relevant, therefore he had decided on a need-to-know approach. Twenty-four years prior he hadn't been quite so influential or as experienced as he was in this day and age, therefore he was concerned that his past actions might not have been quite so tidy in the clean-up department.

Currently seated in the office he had the employees who'd been around at the time, the four brothers: Tommy, Paul, Les, and Sean, he had also invited Marco and his partner's son, Cameron. They just needed Connor to arrive, and they could get on with this shit. He didn't have all day, he had important shipments to arrange. Connor O'Reilly finally entered the room looking slightly dishevelled.

"Sorry I'm late, Jack. There were some unexpected hold ups with the merchandise, it's sorted now though." He explained, then to his son said, "Hey boyo."

"Da," Cameron acknowledged with a nod of respect.

"Right let's move things along shall we? Jack demanded. "I'll cut straight to the chase, since I have a lot of work to do, and we're already behind. I had a visitor the other night and I heard some news that troubled me."

"Is it about Vinnie's death?" Connor asked conversationally.

"No. That eejit was bound to get his ticket punched eventually, throwing his weight around like he was something special. No care about whether he cleaned up behind himself or not. If he hadn't been offed, he'd be in nick now. The police weren't far behind him. He had his uses to be sure, until he didn't. No, I heard Keir Whelan has made an appearance, if my information is to be believed." He announced.

"Wasn't the boy supposed to be dead?" Conor asked.

"Aye he was, maybe he is. I have yet to get confirmation on that." Jack replied.

Originally when they'd arranged for "The Executioner" to deliver the boy to his father, before ending him permanently, the plan had been to allow the boy to live since the debt had been paid in both money and blood. However, after a few days had passed, Jack had felt uneasy about the decision. He had thought at the time that with the lad only being eight what harm could it do to let him live, he would know well enough the cost of crossing them. But then there'd been that little voice nagging him that said he'd seen their faces, could identify them should he choose to, except for Connor and "The Executioner" most of the people present in the room had had dealings with the boy during his extended stay.

He had therefore changed his mind about letting the boy go free and chose instead to arrange for him to be eliminated. He had been assured that this had come to pass. Yet here he was, twenty-four years later, being told that he was wandering about like the ghost of fucking Christmas past. He realised he'd let his thoughts carry him away when he saw the room looking at him, collectively awaiting him to proceed, so he continued.

"I have had Marco here, sending out feelers but as yet nobody has heard anything about him. Nobody called Kier Whelan has reached any of the ears on the ground at this time. I am considering bringing in "The Executioner" though," Jack divulged.

"Achh, no Jack!" Conor exclaimed "We don't even have proof that he lives yet. You may be jumping the gun here. "The Executioner" is a last resort deal, you don't want to be getting too thick with him. He's a loose cannon, so don't fire it without expecting the blowback."

"That's well and good for you, you had no dealings with the lad, I can see why you are less than enthusiastic involving him. I wonder, though, if the rest of you feel that way." Jack said, addressing the room, looking at Marco before he continued," I'm quite sure he'd recognise you, Marco, considering what he saw you do the last time he saw you. What about you brothers? Reckon he'd be unlikely to have forgotten your part in it either." The men shuffled in their seats uncomfortably, and Marco answered first.

"It's been over twenty years now. If he were going to try and shop us, wouldn't he have done it sooner?"

"The eldest of the brothers, spoke up next. "I agree, Boss. Why don't we hold fire to see if he is even alive before we go to extremes. If he is and he does have plans to shop us, then we can call in the cavalry."

Jack didn't like it, he didn't like loose ends and he trusted his gut feelings. He sensed that this boy could be trouble. He supposed though, they did have a point. It had been over two decades ago, chances are they would be drawing more attention to themselves by killing him in the here and now, than copping it for a cold case murder from that far back. There was also the chance that he was indeed dead. Might be best all-around to let sleeping dogs lie until they stopped sleeping. Having come to a decision he spoke once more.

"You might be right, maybe it is better to stay our hand for the time being. Come on, let's get back to work and organise those shipments."

****

Keri stopped what she was doing when her phone rang, seeing it was Cameron she accepted the call and waited for him to give her good news.

"Good evening, my little Keri-blossom. It's taken care of, Da took the bait and the execution has been stayed, no pun intended." he chuckled.

"I knew I could count on you, my heart." Keri cooed down the line.

"I'm on my way home, wait for me." he demanded suggestively.

"I don't know, my heart, I'm a bad girl. I rarely like to do as I'm told. Will I be punished?" She teased breathily.

"Oh, you will be thoroughly punished," he responded, "Soon, my love, I'll be there soon." he warned.

"I'm sure you will," she taunted salaciously.

Keri hung up and smiled to herself. Men were so extremely easy to manipulate. Jack and his motley crew were so busy running around chasing ghosts that they were no longer watching what was happening right under their own noses. It may be about time dear old dad got his just desserts. A spell in prison would be good for him, a chance to repent his sins before he left the earth, lord knows he was getting on in years. Yes it was definitely time for a new era, a new broom sweeps clean after all. With Cameron free to take the reins and her beside him pulling the strings. It really couldn't have come at a better time, the perfect diversion really.

****

Several hours later Marco Salvador had finished helping the boss prepare the shipments and strolled uneasily to his car. Being part Spanish, he was more than a little superstitious and all the talk of ghosts had him on edge. He thought back and remembered what he'd been like two decades ago, when he was younger and had something to prove. He'd been much more ruthless then, short on cash and looking for any way to make money fast. He'd fallen in with the McNamara's who were just starting to make a name for themselves and had wanted a slice of that pie. He hadn't really considered all he'd done to get to the position he now enjoyed and though he didn't regret it, looking back he wasn't sure all of his actions had been completely necessary.

With a family of his own now, a wife and a young son, he did find himself occasionally regretting his part in that particular event. He blamed his age at the time and his drug habit. Young people never considered how their actions may affect others. The others had encouraged it, egged him on and he'd found himself going along for the ride.

His wife didn't like his work, with a young son to consider, she'd been steadily increasing the pressure, urging him to quit and go straight. Maybe the boy's reappearance was a sign that it was time to get out while the going was good. He'd just finish this last job and then have a talk with the boss. Or maybe he should instead work out an escape plan and just disappear. No telling how the boss would react to the idea of him quitting. He could send his wife off ahead of him with their son and then catch them up when he could. He entered the vehicle and as he sat at the wheel and closed the door he felt a pinprick of pain in his neck and the world faded away.

****

Dev woke up with a start. He was bathed in sweat and his heart raced. For a few moments he was unable to move as terror clung to him, though the memory of why eluded him. As he finally managed to slow his breathing from the quick panicked draws he'd been taking when he'd first woken, he felt the panic recede and he looked around. His bed was twisted in disarray, and he found himself wondering why, after so many years, he was once again having the nightmares he had suffered with so long ago. He was dressed and couldn't quite recall why he hadn't removed his clothes. As he pondered this puzzle, he considered that perhaps it was exhaustion. He'd barely slept at all in the last forty-eight hours, no more than two hours sleep and was running mostly on adrenaline. He also couldn't recall if he'd eaten in the last twenty-four hours either. Maybe that had made him more susceptible to his childhood nightmares.

Standing with a swallow, that was more of a gulp down his dry throat, Dev headed to the kitchen for a glass of water, pondering why his mouth felt like the

Sahra on a dry day. Obviously struggling and writhing in his sleep coupled with the sweat he could smell had likely left him dehydrated. But when he stepped into his front room, he stopped short at the sight of his front door gaping wide open. He automatically went on alert and turned on the lights studying the area around him. Carefully he made his way room to room, cautiously entering as he searched. It wasn't until he reached the bathroom and found he was alone that he managed to relax. Returning to face the door once more, he walked to it looking at it in confusion before closing it, and staring at it while he tried to make sense of it all.

Did he leave it open? He thought back but couldn't remember which only frustrated him further. Nothing seemed to be out of place, and he had little worth taking so he doubted anyone would bother breaking in and if they had he wouldn't have slept through it. The only other option he could come up with was sleepwalking, but he'd seen nothing in his case files alluding to the fact that he'd used to sleepwalk when he'd had the nightmares as a child. With a sinking feeling in his gut, he very much hoped that he hadn't because that could prove a problem with him living on his own. Locking the door, he pulled out his phone and pulled up a number he hadn't rung in a long time. He looked at his watch, he considered the late hour before pressing to ring, knowing him, he was unlikely to be sleeping.

"Brother? Is that you? You don't ring for years, and you choose to change that at 2am randomly out of nowhere? What's going on?" His longtime friend from his old foster family, Stephen, questioned into the phone.

"I'm sorry it's been so long," Dev replied, rubbing the back of his neck sheepishly. "But I have something I need to ask. Do you remember when I used to get those nightmares as a child?"

"Yeah…What about them?" Stephen asked.

"Do you recall if I used to sleepwalk?" Dev probed.

"Not often but on occasion, mostly it was shouting and struggling followed by sitting bolt upright with crazy eyes just staring. Kind of creepy actually, used to freak me the fuck out." Stephen answered with concern in his voice, "Why do you ask?"

"It's happening again…" Dev admitted quietly, unsure what to do with this information.

"The nightmares?" Stephen prompted when he fell quiet.

"Yeah. Maybe sleepwalking too." Dev replied, distractedly.

"Have you considered maybe seeing someone about those?" he enquired gently.

"No, I stopped having them for the most part, a good fifteen years ago." Dev explained, "I'd get the occasional one after a particularly nasty crime scene. Figured it was stress, you know?"

"Are you stressed now?" Stephen pressed gently.

"Not especially, I'm actually a lot happier within myself than I have been for a while now, but I do have a particularly strange case at the moment. Can't give details but I haven't had a lot of sleep in the last few days and something about the victim was bugging me." Dev revealed, reluctantly.

"Can you tell me what's bugging you about it? Or is that privileged information?" Stephen teased lightly.

"No, it isn't restricted per say, he just seemed familiar, think it's from another case I've seen but can't quite remember," Dev tried to explain but found he actually couldn't, "I've disturbed you long enough, sorry for ringing at this unsocial hour, I should let you get off."

"If you're sure you're ok and Dev? Don't be a stranger, ok?" Stephen chastised on a more sombre note, "We should catch up soon, maybe grab a pint?"

"Aye mate, I'd like that." Dev concurred and found that he meant it.

"Look after yourself, Brother." Stephen said.

"Aye, you too." Dev returned before ending the call. He sat there for a while, as his thoughts whirred in his mind, before he decided enough was enough and made his way back to his bedroom. Remaking the destroyed bed so it was once again fit to sleep in, he decided he should try and get some more sleep. He'd have a lot to catch up on in the morning and he obviously needed the rest.

Chapter Ten

2nd August 2014

Wren pulled up to the station bright and early in the morning, to be met with the determined face of a local journalist as she was getting out of her car.

"DI Jones? I'm Wendall Miller from the Welwyn and Hatfield Times. Can you tell me anything about the murder victim discovered at Stanborough Park, yesterday?"

"No comment." she answered in a perfunctory tone.

"When will the victim's name be released to the press?" he continued automatically.

"No comment." Wren repeated.

"Do you have any suspects or leads that may identify the killer? Are the public at risk or is it a targeted crime?" He proceeded without missing a beat.

"No comment." Wren said again, beginning to lose patience.

"Who is the senior investigating officer leading up the inquiry and will there be a press conference?" He pressed.

"Sir," Wren began finally losing her cool, "The SIO will be dealing with the press just as soon as they can, they are dealing with many lines of enquiry at the moment and have yet to determine a time for information to be released to the press. When they have decided I'm sure you will be informed. Now might I suggest you allow me to get to work to investigate it, so they might speed that process along and get to you quicker." At that she pushed past him and entered the station. Once inside Wren headed in the direction of the incident room. On arrival she nodded to Matt and then walked over to Jen who was waving her over.

"Morning love," Jen greeted, presenting her with a mug. "I made you some tea."

Wren gave a small squeal of delight and grabbed for it like it was the holy grail, before asking, "Is there anything new?"

"There isn't much more right now, I have managed to pull together a rough timeline of our murder victim's whereabouts of the night in question, if that helps?" She stated, "Obviously, he was last seen at around 10.30am approximately, by yourself, so that's a good place to begin. The trail goes cold for around an hour or so, which I suspect is due to the high volumes of officers in pursuit. I presume he was likely evading police attention, given that he opened fire in broad daylight and attempted to shoot two officers." Jen gave her an apologetic look.

"So, what have we been doing to try and find him?" Wren asked, knowing that Jen would have been trying alternate ideas to get their man.

"I used the notes taken from your notebook concerning your chat with Alma and took a chance, pulling any surveillance footage I could source from the area surrounding the Rose and Crown. It would seem Vinnie decided to pay it a visit shortly after the incident at Alma's. He stayed there for approximately an hour, before he finally resurfaced in the company of the oldest brother, Paul O'Connell. They exited the pub and got into a vehicle before leaving. I zoomed in on the number plate and then used it to try and track their route and here I almost came up empty but then I hit pay dirt." Jen handed her a series of stills she'd printed off, pulled from the CCTV footage, so she could show her what she had found.

"What are these?" Wren asked, looking through them.

"A camera in the area of the McNamara's abode caught the vehicle, and so considering the intel suggesting the ties between them I suspect they may have paid them a visit. I lost the surveillance trail there I'm afraid, which leaves about an hour and a half to account for, which could indicate they were there for that time. These are stills I took from the footage," Jen explained.

"So where did they reappear?" Wren asked.

"The timeline resumes from the account taken from Charlene by Matt, indicating he arrived at her property where he has been residing, at around 2pm. Where he stayed until just after 10pm, leaving as though his ass were on fire, as she so delicately phrased it. I have put in a request for a warrant to gain access to his phone records, Charlene provided us with his contact number and also indicated he'd received a message seconds before his hasty exit from her building," Jen told her and then continued, "Maybe the records could provide us some idea of where he was heading and from there we could find the location he was taken from. Presuming he was indeed taken and didn't willingly go with the perpetrator."

Wren paused to review the information Jen had provided, then asked, "Is the DCI here?"

"He's currently in a meeting with the Super, probably discussing how they will be distributing officers and when they plan to address the press." Jen surmised.

"What about Dev? I haven't seen him yet either?" She queried, gazing around to see if he was here.

"He phoned in ten minutes ago, he appears to be running behind schedule but is on his way in." Jen informed her.

"Riiight," Wren drawled in disgust. He'd only been here a short while and was already waltzing in whenever he felt like it. It wasn't like there was a murder investigation going on or anything. "I'm thinking we have at least two solid lines of inquiry. One being Paul O'Connell at the Rose and Crown and the other the McNamara's." Wren speculated. "As soon as the DCI is free, I'll float the idea of following up on those, hopefully by then, Dev will have dragged his sorry ass in and have graced us with his presence so we can get on it. If not then Matt can tag along for the ride and Dev can swing his pants until he has his own lead to follow." Her tone became snarky as she finished, "You know, if he can fit his job into his busy schedule."

****

Following his nocturnal activities, Dev had eventually relaxed enough to get back to sleep around 4am. Unfortunately, due to his exhaustion, he'd slept through his alarm and was now running behind. He figured though, that since he was already going to be late he may as well make time for a coffee before he got a shift on to the station. He hastily gulped down a cup, the heat of the liquid burning slightly on its way down, then beat feet to get to his car.

Of course, with him being behind he'd failed to factor in the morning rush hour and was then inescapably detained in traffic. By the time he had frantically flown through the door of the incident room, he'd found it almost empty. Occupying her desk, Jen looked up at him with a reproachful look.

"Well, aren't you a little worse for wear this morning? Perhaps consider straightening your tie and doing something about that shirt, are the buttons done up wrong? Sort yourself out. We are supposed to be professionals here, you know."

"Aye sorry, I had a rough night." Dev said, penitently.

"Anyone I know?" Jen cajoled, playfully.

"No, nothing like that, just had a hard time sleeping, a lot playing on my mind. I managed to fall asleep in the end, only to oversleep, you know how it is." Dev explained defensively, before asking. "Where is everyone?"

"The DCI had a meeting first thing and is now in his office preparing a statement for the press. Ash has gone out to speak to the good Samaritan who found Vinnie's cell phone. Charlene stopped by this morning to hand it in. According to her, the man found it and though it was locked he decided to try the emergency contacts section on the lock screen. He dialled a number there and got Charlene, before arranging to drop it off with her. Ash is trying to locate him so that he might discern what area the phone was found in. He thinks it could be Vinnie's last location before he was taken. Presuming he was taken and didn't go with the killer of his own free will," Jen told him.

"And where's Wren?" Dev asked.

"Wren has gone with Matt to the McNamara's residence and then will be following that up with a trip to the Rose and Crown to speak with Paul O'Connell, following updates to the likely timeline of our victim. Which is where you would've been if you had made it here on time." She finished, giving him a pointed look of disapproval.

"I can't apologise enough," Dev replied, sending her a remorseful, sad puppy look, "What do I have to do to make amends."

"Oh, save that look for Wren, it's wasted on me, Wren is the one with her nose out of joint. She's also the one you'll have to answer to when she gets back here." Jen warned. "However, if you want to have any chance of redeeming yourself, maybe taking the edge off of her wrath, you could help me sift through the messages on Vinnie's phone once I've collected them from the device. Maybe if we find something *really* good she'll forget to be mad at you."

"Aye, put me to work." Dev replied, eagerly. He wasn't particularly fond of the idea of facing Wren in a tizzy.

****

Wren had spent the entire half an hour, while driving over to the McNamara's home, bitching extensively about Dev's poor timekeeping. She'd only realised how much she'd vented, when Matt had taken the opportunity between breaths to jump in and say, "You know, Wren, it's not exactly polite to be so upset that you 'got stuck' with me, when I'm the one you are whining too." He mocked, putting his hands dramatically over his heart before adding, "You're kinda hurting my feelings."

Wren frowned, then guiltily explained, "You know that I didn't mean it that way, it has absolutely no reflection on you in the slightest, I just expected more from him, is all. We're working on a murder investigation, not planning a trip to the seaside. Seems to me to be a good reason to clear your schedule and make it in on damn time." Winding up to begin her tirade again she was stopped by Matt's reply.

"Do you miss him already? Is that why you are behaving like somebody pissed in your cornflakes? He overslept, shit happens, you'll see him later, don't fret." Matt teased.

Wren gave him a glacial stare and flipped him off before flouncing out of the car, Matt's laughter following from behind her. He emerged from the passenger side and walked around to meet her at the front of the vehicle. Due to the fact the Rose and Crown would unlikely be open at this hour, they'd opted to instead begin their inquiries here. They made it as far as the gated entrance and Wren pressed the buzzer.

"Who is it?" A cold voice came over the loudspeaker above the buzzer button.

"Sorry to trouble you ma'am, we're police. I'm DI Jones and my associate is DS Ainsworth. We have some questions if you don't mind." Wren responded to the voice in the box.

"Very well, I'll send someone down to collect you."

A short time later, a burly man arrived at the gate and led them to a garden area at the back of the house. Sitting ahead a ways, perusing them with bored disinterest, was Mary McNamara. She waved at them to sit before addressing them.

"Good morning, detectives. I hope you don't mind sitting here in the garden, we're having some work done inside and it's in a bit of a state at this time. Is this going to take long? Only I have to leave shortly, I have a hair appointment to get to." She greeted, belligerently offering them a sour smile.

"I'm sure it won't take up too much of your time, Mrs McNamara. We wouldn't want to inconvenience you, we know how precious your time is." Wren replied with saccharine sweetness, politely offering an insincere smile in return.

"Very well, ask away," she said and waited for them to begin. Matt took out his notebook and nodded to Wren to say he was ready.

"We have reason to believe that Vincent Walker and Paul O'Connell were in this area yesterday at approximately 12.30pm. Could you tell us if they perhaps paid a visit to you here at that time?" Wren queried.

"Why would they have been here?" Mary returned innocently.

"We have it on good authority that they are acquaintances of yours?" Wren explained and then pressed, "With that being the case it is safe to assume if they are acquaintances and in the area, they may decide to pay a visit."

"You know what they say, detective, to assume makes an ass of you and me." She derided, "We are acquainted with Paul, yes. Vincent not so much; he isn't exactly the type of man we usually entertain. More of a passing acquaintance if you will."

"So, they weren't here yesterday?" Wren repeated, deflecting her attempt at evasion.

"Not as far as I'm aware, I'm afraid." Mary hedged once again." They may have been in the area but whatever they were doing, they weren't doing it here. I'm sure Paul could have some idea though since he was the one in the area. Have you asked Paul?" She smiled again but it didn't reach her serpent-like eyes, which remained cold and unblinking.

"We will be speaking to him, yes," Wren confirmed.
"Then might it be a better use of your time to start there?" she inferred, smugly.
"As I said, we intend to, before we go though, is there anything you can tell us that might help us with our enquiries?" Wren tried one last time.
"Such as?" Mary asked, her tone indicating she was out of patience.
"Anything you may be able to give us in connection with Vincent's recent movements? Anything that might be relevant and could offer leads that may open other avenues for us to explore." Wren probed.
"I'm afraid not, like I said, I don't really know the man." Mary stated, unmoving.
"In that case, Mrs McNamara, we're sorry to have troubled you. One last thing. Is your husband here?" Wren pried.
"I'm afraid not, he's out at this time. I'm sorry I couldn't be of more help. I do hope you find what you are looking for." She said dismissively, indicating she was done, then directed her attention to the burly man who was still in attendance not far away. "Be a dear and see them out, would you?" She instructed before giving a final look and sauntering off.
Once they'd been escorted back to the gate, left the premises and were out of earshot Matt muttered, "Well that was a monumental waste of our time."
Wren nodded before adding, "At the very least, if we find cause to contest her statement, we could arrest her for obstruction. That is something we can hold on to."
Matt laughed. "Yeah, that would certainly make the trip out here worthwhile.
Wren checked the time and deliberated aloud. "Do you suppose that the Rose and Crown will be open now or

do you think it's still too early? If so, we could stop and get some tea while we wait."

"I think it's better to give it another half hour or so just to be sure, I wouldn't say no to a cuppa, and I wouldn't turn down a bite to eat either." Matt replied thoughtfully.

"Moreno's Café?" Wren suggested.

"I think that's a fine idea." Matt concurred, enthusiastically.

****

Jen had finally managed to recover the text messages from Vinnie's phone and was passing pages she'd printed off over to Dev. He was sitting next to her sifting through them, while she loaded up the search on her monitor in case they found anything they could use. Dev decided it best to begin with the last message he'd received and read aloud. "They're coming." Dev paused, confused, "What do you suppose that's about?"

"I'm not sure." Jen replied while logging onto the system, and typing in the number as she did, "but the number isn't registered. It's a burner."

"Ok, so was someone warning him or threatening him? If they were threatening him, we can presume he knows who it is. If not and it's a warning, who were they warning him about?" Dev debated.

"Hard to say, considering he was murdered shortly after. We were closing in, without the warning we likely would've caught up to him at home. If they knew we were searching for Charlene's address, they could have assumed we would have been along sooner or later." Jen surmised then frowned and said, "but how would they have known that? Could we have a leak?"

"Let's not borrow trouble on that front just yet, we haven't even figured out if it was warning him about us or somebody else. We can worry about that when we have more to go on." Dev replied, looking at the messages above it and began reading the next one. "I need to see the boss."

Jen looked at the call logs to where the number of the phone logged as the text's recipient was displayed. Vincent had received a call-in response from the same number, not long after. She ran the number through the system and shook her head again.

"I've got nada." She grimaced. "Could we assume the text refers to Jack McNamara? Would he be the 'boss' he mentions?"

"Aye, we could assume it, but we can't prove it." Dev shrugged and moved on.

"Rose, this is Vincent. I'm trying to reach Marco, but he isn't answering. Can you pass him the message, it's important he contacts me." He recited, and a feeling in his gut told him this might be the message they'd been looking for, "We have some names, don't suppose you can find who they belong to in that computer?" Dev probed.

"On it!" Jen said, nodding as her fingers tapped keys at an alarming rate as she searched. "Bingo! Marco Salvador fits the criteria, he's affiliated with the McNamara's and has a sister named Rosa." she crowed, victoriously.

"Do we have addresses to go with these names? Dev asked hopefully.

"We do indeed." she smiled smugly, "I'll write them down for you."

"Marvellous! You're a star. So, I'll update the Super and then if you fancy it, we could go for a drive?" He suggested.

"If it's all the same to you, love, I would be best working on this end, following up on the leads we have." She declined kindly, before indicating Ash who was approaching them, "looks like Ash is free though."

"Free for what?" He asked, catching the tail end of their conversation.

"Jen will catch you up," Dev said, "I'll go and see the Super." Standing quickly, he headed for the door without delay.

Chapter Eleven

Marco woke with his head swimming and feeling as heavy as lead, what had happened? Was he ill? He fought the wave of nausea that hit him as his mind whirled around disjointedly in a combination of confusion and chaos. Slowly the spinning subsided enough for him to refocus his thoughts on his current situation. He didn't recall feeling ill earlier when he'd left...wait, where had he left? Another wave of nausea rose, and his mind clouded over, and suddenly he was unable to find the will to chase the train of his thoughts. Darkness overwhelmed him, and he fought for a few long moments, drowning in it, before he let it take him.

When Marco roused again his dizzying mind had slowed. How long had he been out? Had it been hours? Days? He took a few steadying breaths and cold air filled him, he WAS ill. He shivered as the cold air crept along his veins, settling into his weary bones and he found that he didn't have the strength to shake it off. As he lay there, for how long he couldn't say, the cold finally gave him clarity. Where was he? He fought to open his eyes but found that he couldn't. He tried again....nothing. He finally accepted that he was unable to do so and allowed his mind to go back, if he couldn't ascertain where he was, where had he been? At last, he had a fleeting flash of memory; he'd been leaving the meeting and entering his car, that was when the dizziness had begun. But how did he get from the car to here? He surely hadn't managed it himself. Maybe somebody had assisted him? Called an ambulance? Where were they now? He paused to listen...the silence was deafening...so he wasn't in a hospital. He strained to listen more closely.

Dripping.

He could hear dripping. He tried to move but he couldn't, so he tried once again to open his eyes and this time he felt a tug of resistance. What was that? He tried again putting more effort into the action and again he felt a pulling sensation at various points across his eyelids. He cast his mind back, trying to remember if he'd felt it the first time he'd gained consciousness. He tried once more; the strange sensation felt familiar. As his mind raced trying to puzzle it out, it dawned on him, and ice cold fear took hold of him. Panic made the air lodge in his throat and he fought to move, to claw at it, but his struggles were to no avail... He wasn't too ill to move, he'd been restrained. He battled for breath, his chest heaving with the need to get oxygen into his lungs and as air whooshed in he took it in sharp, tight pants. The realisation that had struck him, stealing his breath in terror, hit him a second time. His eyes were unable to open not because he was too weak to do so but because they'd been sewn shut.

****

Wren and Matt walked into the Rose and Crown and were greeted by the unfriendly stares of its patrons. As they approached the bar they found one of the O'Connell brothers waiting for them, leaning with his palms on the bar surface and as they neared he addressed them.

"What can I do for you fine officers this morning?" he said with an underlying note of sarcasm and more than a little unfriendliness.

"I'm sorry to trouble you Mr O'Connell, sorry I'm not sure which one you are…" Wren began and waited for him to give her his given name. It never came though so she continued, "I am DI Jones, and my colleague here is DS Ainsworth, and we would like to speak to your brother Paul if we could."

"Why?" he asked.

"We are following up on intel we have in regards to Vincent Walker, and we have reason to believe that at approximately 12.30 yesterday afternoon he was with your brother Paul, heading to an unknown location and we would like to determine where he was for the purposes of our enquiries." She answered, then asked again, "Could we speak to him?"

The brother didn't reply, instead leaving the bar and heading into the back.

"Was that a no?" Matt joked. When he'd been gone more than a few minutes Matt asked. "Do you think he's coming back?"

Before Wren could answer, the elder brother appeared and gave a jerk of his head to indicate they should enter the back. Wren looked at Matt unsure, but when he shrugged and moved to enter she followed.

"My brother tells me you have some questions." Paul stated as they entered a kitchenette.

"That's right, Sir." Matt answered.

"What would you like to know?" He asked.

"We are trying to ascertain Vincent's movements yesterday. We have it on good authority that he was with you between 12.30pm and 2pm. Could you tell me what you were doing at this time?" Wren probed.

"He wanted to see me because he thought he saw a ghost." Paul laughed but Wren didn't get the joke.

"I'm sorry?" she said, hoping he would enlighten her.

"He thought he saw someone who was dead." Paul rephrased but it changed nothing, she still didn't understand.

"Who did he think was dead?" Matt chipped in, helpfully.

"Some kid who died about twenty-four years ago." Paul replied.

"Do you have a name?" Matt asked, while Wren was still trying to figure out what this had to do with their whereabouts.

"Na he didn't say. He was freaked out and said he saw a ghost and we went off to check out an old area so I could help calm him down. Convince him that he wasn't being haunted." Paul reeled off.

"Were you aware that he was averting arrest for using a firearm in a public place with the intention of causing harm to the officers there?" Wren asked confrontationally.

"Why would I know anything about that? He didn't tell me he had, just came to tell me he could see dead people." Paul joked.

"Ok, so do you know of any reason somebody might want him dead?" Wren pressed, trying a new approach.

"Yeah, plenty. He wasn't exactly a popular guy. I've no doubt you have quite the list of suspects without my help." Paul answered.

"We do," Wren confirmed, "Can you think of anything that might have happened recently, like within the last week or so?"

"Not really, I don't envy you trying to figure it out either. Vin upset so many people, it would be a shorter list if you were to ask who didn't want him dead." Paul said.

"Right… Is there anything you can tell us that can help our enquiries at all?" Wren asked with exasperation.

"If I could, I would've said so." Paul remarked.

"Going back to the dead person, where did you go to help convince him he wasn't seeing dead people?" Wren asked, trying to better fill in the strange testimony that was still baffling her.

"Cemetery, the kid's buried there." Paul shrugged.

"Ok then," Matt said, "I think we're done here, thank you for your time."

"No worries. I'll show you out," he replied politely and opened the door back into the bar.

As they left the bar, Wren grumbled under her breath.

"What did you say?" Matt queried.

"I said, that was the weirdest fucking excuse I've ever heard." She fumed.

"Sometimes, the weird answers are the most truthful ones," Matt countered.

"You believe him?" Wren asked in disbelief.

"I think there was some truth there, was it the whole truth? Probably not, but I didn't get the sense he was entirely fabricating it either."

Wren said nothing, she didn't even know where to begin with that.

****

Marco had been at this for hours, his wrists were raw and bloodied from attempting to get loose from his bonds and he'd likely pulled a muscle in his legs. Thrashing in a bid to free himself, they now throbbed painfully as he lay still. Exhausted and desolate, his thoughts turned to something other than escaping. Who had done this? He knew he had enemies, but would any of them be this bold, to dare this? When the others learned of it there would be hell to pay. A path of destruction and death, the likes of which they couldn't even begin to fathom would follow and when they were found, the price would be a costly, and painful one. However, not even this could offer him any solace, as he was unlikely to be there to bear witness to it.

"Hello?" He called out for the umpteenth time. He had yet to see his assailant.

When no answer came, he gave himself a mental shake, all was not lost yet. There was still a chance he would be found, maybe he had something he could offer for his release? No, he soothed himself, until he knew who and why, it wasn't over, nothing had been done that could not be undone. It could be that this was a demonstration of power to garner his attention and make him understand that they were playing to win. The cost of his freedom could very well be compliance, if so then they would have his undivided attention. Once he was free he could concern himself with how he planned to repay that favour, but until that time he needed to remain calm and be patient.

A noise startled him from his thoughts… the sound of slow approaching footsteps. Finally! It was about time they made an appearance.

"Who's there?" He demanded.

The steps stopped and an acute feeling of being watched hit him, but no answer came. He waited with bated breath as his captor resumed their movements. Strange sounds he couldn't distinguish passed in a flurry of motion and in a rush to slow it, he once again addressed air.

"What do you want?"

Again, no reply followed.

"Is it money? I have money!" His companion continued as though they hadn't heard.

"Not money?! I…i…information? D...do you want information?" He stuttered over the words as they tumbled from his dry mouth in desperation. When he was met with more silence, frustration and anger bubbled up and he all but shouted. "WHY AM I HERE?!"

Quietly his keeper drew in a breath and began humming an eerie, familiar tune. It danced along his nerve endings, chasing down his spine in a slow macabre waltz. What were they doing? When the humming stopped he was breathing hard, unable to quell the feeling of dread that assailed him. This time, on a small, almost pleading note, he tried once more.

"Why?"

And then his tormentor sang. "Humpty Dumpty sat on the wall."

With the voice came the realisation, Marco knew his jailer.

Slowly, almost sweetly, the rhyme continued, malevolence coating the once innocent words as they did. "Humpty Dumpty had a great fall."

Panic crept up, swallowing him as it went, making the hairs on his arms rise and prickle as though they had divined the future and knew what was coming.

"All the king's horses and all the king's men…"

No, it couldn't be! It couldn't, Marco thought as the familiar voice went on.

"…Couldn't put Humpty together again."

The rhyme ended and a soft malicious chuckle resounded into the silence, as fear paralyzed him in place and he knew without doubt who held him. His last thought, before the screaming started, was that without doubt, without question, he would not be leaving alive!

****

Ash was parking the car, while Dev tried to get the lay of the land, he'd be happier when he knew the area well enough to drive, but until then he would just have to lump it.

"Is this the place?" Dev asked, looking at the apartment complex in front of them.

"It's the address Jen gave us," Ash replied.

Before they'd left the station, they'd had two addresses to check out. They had been by Marco's place, but no one had answered. He'd assumed Marco was likely at work, doing whatever it was he did for the McNamara's but had thought his wife might be home with their child. Ash however, had suggested that perhaps the child would be at nursery and the mother either working herself or doing whatever mother's did while their child was at nursery. With that decided, they figured they could check back in at a later time when they were more likely to be home.

They were now trying their luck at Rosa's apartment. Dev hoped they'd have better luck finding someone home. He really wanted to get something they could use and then maybe, just maybe, Angel would be less likely to incinerate him for his late arrival this morning.

They got out of the vehicle and walked the short distance to the apartment building. Ash checked the piece of paper and briefly studied the numbers on the intercom system. He pressed one and we waited.

"Hello? Who is it?" A melodic voice, with a Latino lilt, came back.

"Good afternoon ma'am, it's the police, could you please buzz us in? We'd like to speak to you?" Ash asked.

"Tell me your names." she demanded.

"DI Devlin Doyle and DC Ashley Carter, ma'am?" Ash complied dutifully.

There was silence for a moment and Dev wondered if she was going to speak again at all.

"Just hold on for a few minutes, I'm calling 101." She informed them.

Dev looked to Ash, who had a look of admiration on his face. "She's smart," he murmured, as they continued to wait.

"You can come up now," she announced, and the door buzzed. They entered the building and took a glance around to search for her apartment number, finally Dev's gaze caught an open doorway with the number they were searching for on one side. Standing in the entrance was a mature woman, perhaps early forties, with straight dark hair that flowed to her waist. She had olive skin, a petite frame and was giving them a wary, assessing look as they began to approach.

"Miss Salvador?" Ash asked politely, a hint of colour flushing in his cheeks. Dev frowned slightly, the officer was nearly half her age, but it appeared Ash wasn't concerned about that fact. He was surreptitiously eyeing her up with interest.

"Yes?" she said, giving Ash a pointed look, her frown matching his own. Ash appeared to have lost signal to his brain and Dev tutted, giving him a sharp dig to the ribs with an elbow before addressing her instead.

"Good afternoon Miss Salvador, I'm DI Doyle. I have a few questions I'd like to ask if you wouldn't mind? Could we come inside?" He asked, while Ash looked down at his feet like a naughty five-year-old.

Her gaze swung from Ash and for the first time focused its attention on him and she blanched. Dev stiffened and they became locked this way, frozen in time for what seemed like an endless moment. A myriad of emotions flashed across her features, one after the other, and a strong sense of déjà vu hit Dev full force. Neither of them appeared able to break the connection.

"Sir?" Ash's voice seemed far away, confused and if Dev wasn't mistaken, a little irritated. At his tone Rosa returned her gaze quickly to Ash before looking back to Dev and addressing him quietly.

"Have we met?" she whispered, almost like she was hoping he wouldn't answer but couldn't quite refrain from asking.

"Not that I can recall, Ma'am." Dev replied, equally disorientated, as he tried to find the source of the discomfort that was creeping through him.

Rosa released a breath and gave a nervous laugh, dissipating the tension, and the awkwardness of the moment thankfully passed.

"Perhaps we met in a past life." She joked weakly, before explaining, "It's just you just look so much like someone I knew when I was younger, that I was thrown for a second. But that was a long time ago and it couldn't possibly be you, if it were then you'd look well for a man over fifty."

As Dev tried to make sense of her rambling, Ash cleared his throat to get her attention. "Miss Salvador, I'm sorry to interrupt, but we were hoping to ask a few questions." Ash prompted to remind her of the reason they were there.

"What?.. Oh yes, sorry. Come in." She murmured, giving one last look at Dev, then shaking her head, and stepping aside to allow them entry. They walked inside and Dev immediately assessed the area around him. They'd entered into a large open living room, it had a cosy feel to it with a comfortable couch and matching armchairs. A coffee table in the centre was situated between the arrangement and a tv stand with a small television on top was in a corner.

Off to one side was an open doorway with no door that led to a small kitchen area, and on the opposing wall he noted another entryway, which he assumed led to a bathroom and likely one or two bedrooms.

"Take a seat." Rosa invited, pulling him from his inspection. Dev sat, nodding at Ash to continue, silently communicating for him to take the lead, while he observed. He didn't want to be sucked back into any more strange interactions with this woman and decided it would be the best course to take. Ash, understanding his gesture, gave a chin lift to him in acknowledgement before fixing his gaze on Rosa.

"Miss Salvador, my colleague and I are here because we are looking into a case regarding Vincent Walker," he began. "During our investigation, we came across a message he sent to you, that you would likely have received yesterday around midday. It asked you to pass a message to your brother, Marco."

Rosa gave a look of disgust and remarked, "I do not like that man. I have no idea how he obtained my number, my brother has terrible friends."

"Did you pass the message to Marco?" Ash asked.

"No. I'm not his personal secretary and I do not wish to have any further dealings with those people." She declared, passionately.

"Those people?" Ash reiterated in question.

Rosa closed down and didn't answer.

"Are you referencing your brother's connection to Jack McNamara, Vincent or both?" he pressed.

"I refuse to have anything to do with any of Marco's associates," Rosa confirmed carefully. "They are not good people."

"What makes you say that?" Ash pushed gently, "Is there something you know that perhaps we should be aware of? We could help you if you need it…"

"Nothing that would help you with Vincent." Rosa hedged, uncomfortably shifting in her seat.

"Maybe something else though?" Ash asked persistently.

"I'm sorry, I can't help you." Rosa insisted, almost pleading with him to drop it.

Ash conceded, accepting that line of inquiry would get him no further and changed tack.

"Can you think of any reason someone might want to do Vincent harm?" He prompted.

"Yes. He hurt women." Rosa declared without hesitation.

"Hurt women? Is that something you know from experience or have seen with your own eyes?" Ash asked quietly.

"Only by observing his treatment of his wife, some rumours, I hear things sometimes," She explained.

"Did you have much interaction with him?" Ash questioned.

"Not for a long time, Detective, some in the past at the beginning, but I could sense his evil. I did not like to be near him," Rosa said enigmatically.

"At the beginning?" Ash repeated.

"When Marco first started working with the McNamara's," Rosa clarified.

"What does he do for them?" Ash probed.

"He doesn't tell me, and I don't ask. I didn't have a lot to do with him for a time, not until his wife had his son. I like his wife, she'll lead him to better choices. She is good for him, and wants them to move from here. I hope they do… Perhaps I will also," She finished.

"Do you have any names you can give us of people who may wish to do Vincent harm?" Ash asked.

"I know he is not liked, I suspect there are many who would not cry over his loss. However, I have no names to give you," she told him. There was a moment of silence, while Ash considered if there were any more lines of inquiry to travel when Rosa spoke again. "Will you be speaking to my brother?"

"Yes ma'am, we intend to head there when we leave," Ash confirmed.

"Good," She nodded, satisfied. "Maybe you can give him the push he needs to follow his wife's advice."

"I'm not sure we have that kind of influence to offer, but you never know," Ash replied. "I think that will be all for the moment, ma'am. Thank you for your time. We can see ourselves out."

He stood and Dev followed his cue, as Ash walked to the door, he paused for a moment before speaking for the first time since they'd entered.

"If you have anything to add or need our assistance, call, and ask for me. DI Devlin Doyle. They'll put you through and we'll come," he said, waiting for her to indicate that she understood.

"I will," She agreed quietly, giving him one last curious look.

Dev turned and joined Ash at the door, leaving Rosa to the rest of her day.

When they reached the area outside, Ash spun on him and blurted, "What the fuck was that?"

"I'm sorry?" Dev flinched, caught off guard by his question.

"When we first arrived…that weird thing you two had going. What was that about?" Ash asked.

"Honestly, I'm as confused by it as you are. I can't remember ever meeting her before, but there were a few moments where I was almost sure I had." Dev tried to explain though he didn't quite manage, since he couldn't comprehend it himself.

"It was weird though, right?" Ash continued to pry.

"It was," Dev confirmed.

"Will you be checking that out?" Ash asked and Dev didn't understand the question.

"Checking out what?" He continued, confused.

"What would cause her to have that reaction to you, like you were a ghost coming to haunt her." Ash answered matter of factly.

Dev agreed, "She did have an odd reaction…I'll think about it, maybe I can figure out why," he answered, conceding that Ash had a point.

"If it wasn't you, whoever she thought you were freaked her out. Speak to Jen, maybe she can have a dig into it." Ash suggested.

Dev considered that thoughtfully on the drive to Marco's residence. As they began walking to the door, a sharp, trilling sound came from his pocket. He patted it and reached inside. Accepting the call, he said automatically, "Doyle."

"Dev, it's Jen. You need to get to the hospital immediately," She informed him, urgency lacing her voice.

"Why? What's going on?" He asked.

"Marco's mother has been rushed there, after being found unconscious. Marco's wife is hysterical, the staff are trying to calm her down. But her son, Alexis, has gone missing," She clarified, and Dev was suddenly beginning to understand her concern.

"Marco's son? How long has he been gone?" He asked.

"They don't know, the mother is too distraught to get any sense out of her," She replied.

"We're on our way," Dev said, all but running to the vehicle, Ash quick on his heels.

Chapter Twelve

January 23rd, 1990

The two children sat huddled together over the nursery rhyme book their mother had been reading to them. The boy quietly read to his sister, picking up from the last place their mother had read before she had left two days ago. After the bad man had left she'd been sick and was taken to be "fixed up." At least that's what they'd been told by the kind lady, Rosa. The lady herself stepped in the door, causing the boy to stop reading and stride across the room to confront her.

"Where is my Ma? It's been days, and I want to see her!" he demanded.

"She'll be back tomorrow," Rosa said calmly. She was only a young woman herself, at just nineteen. Her brother worked with the boy's Da, and Marco had asked her to watch them while the mother recovered. She hadn't wanted any part of it but seeing the two precious children, too young to be left alone with these monsters, she'd agreed against her better judgement.

She bustled in and began getting the children cleaned up as best she could and was brushing the little girl's hair when Jilly entered. Rosa didn't approve of any of the people in this abode, but she loathed Jilly. She was everything Rosa couldn't abide in a woman; bitchy, devious, fake and had the morality of an alley cat.

"Where is he?" She asked expectantly, "Is he with that dog of a wife?"

"I couldn't tell you whether or not Jack is with his wife, though I believe it is customary for that to be the case when you marry someone.." Rosa remarked with disdain, turning her back on Jilly. She continued to

brush the girl's hair and ignore Jilly, soothing the girl who had tensed beneath her.

"You have beautiful hair, mi Cielito" Rosa cooed to the six-year-old, while her brother watched Jilly with wary eyes.

A slap connected with her cheek so hard she was knocked to the floor. Jilly, with a pair of scissors in one hand, grabbed the little girl by the hair and began hacking into it as the boy launched himself at her to try and get her off. Rosa lay stunned, watching in horror before clambering to her feet and helping the boy to drag a crazed Jilly away, as the little girl wailed in terror. They managed to subdue her between them, but the damage was done, clumps of fiery red locks lay strewn on the floor. Rosa turned to Jilly, eyes wide with the horror of what she'd caused.

Jilly smirked and said spitefully, "Maybe next time, you'll understand the pecking order a little better and show me some respect, you high and mighty little whore. Look down your nose at me, will you? Maybe this will remind you of your place!" With that she flounced from the room while Rosa gathered the poor girl in her arms, and they cried together at the cruelty of the woman.

Chapter Thirteen

Wren got the call about the Child Rescue Alert from Jen as she and Matt headed to the hospital. Jen told her Dev had been following up a lead that was connected to the boy's family, so he and Ash were also on the way. The DCI was orchestrating the operation from the incident room and officers had been dispatched to the grandmother's home whilst others were being assembled trying to locate the boy.

As they got to the hospital, they stopped at the reception desk and were now heading down the corridor where hospital staff were waiting there, trying to calm Geena Salvador. She was beyond hysterical by this point, on her knees sobbing and incoherent, visibly shaking. Staff were trying to help her up, and by the looks of things, were considering giving her a sedative. She approached Geena with a calm she herself wasn't feeling.

"Mrs Salvador, can I call you Geena?" Wren asked gently, the woman didn't seem to hear her and continued as though she hadn't spoken, so she tried again a little firmer. "Geena, I'm DI Serenity Jones, I'm with the police, can you hear me?"

This time the woman met her soothing gaze and quietened before muttering "Ha llegado un ángel!" before clutching at Wren's legs in desperation and sobbing. Wren looked down in surprise, giving Matt a questioning look. He mouthed something to her, but she didn't catch what.

"An angel has arrived," Dev's voice came from behind her translating the sentiment. She couldn't see him, but his Irish lilt couldn't be mistaken. He walked around her and sank to his knees to attend to the woman inconsolably sobbing at her feet.

"Mrs Salvador. We are here to help find your son. Nod if you understand." She nodded, her sobs easing a little. "Now I want you to take a few deep breaths with me. I need you to dig deep if you are going to help us, can you do that for me?" he asked and she nodded again.

  He proceeded to breathe with her for a minute, maybe two and Wren was released from the death grip on her legs. Looking down she saw Dev had taken Geena's hands much the same as he had with Alma, then he released them and gently swooped her up before striding to the chairs in the waiting area and setting her down. Kneeling before her, he kindly wiped the tears from her face. Wren felt her heart tug in her chest and her breath caught as she watched this giant beast of a man tend soothingly to the woman in the chair.

"Good. You're doing so good, Geena. Can you be strong for me and answer a few questions? Your son needs you. We need you to be able to answer our questions if we're going to find him." He pacified her, encouraging her to meet his gaze by lifting her chin, her broken one met his reassuring one, lending her his strength and her spine straightened when she nodded again. He gave her a proud smile, dimples appearing in his cheeks and said, "That a girl!" before becoming solemn again.

"Can you tell me when you last saw your son?" he asked softly.

"Yesterday afternoon." she croaked, her voice hitching with emotion. "He was going to stay with his Abuela for the night until I could pick him up."

"What time did you arrive to pick him up today?" Dev probed.

"3.30pm. I finished work at 3pm and drove over to collect him as arranged. I used the key his Abuela had given me and…" she broke off here and began to hyperventilate a little.

"Easy Geena, breathe…take your time." Dev soothed and Geena's breathing slowed once again, before she continued.

"When I got inside I found her unconscious. I rushed to her and called for help. Then I remembered my Alexis. I looked around for him, but he wasn't there." A sob escaped again, and she buried her head into Dev's chest. He stroked her hair and murmured low, a sweetness lacing it, but Wren couldn't catch the quiet words he spoke, but Geena calmed again.

"Geena, I have another question, think really hard for me. Since you last saw him and when you arrived to pick him up, have you spoken to your mother-in-law or your son?" Dev enquired. His intention was to gauge how much time had passed since she'd last spoken to him and when she had found him missing. Geena was quiet, hitched hiccups came from her sporadically while she fought against her distress to think about his question. Finally, she nodded.

"Good. That's good. Can you tell me what time that was?" Dev pressed.

"I called. I think it was sometime around 6pm. He usually goes to bed at that time." she answered.

"Marvellous. That's incredibly helpful, Geena. One more thing. Do you happen to have a recent picture we might have to help us find him?" Dev asked. She nodded her ascent, looking around for something but not finding it. As she started to panic, a hospital staff member stepped forward handing her what Wren assumed to be her purse. Geena snatched it unceremoniously, rummaging furiously through the inside and pulling a small photograph from the opening which she handed to Dev.

"Now I'm going to leave you for a moment to hand this to my colleague." He explained. "Can you wait here for me?" She silently agreed as Dev got awkwardly to his feet and made his way to Wren. Their eyes met and her heart caught in her chest at the expression on his face, it seemed so sad, heart-wrenchingly so, that Wren got choked up for a moment and cleared her throat. He held his hand out offering her the photo without speaking.

"Geena!" a voice exclaimed, and a woman tore toward her. Ash had been escorting her in but upon seeing Geena in the chair, she'd rushed to her side.

"Rosa?" Geena whispered, her voice cracking as she was swept up in the woman's embrace.

"I'm here mi Corazón." Rosa replied, cradling her. With Geena occupied, Wren called into the station, relaying the information they'd been given. Dev returned to Geena and Rosa, while Ash hovered nearby, watching them. It was time for Wren to get to work and time was of the essence.

****

Jack McNamara had been with his mistress, Jilly, getting his end away when the call from Cameron had come. He was now back in his office processing the news. He'd tried to reach Marco but had had no success. He sat back in his office chair and quietly seethed with rage.

To summarise; Marco was missing, his son, Alexis, was also missing and Marco's bitch sister had been visited by the police, which he didn't like. Rosa had no love for them, he knew. Everything appeared to be going to hell in a handbasket, but Jack was the king of the underworld. He would do whatever it took to get this shit straightened out.

He'd put out word to all the corners of the area, Marco was to be found and the person responsible was to be delivered to him, whoever had decided to rock his world, would die drowning in their own piss. By the time Jack was finished with them, they would wish they'd made it to hell quicker.

****

Keri McNamara smiled to herself. So much chaos in so little time. Their plans were going smoothly, the timing of all of this, really couldn't have worked more perfectly in their favour. With Jack's attention more than a little occupied, they'd skated unnoticed under his usually watchful eye. She'd been practically skipping while she worked. Jack had been insistent she study medicine when she was younger. He'd wanted a trained medical professional on staff to take care of any medical needs that needed attending to and having her meant they could be kept off the record, after all nobody got a free ride. He'd said that she had to do her part if she was to earn her keep, and given her the choice between medical school or sexual services. Keri had made the smart choice and bided her time.

She'd handed in her notice at the hospital just this morning and was happily going about her day, pleased she was finally leaving the hellhole, when she'd seen him and the smile had slipped from her face. A gasp escaped from her mouth, and her face paled. She felt a small crack appear in her cold, twisted heart, which surprised her as she'd long since believed her heart was encased in stone. Of course she had a lot of affection for her fiancé, but it wasn't anything she couldn't live without if she had to. However, as she stood, her eyes fixed on the apparition before her, one lone tear escaped and trailed down her cheek, astonishment compelled her to catch it on the tip of one fingernail and she studied it with disbelief. Perhaps the "Ice Queen" wasn't quite as cold as she'd thought.

****

August 2nd, 2014, 11.30pm

   After a long day running around doing his best to find any sign of Alexis Salvador, they had come up empty. They'd gone on long into the twilight hours, until finally the Super had called time, stating that nobody would be able to work effectively if they didn't rest. Dev had fought it, the repeating image of Geena Salvador's heartbroken sobs disturbing him with such sheer force he couldn't shake the lingering horror. When he'd finally given in to the Super's command he'd gone home, only to find that he couldn't settle. Beyond agitated he'd paced and grabbed his jacket, heading to the first bar he could find.
  "What can I get you?" The barman asked.
  As he was about to answer, his eyes fell on a familiar figure leaning over the bar. There was no mistaking

Angel, her hair flowing loose, giving an iridescent glow as the lights changed to the music on a dancefloor nearby, they caught the white of her hair and made it come alive with vivid colour. As he watched, a small smile curled his lips, the first he'd had in hours and the agitation eased. She called to him, her light beckoning him to her, and he mindlessly moved to her side. As he did, she looked at him and spoke over the music thumping in the background.

"You couldn't sleep either, huh?"

Dev shook his head in reply, not even attempting to talk over the music.

"I was about to order a drink, but I forgot it was disco night," She all but shouted, "I know a quieter bar… wanna keep me company?"

Dev nodded this time, watching as Angel grabbed her bag, before they left the noise behind and stepped out into the mild, summer night. A few feet down the road they entered the quieter bar that she'd promised, neither one in the mood to chit chat or make small talk. They found a table, which in itself was a miracle on a Saturday night and Dev asked Wren what she was drinking. Quickly striding to the bar, he came back with a tray that had two of her own order on it, alongside two whiskeys on ice, if the rock glasses were any indication. She thanked him and they sat, worn and weary, in companionable silence while they slowly drank through their first drinks.

As Wren lifted the second glass having drained the last of the first one, she paused mid-lift to give him a sharp look as though trying to solve a puzzle. He said nothing, allowing her to weigh him up in her own time. "So, what's your story, Dev?" she finally asked, curiously sipping on her drink.

"I'm not sure what you're asking, exactly," Dev said, a half-grin spreading on his face but not quite reaching his eyes.

"Ok, I'll lay it out for you. You get sent here because of some big fuck up and I'm expecting this loudmouthed, jack the lad, who thinks he knows it all, dickhead. Instead, I meet this quiet, observant, hawk-like man with sharp, intense eyes who watches everything almost too closely and I'm surprised. It goes like that for weeks…" Wren pauses taking a sip of her drink before continuing, "…Then out of nowhere we get a different Dev. This one is like the epitome of the typical Irish man, charming, a little cocky, snorts through his nose while he smothers laughter and flashes his Dimples at older ladies to put them at ease."

Dev shifts uncomfortably at her assessment, knowing from her tone that she wasn't done yet.

"Then we get the third Dev, and he is also a completely different person. This one gets on his knees to wipe tears from a distraught woman's face, before carrying her to a chair, and stroking her hair. While he tells her what she needs to hear to find the strength to do what she has to. In short, Devlin, I have been married and work in a job pretty much surrounded by men most of the day and it doesn't wash, unless you have a story. I'll ask again, Dimples. Who the fuck are you?" She concluded.

"I wish I fucking knew!" Dev laughed bitterly at the irony of that last statement but didn't explain the joke.

"I don't understand you Dev and I like to think I'm a shrewd judge of character, I can usually see a person's intentions and motives long before others finally catch on. I don't trust what I can't understand," she finished.

"Well, when you figure it out, clue me in too because I understand myself even less than you do," He returned with a self-deprecating laugh and looked away, feeling a little sore at her assessment.

"Don't do that," she said, her tone changing, softening. She reached to take his face in her palms and pulled his gaze back to her, looking him dead in the eye. "You misunderstand me, I may not trust you, but I do like you." She murmured trailing off. They stayed locked like that, Dev felt a sudden urge to lean forward, his eyes tracing the line of her soft, inviting lips before returning to her intense, inquisitive stare, looking for something but couldn't quite find it.

However before he could make up his mind whether he should follow his instinct, or not, she was standing. She leaned down, kissed him gently on his forehead and took her hands from his face before saying, "Enjoy the rest of your night, Dimples, but you best be in bright and early tomorrow to make up for your late appearance this morning, don't you think?" Then downing the remaining liquid in her glass, she placed it on the table, and gave him her back while he watched, still frozen, as she sauntered away.

Chapter Fourteen

August 4th, 2014

   Marco wasn't sure how he was still alive...the pain was excruciating. His heart thumped so hard and fast he didn't know how it still beat in his chest. Remembering all that had been done to him made his stomach turn over, even as he tried to block it. He'd long since given up hope on being rescued, and had long ago prayed for his death, begged for it, screamed for it until his voice was hoarse, broken and all but gone, but still his torture continued.

   There were sharp stabs of pain, like hundreds of nails being hammered into each joint and he wondered what more there was, what more there *could* be. He'd endured hacking, sawing and cutting until he'd lost consciousness, over and over, yet every time he thought it was over, he woke again and again...it shouldn't have been possible. Now he lay spent, verging on death's door but always eluding its final grasp. He'd been numb and deadened to the pain, but not quite dead.

   The constant humming of the damn rhyme while his tormentor had worked stripped him of any sanity, breaking his mind; where the physical torture broke his bones and tore at muscles leaving him reeling on the edge of the precipice but never quite tipping him over it. Would it never be over? Marco thought dejectedly.

   Suddenly there was a new sound; a click then a whirling and his breath caught. Was he back? A youthful voice filled the air, not the merciless relentless humming of before but scared and small.

   "Daddy?" It sobbed.

"Where's my Daddy?" It asked, with more gulps and quiet sobs.

"I want my Daddy, PLEASE!! NO!! DADDDDYYY!"

In what was the sheerest fright of his existence, beyond all he had already suffered, he wrenched his eyes wide, unthinkingly and with such force, he felt skin pull and rent and the flesh of his eyelids flapped, wrested away from their place. His sight clouded and wavered until shapes manifested in the dim light. Horror overtook him and where he had, in the beginning, thought blindness to be the very essence of fear he knew his now permanently open eyes proved to be a far worse fate, as they fixed on a screen with his son, Alexis, screaming.

He averted his eyes, turning his head away and in doing so saw his limp arm stretched beside him. Neat sutures held it together; at his shoulder, elbow, wrist, and as his eyes followed it down, they even held every finger on his right hand together. If his eyes could've stretched further open in terror, they would have then. Now he wished to be blind once more.

****

Dev was in the incident room, bright and early the next morning, not because Wren had insisted but because after another terrible, nightmare ridden night, one question continued to plague him. Where was Marco Salvador? When Geena had given him her statement and he'd asked, she had told him that he was out of town for work. When asked how she knew this information, she told him that she had called Jack McNamara's home and that was the message which had been relayed, with the reassurance they would get him to call as soon as he'd been contacted. It had seemed plausible then but now, all these hours later, why had he still not shown up?

Where was Marco Salvador? Over and over, it turned in his mind. If he were not in fact working, why had he not come running upon learning of his son's abduction? Could he be the person who'd taken him? Then why would he attack his own mother, wouldn't she have just handed him the child and let him go on his way? It didn't matter what way Dev spun the questions around and tried to explain it away; he couldn't get over the gaps in the pictures.

He asked himself again, Where was Marco Salvador? What if he too had been abducted? Then why would McNamara's crew hide the fact that he was missing? How could it possibly benefit them to hide this information? Were they telling the truth and he'd lost his phone, had an accident? Where the fuck was Marco Salvador? Dev growled in frustration and slammed a hand down on the desk in front of him.

"Wow… What did that desk do to you?" Jen asked in surprise, taking a seat at her own desk.

"WHERE IS MARCO SALVADOR?" He shouted aloud startling Jen, who spilled her tea everywhere in shock. She began nervously mopping up the mess, while Dev continued unaware of her alarm. "Tell me! Where is he? It's driving me insane!"

"Somebody needs a caffeine break… Dev with me," Wren ordered, from the doorway, "Jen, be a dear and do some digging and see what you can find on Marco Salvador before *someone* has an aneurysm." With that she swung around and headed to the canteen not bothering to check if Dev followed, since he damn well better be.

She entered the canteen and began making drinks, sensing the tension from Dev behind her. It was still early, and they were alone, so she busied herself pulling cups from the cupboard and placing them on the counter. She waited for the machine to start whirring before doing a swivel on one foot getting straight to the point without any preamble.

"What the hell was that?" She snapped furiously, "this is a police station, not a football match and you are a detective, not a hooligan. Act like it. If you get frustrated take a fucking walk but do not shout like an imbecile, scaring the crap out of the staff. Do I make myself clear DI Doyle?" She finished coldly.

"Aye, you do. I'm sorry. I didn't think—" Dev began.

"Too right you didn't think, do better." Wren cut in. "Now finish making the drinks and you better replace the one you made Jen spill when you scared the bejesus out of her." Then she stalked back to the incident room without another word, leaving him alone. Dev sighed and ran his hand over his face, before moving to the counter to do as she'd demanded.

"Morning," Matt said cheerily, as he strolled in. " I hear you're having a super morning."

Dev groaned before saying, "Jen told you?"

"Na mate, was listening at the door" he needled with good humour, "we're a nosey lot, detectives, didn't you know? When Wren said make the drinks…I was included, right? Because I could murder a cup of coffee about now..."

"Aye." Dev said reluctantly before placing another cup on the counter.

"Morning," Ash greeted. "One of those for me? You aren't going to make me throw it everywhere, are you?" he joked.

"Listening at the door?" Dev asked, resignedly.

"Na mate, Jen told me." He laughed. "We gossip too," he winked, laughing loudly as he skipped out the way of a well-aimed, wet tea bag.

"Feck off, ya eejits!" Dev snarled, only half serious, before he turned his attention to the drinks so he could hide the wry smile turning his lips up.

****

Wren sat at the desk next to Jen, while the boys were busy in the canteen. Her fury at Dev's behaviour had burnt out pretty much as soon as she'd left the canteen, because the question he'd been shouting, unfortunately, had brought up a very good point and taken some of the wind out of her sails.

"So…" she asked Jen. "Got anything on our friend, Marco?"

"It's been less than fifteen minutes," Jen answered, rolling her eyes, "I'm good but I'm not that good. I can tell you though, that his phone has had no calls or messages since Thursday afternoon. Which could mean he's turned it off or could also mean it's out of battery. Either way, he's made no communications with it since then."

"So potentially, we could have two missing persons," Wren said aloud.

"Yep," Jen confirmed, popping the p, for emphasis.

"Well, damn. I'm kind of feeling Dimples on this one." She stated with frustration.

"Oh, you wish, sweet cheeks," Jen teased, and Wren swatted her.

The phone on the desk rang beside her and Jen's laugh froze in her throat as she put the receiver to her ear and listened to the voice on the other end.

"The boy's been found." She informed Wren covering the phone with her hand so she couldn't be heard on the line. Wren jumped from her seat and asked in relief.

"Where?" Watching as Jen spoke into the phone and covered it again.

"Rosa's apartment complex. The buzzer was pressed but no one spoke. When she went outside the boy was blindfolded and bound by the doorway. It happened in the early hours of this morning. She would've rung sooner but she was dealing with him and trying to get hold of Geena. She has only just gotten around to it."

"Tell her we're on our way." Wren called, already running for the canteen.

****

Keri McNamara fluctuated between happiness and violent rage. She'd been feeling this way since she'd seen him. She wasn't sure what to do with these feelings since she couldn't recall the last time she actually cared about anything with this degree of emotion. Well, not recently anyway. And not for an exceedingly long time. On the one hand, she was happy that he'd lived but on the other she was beyond enraged that she had only just found out. There was a lot she had only just discovered, and she was frothing, seething even.

She'd followed him yesterday, observing from a distance, not completely sure why. She'd watched as he had comforted Geena and it'd had an uncomfortable effect on her. When she'd seen his expression as he'd gone toward the weird, white-haired woman, she found herself wanting the missing boy to be reunited with his mother. She was truly horrified by this turn of events. She was having these ridiculous feelings, and she didn't like it. Not one bit. Honestly. Ok, maybe she liked it a little bit, she could admit to herself, but otherwise not at all. This would not do. It would not do at all. However it changed nothing, the plan remained the same. All that had changed was that she wished just a teensy-weensy bit, that things might have been different.

As she sat in her car, some distance from the station, she vowed that tomorrow she would put this new stalking obsession to bed and stop watching him…Yeah, tomorrow.

****

Dev couldn't remember a time before now, when he'd had such an awful start to the day, that had morphed into one that brought such a feeling of unexpected elation. He'd had his share of wins whilst on the force but none that rivalled this feeling of relief, that things had worked out in the favour of the "good guys." They'd sat with Rosa and Geena, who'd been overjoyed to have the boy back in their care. Geena hugging him a little too close, the lingering fear he may vanish, causing her to cling that little bit tighter.

They had hoped maybe they could garner some small amount of information from the boy, but he was too young to help them fill in the missing pieces from his time with his abductor. It also left Dev with another two unanswered questions to add to the one that had been nagging at him all morning. Why had he been taken and then so suddenly returned? No money had been exchanged, no demands had been answered, he couldn't understand the motivation for it at all. By the time they left the apartment, he was more confused than ever. What in the hell was going on?

He and Wren walked towards the vehicle and were heading back to the station to see what new information had been found. He wanted to see what Jen had found on Marco now that the boy was safely in the arms of his mother, he also hadn't been keeping up to speed on Vincent's murder and was interested to know where the DCI was on that.

Everything had been so chaotic, that the station was spread thin trying to cover the caseload. As they got to the vehicle, he noticed a piece of paper on the windscreen and thinking it to be a flyer he took it off and gave it a glance. He started and dropped it like he'd been stung, looking down at the ground in disbelief. Wren, noting the change in his body language, bent down without touching it to see the words glaring on the page in large, typed font.

REMEMBER ME?

Chapter Fifteen

August 5th, 2014

Marco is heavy. It was quite a pity that he died before the main event. The hope was that he would stay alive for this part. But that's the difference between imagination and reality one supposes. Sometimes the reality just doesn't meet the expectation you have hyped it up to be in your head. Oh well, it had still been executed to a satisfactory standard. That would have to do. Finally made it. Looking down, it does seem like the finish at least will live up to the hype… Bye Marco.

****

After the strange note left on their windscreen the afternoon before, Dev and Wren had returned to the station, while deliberating its strange message. Jen hadn't managed to uncover much more on Marco, and nobody seemed able to locate him. Vincent's case had also slowed with not much more to go on and they had eventually called it a day, hoping more would surface with time. He'd gone home this time more settled; knowing that at least Alexis had made it home. He'd had some food, if he could call what little he'd had in his fridge food. After a quick shower, Dev had fallen onto his bed, deciding that an early night was just what he needed. The lack of sleep lately was leaving him weary and disinterested in anything other than sleep.

He'd once again woken in the night with a start— the nightmares had resurfaced with a startling regularity this week— for reasons he couldn't explain. Despite

that, he'd still managed to get enough sleep to call himself refreshed. That was until the phone rang.
"Hello?" He asked.
"DI Doyle?" The Super said through the line. "DI Jones is coming for you, she knows the area and will get you here faster, there will be no time to stop at the station. We have another one. Get here and get here fast." The line was dead before he got another word out.

****

Wren pulled up to Dev's address, looking at the small two up two down that he now called home. She hadn't picked him up here until now, but she knew the area and that there would be no time for tea this morning. She rang his phone, but he didn't answer. Instead, the front door opened, and he walked with purposeful strides towards the car, opening the passenger side he sat, and she'd left the drive before he had even put on his seatbelt.
"Where are we going? Dev asked.
"The viaduct," She answered.
"The viaduct?" Dev reiterated.
"Yep," she confirmed.
"Do I want to know?" Dev enquired.
"Even if you did, I couldn't tell you. The only information I have is that there is another murder and it's at the viaduct. Your guess is as good as mine. Well, mine's probably better, but you catch my drift I'm sure." She joked lamely, in an attempt to lighten the mood.
When they arrived they found the expected perimeter surrounding the area, what they were surprised by was

the fact that there wasn't a tent set up. They made it through the scene guards and pulled up in the area they'd been directed to and found Matt waiting.

"The Don said to tell you to get to her post-haste." He said without even a good morning, his usual easy smile missing.

"Where's the tent? Are they still getting it set up?" Wren threw behind her, as she began to move in the direction indicated.

"No tent. Too many pieces." Matt responded with a grim expression.

Wren stopped where she was. "What?"

"You'll get it when you get there, now go!" he replied, hurrying them along.

"Too many pieces…" Dev repeated quietly as they moved.

As they located the Super they noticed that the SOCO team had beat them there. And they were…everywhere. Wren wasn't sure she liked where this was going.

"You took your time," The Don said, as they approached, "It's a goddamn circus. The SOCO team are having a meltdown trying to isolate the body parts and keeping the scene as undisturbed as possible. Which frankly is going to be hard considering the distance they're covering between pieces."

Wren could hear the words but was having problems making them make sense. Clearly there were body parts, and they were in several places, she got that part. "How many bodies were there?"

"We don't know. Could be one. Could be many. Until we have all the pieces we won't be sure." The Super replied and Wren realised she'd spoken aloud.

"Jesus." Dev remarked.

"Jesus couldn't even help them now. Even if a resurrection were possible, the pieces would be too hard to piece together." She muttered in irritation.

Dev winced and Wren looked at the Super in question. "If it's going to be a while before SOCO is done, why was it so urgent that we got here?"

"Good question, Jones. Here's your answer." She pointed to the floor just behind her where the pathologist was waiting to bag something for transport. "Are you familiar with Marco Salvador, DI Jones?"

"Yes, ma'am." Wren said, waiting for the answer that was promised.

"Good. Take a look." She directed her to the pathologist, who stood back a little and revealed a head on the ground.

They both looked at it with shock before Wren looked closer and nodded. "Yes ma'am, it's him. Well.. I'm fairly sure, you know if you give him some…eyelids.. in your head," she said stuttering.

She stepped away and Dev continued to stare, with a look she couldn't interpret on his face. She watched him, wondering what he saw that she didn't. And thought to herself that this was going to be a very long day.

****

As expected the day had been a long one. It had taken the SOCO team an extremely long time to get the scene completed. After a good portion of the morning the Super had finally told them they could go and gave them several directives. The first had been to inform the family. With the mother still in hospital in a critical but stable condition, that particular trip would be dealt with at a later date. However, there were still two other trips they'd had to make. Rosa and Geena. The two women had had opposing reactions to the news. Rosa's had been one of acceptance. She had told them they hadn't been on the best of terms and Dev suspected she had some idea of what he did for a living, therefore had no surprise it had ended this way. Of course, she didn't have the details, although at this time they were thin on the ground while SOCO worked to uncover the extent of it all, it was pretty clear though, that it hadn't been a pleasant end.

Geena's reaction by comparison was one of extreme distress, not quite the same as she'd had when finding out Alexis had been missing but close. When they'd finally left, the elation from the previous day had dissipated and he once again felt annoyed at himself. Marco he suspected hadn't been a good man, however Dev had known something wasn't right about him not being present and it had taken him much longer to start questioning it, than it should've. Perhaps if he had got to that nagging feeling sooner, this end could've been avoided, they may have located him before it had come to this.

The next directive had been to speak with Jack McNamara. He'd told Geena that Marco had been working, not told them he was missing. They needed to speak to him directly so they could wade through the accounts and decide if they had intentionally misled them or if they genuinely thought he was alive and would eventually check in. Also, it would be nice to know what "job" he'd been doing and where he had been going so that they may try and find his last location. Tracking his movements might help them uncover who's path he may've crossed. They needed a starting point if they were to investigate it and until the SOCO team could give them the preliminary report, they didn't have much more to go on other than the fact that he hadn't communicated with anyone since Thursday.

Unfortunately, Jack McNamara was a hard man to pin down. They had run around most of the day trying in vain to find him and he suspected he was purposely making that the case. When they'd finally made it back to the station he'd been beyond frustrated. Wren was quiet and he could feel her contained rage, seething beside him. He suspected she too shared his frustration. The DCI was outside trying to fend off the press and, while he tried to field their questions, Dev and Wren slipped past into the station and made their way to the incident room, deflated.

"Any joy on your end?" Jen enquired as they entered.

"Not really." Wren muttered, "That dickhead has given us the runaround for the best part of the day."

"I tried your phone a few times, Dev. Is it off?" Jen directed the question at him.

"Aye, the battery died a while ago. It needs charging. Did you have something for me? I was with Wren, you could've tried to reach me on her phone." He'd perked up hoping she had something, anything, to give him.

"Not much I'm afraid, we were going to get some food in, but when you didn't answer we figured you weren't likely going to be back for a while and went ahead without you, sorry." Jen explained.

"Oh" Dev replied, disappointment flashing through him, and his shoulders sagged in defeat.

"I did trace the location of the last communication received on Marco's phone though. Strangely it was here in Welwyn. Which means his phone has been off since he left for wherever he went. Assuming he actually went anywhere." Jen said.

"Is the SOCO team finished at the scene yet?" He asked while he pondered that small amount of information.

"The body has finally been removed from the scene, the pathologist believes the parts all belong to Marco, that does make this slightly better. Only one victim, it's not much of a bright side though, is it? The rest of the team are finishing up searching the surrounding areas, but they aren't quite finished yet." Jen informed him.

The phone on the desk rang and Jen picked it up. Dev checked the time; it was nearing 8pm. He ran through the events of the day while Jen spoke on the phone, not paying much attention to the one-sided conversation. He thought back to the moment he'd seen Marco's head on the ground. The moment had joined many nagging moments he'd had through the course of this week. He wasn't sure what to do with it all. It had been happening since the first time he'd laid eyes on Vincent in the street. The overwhelming sense of familiarity, recognition. He couldn't place it, but he had definitely seen these people before.

First Vinnie, then Rosa and now Marco. It wasn't hard to guess that if he had in fact come across them at some point, he would be familiar with them all since they were all inescapably connected, but the fact that he couldn't quite pinpoint the case it pertained to was really frustrating him. Lost in his thoughts, he was surprised when he felt Wren's hand on his arm.

"Something on your mind?" she asked.

"I can't seem to shift the feeling that I've seen these people before." He answered, hoping using her as a sounding board might pry something loose from his mind and help jog his memory.

"Know them from where?" she asked the question he suspected she would. So, he divulged the issue plaguing him.

"That's just it, I can't put my finger on it. I suspect it was a case, maybe a cold case. If it had been recent I would remember, so it must have been some time ago. I think maybe I have worked on a case involving them before. I have Alec, back in London, looking into it for me. I should check in with him when my phone's charged, whatever it is, it's playing on my mind. Maybe that's why the nightmares are back, perhaps the strain of trying to lock down the information in my mind is causing too much stress and they are the result of overthinking it." Dev said thinking out loud, then realising he'd said more than he'd meant to.

"You're having nightmares?" Wren immediately latched onto the one part of his statement he didn't want to get into.

"That's not the part you should focus on. But, yes I have nightmares, it's a childhood thing. I don't know why because I can't remember. And that's all there is to it. The case I can't remember is the part that's bothering me," Dev reminded her, trying to get her back on point.

"But don't you think you should maybe see someone to try and stop the nightmares?" She pursued, making Dev sigh with exasperation.

"They don't happen all the time, mostly they stopped happening when I turned eleven, occasionally and it really is occasionally, they make an appearance from time to time, when I'm under pressure and not getting much sleep. Like this week…Ipso facto… nightmares.

You know what? Never mind… It'll come to me. Let's drop it." Dev said dropping the subject and turning his attention to Jen who had finished on the phone. "Anything we need to know about?" He asked in reference to the call she just finished up with.

"It was The Don. She said that it's going to be a while and to tell everyone to wrap up for the day, pick it back up in the morning when there's more to go on." Jen recounted.

"Right. In that case, I'll head home. I need to charge my phone and catch up with Alec." Dev replied leaving Wren watching him speculatively, as he left the room.

Chapter Sixteen
January 26th, 2014

   The mother had finally been returned to the room with the children. Her face, still wearing bruises of various shades. The children were happy to see her, even though seeing the little girl's hair had made her cry. They now sat in the room near the window, which was open, and the cold wind was blowing in but the two guards on duty refused to close it. They were smoking weed, and the smell was pungent. The boss didn't approve so they'd opened it to air out the smell.
   The mother was reading from the nursery rhyme book and had just started to begin Humpty Dumpty.
   "Humpty Dumpty sat on the wall—" she began and the one called Marco leaned in and blew smoke into her open mouth. He laughed as she sputtered.
   "Must you do that? There are children here!" She snapped, forgetting herself for a moment.
   "What did you fucking say to me?" He asked with anger flashing furiously on his face. He snatched the book from her, and she grabbed at the air, trying to take it back. "What is this shit?" He looked at it in disgust.
   "If you'd bothered to attend school, you'd know." The mother muttered under her breath. Marco heard her and his friend laughed.
   "You gonna let her talk to you that way?" the other guy asked.
   Marco's face turned from angry to enraged. Then something happened and he smiled a wide, evil grin.
   "You're right. I didn't much like to read. I always preferred to watch it on TV. Don't got no TV here

though, so we might have to do a re-enactment instead."

Before the mother could follow his meaning he'd grabbed her by the throat and put her on the window ledge. The boy ran to get to her, but the friend was quicker. Holding the boy firmly, he watched the scene before him unfolding with delight.

"Humpty Dumpty sat on a wall, Humpty Dumpty had a great fall," he recited, shaking her a little over the edge, and making her squeal. He and his friend laughed, which made the boy struggle harder to get free with no avail.

Neither of them noticed the little girl until she bit Marco's leg. Startled, he released his grip on the mother and her weight toppled backward and she fell from the window ledge. The room was a long way from the ground floor. The sound of her body connecting with the concrete below, was drowned out by the screams echoing from above.

Inside the room the men looked scared. The screams of the children continued, and Marco grabbed at the boy and gave him a swift back hand to the face. The boy quieted, a look of petulance on his face mixing with the visible distress from watching his mother fall from the window. The girl continued to scream behind them. Marco whirled to her and spoke. "If you don't stop that screaming, I swear you will join her!" The room was silent for a moment before the other man said quietly.

"What are we going to do?"

Marco thought for a moment and replied, "Tell them she jumped."

Chapter Seventeen

Dev walked into his home and put his phone straight on to charge. He really did need to catch up with Alec, see if he'd yet had time to look into the case he couldn't remember. There had to be one, because he couldn't for the life of him understand how he could have such a strong sense of knowing people with no recollection of the exact reason why. He opened his fridge and realised he also needed some supplies. He was running low on food, and he couldn't remember the last time he'd actually had real food. With that in mind he decided it might be wise not to put it off any longer and headed for the local supermarket.

He returned a short time later, unpacking his bags and began to cook up an omelette since it was quick and easy. It had been a long day, too long since he'd eaten, and he didn't have the energy to make anything more substantial after his jaunt to the local shops. He polished it off in short order and cleared away the pots before flopping down in his chair in the living room. He awoke a short time later and realised he'd dropped off. Looking for his phone he remembered he'd been charging it and decided he had better check his messages and get hold of Alec to check in. He picked it up and waited as the screen loaded and his phone let off several alerts to tell him he had messages. He pressed to listen to the first. It was Jen.

He absent mindedly listened to her voice. It was the food order thing she'd mentioned earlier. Clicking the phone he skipped to the next one. It was the Super telling him to call it a day. Must have been why she'd rung the incident room instead, he supposed. Skipping again, he found a message from Alec. He listened intently until Alec relayed that so far he hadn't found anything about the case he was looking for, but he would keep looking into it when he got a chance. Dev sighed, well that was a bust, but at least he didn't need to call him. Skipping to the next message he froze.

"DI Doyle? I hope I dialled this number right. It's Rosa. I know you are probably busy, what with my brother's…well with your investigation but I wanted to talk to you. Geena and I, we've been talking, and we think it might be best if we left town. We feel that with all that's happened with Alexis kidnapping and Marco's death, we should get out for Alexis' safety and our own. I will obviously inform you when I know where we're stopping, but it really would be in our interest to get out now. Especially when there's no reason to keep us here. Mama… Mama passed today so… Anyway, I'm getting away from the point. I want to speak to you before we leave tomorrow. I have things that it is time to say but didn't want to for fear of what could happen. I'm hoping with us leaving, that now is the time to do this. Please come."

Dev listened to the message once more before he scooped up his phone and ran for the door, it seemed the day wasn't quite over for him yet. Getting into the car he paused to call Wren, but no answer came. Leaving a message for her he drove into the night for Rosa's apartment.

****

Jack McNamara was at the end of his rope. He wasn't sure when he'd lost a handle on the situation but by

Christ he was going to get a tight grip on it now. He'd had word that Marco had finally surfaced…or hit the surface…from a great height it would seem. And that bitch Rosa was beginning to loosen her tongue. He needed to shut her up once and for all, now that he didn't have Marco keeping her in check.

   He'd heard no more on the Keir front either, however he'd had some alarming messages throughout the day of his "ghost" or his "doppelganger" stalking staff, interested in his whereabouts. Since he was currently keeping a low profile at his mistress' place, he hadn't answered any calls, he was also avoiding the police attention he'd been warned about. Until he had a handle on it, he wasn't prepared to feed the police the bullshit he intended to feed them. He couldn't feed them bullshit that would stand up to scrutiny unless he knew what the fuck was going on and at the moment he didn't. So he would be staying right here until he fucking did. Then and only then would he be making an appearance and when he resurfaced, heads were going to roll.

****

   Dev had buzzed Rose's apartment a few times before realising she wasn't going to answer, he'd called for back-up, but they were still en route, so he pressed the special assistance button and waited.
"Hello, this is the help desk, how can I help?" A woman's voice croaked over the telecom.
"Good evening Ma'am, it's the police. I'm DCI Doyle from the criminal investigation department and I'm responding to a call made from apartment 3c but

there's no answer, I would like to gain access to the building please."

"Ok..." She began and some shuffling sounds were heard before she spoke again " if you could please hold your I.D. up to the camera monitor so I can see your credentials and I will be able to permit you entry."

"Thank you, there should also be a response team following shortly" he informed her as he held his badge up to the screen.

A minute later he heard the sound of the door humming as it granted him access, more than a little concerned for Rose' safety he continued. As he headed to her apartment he noticed the door slightly ajar. Picking up his pace, he quickly reached his destination and paused hesitantly. Reaching for his two-way radio, he bit off a short update on the situation.

"Doyle, back up is five minutes out, wait to enter." The commanding tone of The Don, filling the air space.

"She may be injured and in need of medical attention, paramedics may be needed too, I should take a look—" he started.

"Doyle. There may be a perpetrator on the premises, wait for backup" The Super said sternly.

"I'll proceed with caution, backup can't be far behind now..." He pushed.

"Damn it Doyle! Fine." she conceded after a small pause, "they're almost with you but, if you see anything and I mean *anything,* to indicate there is an intruder you are to evacuate *immediately*! Do I make myself clear?"

"Crystal," Dev muttered.

He pushed the door gently and peered into the dark. The hallway was quiet, and he could see no movement as he took cautious steps forward, heading for a doorway. He stopped at the edge and examined the area before entering. The apartment was neat and clean, some magazines lay strewn across the coffee table at the centre, but nothing too far out of the ordinary as he flitted his gaze across scouting for any sign of life.

At the light tap on his shoulder, he swayed and twisted, only to find three officers he didn't recognise behind him, the first putting a finger to their lips to indicate he should hold his silence. Relief flooded him and he resumed his task and moved onward, continually surveying his surroundings. His eyes came to rest on a small, strange luminosity under one door to the side. He nodded toward it to signal his intention and they split off, one following his lead the other two heading off to broaden the search.

They silently took position, one on each side of the door frame he'd chosen, and after a brief communication without words, he reached down and quietly turned the handle. The door parted, leaving it open a fraction while they prepared to go in. With slow, concise movements he eased inside preparing for an oncoming onslaught but stopped dead in his tracks, his team mate on noting his countenance moved around to get a clearer view of the scene.

"Jesus," he murmured.

Before them lay a grisly picture; Rose lay half submerged in a bath of blood, face twisted in pain, her eye sockets empty and gaping with what appeared to be something akin to spider threads dangling from what remained of her eyelids. While her mouth was open in a silent scream. The dim light emanating from above had blood coating it, casting an ominous red glow, as though the room ran red with a river of gore, and one

155

couldn't tell if the walls and water contained it, or the effect just made it appear that way.

"What's in the water?" The whispered question came from his side, and he was released from his frozen demeanour. He leaned closer and on further inspection, Dev saw what he had observed. Flowers had been scattered in the water, the colour indistinguishable in the current lighting and whether they were in offering or a taunting farewell, he couldn't say. As he prepared to speak another voice filtered in from the hallway.

"The rest of the apartment is clear."

He turned and light flooded the hallway, letting his eyes fall upon the opposing wall and he cursed violently.

"What the hell?" Another spat.

The words, YOU CAN'T SEE ME BUT I SEE YOU, stared back at them in what looked suspiciously like blood.

****

Wren rushed to Rosa's after receiving a call from the Super. She'd missed Dev's call because she had decided to have a soak and wash the day away, but now she was kicking herself, since the day clearly hadn't been over. Dev had been left whistling in the wind because she'd been playing with bubbles and having a glass of wine. If she had answered he would've waited, and he wouldn't have had to go in alone. She also wouldn't have had to listen on the two way to the Super letting him risk his life entering a property in an attempt to rescue Rosa.

Her heart had been in her mouth, she'd even prayed, while she raced across town to get there. She'd finally drawn breath again when it became clear a team had been hot on his heels and he wasn't about to die at the hands of a serial killer. That's what they had now. Four murders. Whether it had been the killer's intention to kill Marco's mother or not remained to be seen, but regardless she had still died. They had to all be connected somehow, given that almost the entire Salvador family had now been eradicated. Which made young Alexis' return even more of a puzzle. If the perpetrator had taken him, why had he then been returned unharmed, while the rest of his family met their demise? Why was one lone boy spared?

Racing from the car, up to the apartment building she found it sealed off, the SOCO team—having not long finished at one scene—had doubled back a short way, and arrived ahead of her. The scene was now locked down until it had been processed, looking around her she looked for the team so she could get updated. She caught sight of Ash and Matt just outside the perimeter, who appeared to be having a heated discussion, but upon seeing her Ash stepped away and took a walk. Matt approached her.

"Wren, you made it then?" He asked the rhetorical question before continuing, "I'm going to be honest, listening to the two-way on the way here…it was intense. I thought our boy was going to have a sticky end for a time there. When they patched him through to the incident room and The Don was talking to him, I damn well almost had a coronary." He stated dramatically.

"Yeah, we have Jen to thank for that. She somehow hooked us in on the line for the same conversation, so we could follow what was happening. I don't know whether to hate her or love her for that at the moment. Where is he?" she asked not needing to use his name because they both knew who she was referring to.

"He's with the Super," he answered, "I wouldn't be surprised if she weren't giving him a piece of her mind. I know the boy doesn't have a family, so he probably doesn't understand the drill. But when shit is hitting the fan, you call your family."

"He doesn't have a family. When did he tell you that?" she queried, unable to help herself from prying.

"Guy's talk to you know, not in the same amount of detail you lot do but still.." he joked.

It was at this point Wren realised she'd gone off on a tangent. Remembering her priorities, she flipped back to the here and now.

"He called me, but I didn't hear it," she admitted, "what do we have?"

"What we have here is what an ex-military man, like me, would call fubar," he stated.

"Isn't that an American military term?" Wren pointed out.

"It may have started that way, but word gets around," he chuckled.

Wren supposed he was right though, this was fucked up beyond all recognition, she wasn't sure they were even close to a resolution either. What they needed was a goddamned break. Something to give them a clue as to what they were looking at here.

It was then she saw him, Dev was walking with angry strides towards the exit of the perimeter. His fury vibrating with every step he took, he looked set to go off. She walked into his path and their eyes met as she said softly.

"God, Dev, I'm so sorry." She began, and his anger seemed to temper some. He stood lost and as though he was unsure of what his next move should be. She helped him out of his indecision by pulling him into a hug, which wasn't exactly professional behaviour, before saying "You took a year off my life! When I realised what was happening I came as quickly as I could. Don't do that again, ok? You may be new here, but we have each other's backs. If you can't get hold of me you ring Jen, and she'll sound the alarm."

Dev looked like he didn't know what to do with that information so he nodded, and gave her a reassuring squeeze that may have lingered a little too long, before letting her go with a small grin and saying, "Aww you do care…" attempting to play off the moment by adding some levity.

"Na," she said playing along, "If you die I'll have to break in another one and I've only just broken you in."

"Thanks Angel, always good to know where you stand," he replied wryly.

Wren paused at his use of the nickname, before shrugging it off and getting to the crux of the matter.

"So," she began, "Since you got eyes on our crime scene first, tell me what we have in there."

Dev relayed the scene as he'd found it, in all its uncensored detail. Wren turned it over in her head. "So, the perpetrator is communicating with us now? What do you think that tells us? Do we think that the note on the car is related?" Wren speculated on the possibilities. "Why now? What changed?"

"Or maybe they have been all along, and we just didn't know what to look for until they made it clearer," Dev considered. "Maybe somewhere in all of this, there are messages we haven't picked up on yet."

"Well, isn't that unfortunate, guess we'd better have a second look over everything, while we wait for preliminaries on both scenes to come back."

"With two going, who knows how long before we get that report." Matt whined, from not far beside them.

"Will you quit it with the eavesdropping, you nosey bastard?" Dev cajoled.

"It isn't eavesdropping, I'm a detective, it's gathering intel." Matt countered.

The Super walked towards them as they were deliberating, and gave them all a sombre look, when she finally reached them.

"It's looking as though it's going to be a while. You should all get off. If we're lucky maybe the pathologist will have something for us, at least on the viaduct murder, by morning. This one might be a while longer. It's late. Some of us should at least try for some rest, so they can carry the rest of us stuck at the scene when we're falling asleep on our feet tomorrow. CID has arrived, so get on with you."

Chapter Eighteen

August 6th, 2014

For the first time that Dev could recall, his nightmares had faces. He wasn't sure if that was a good or bad thing. Good that he could recall them or bad that they were no longer remaining in his subconscious. In his sleep he'd seen Rosa, Marco, and Vinnie; although they seemed younger. Before time and of course a serial killer had ravaged them. There were new faces though that he hadn't recognised. All in all; this new development disturbed him a lot.

Finding Rosa that way had been devastating, he'd failed her. He'd failed them all, something had been gnawing away at him and he couldn't figure it out. Yet, he was almost positive it would make all of this make some sense. Either that or he was clutching at straws because he had nothing else to focus on, no clues to sink his teeth into. What he needed was fresh information. So, he got up and before the sun had even risen he headed into the station.

That was how he'd been there when Marco's preliminary report had come through. At some point during the course of the evening, he suspected the DCI had visited the pathologist for a general outline, but the preliminary report wasn't guesswork, it was something solid to work with. He was about to start reading through it when Jen appeared at the doorway.

"And I thought I was keen," she said looking at him in question.

"Couldn't sleep," he said, shrugging.

She noticed the printouts he had in his hand and looked at them with interest. "What you got there?"

"It's the preliminary for Marco," he answered.

"Oooooh, I wanna see!" she exclaimed, like a child at Christmas, as she hurried to his side and sat down while making grabby hand gestures.

"Easy tiger, I'll put it down so we can both read it," Dev said with a chuckle.

They sat quietly reading the report, documenting the catalogue of injuries both antemortem and posthumously. They'd been at it a while, when Jen's face suddenly got animated, before she rushed to her desk and began typing furiously. Dev was pulled from his concentration as looked at her, watching, and suddenly picking up the excited vibes coming off her in waves.

"What did you see that I didn't?" he asked.

"The thing about being a nerd is you take in information super-fast," Jen began to explain between typing, "You probably didn't get to it yet but if I'd waited to look I might forget that I saw it. He had "Humpty" etched into his torso."

"As in "Humpty Dumpty" the nursery rhyme?" Dev enquired.

"Yeah. Look at the report, really look at it. He had amputations at all the joints, with his head removed from his neck and the signs of stitches as though they'd removed it only to repair it again. Some of it was done while he was still alive, by the way, ouch. His fingers, wrists, elbow joints, it's like the joints in a doll, except he's Humpty. He was thrown off of a bridge and there wasn't much chance of putting him back together again, what with his being dead and all. I think their message is pretty clear. Then I wondered, how did that correlate to Vincent?" She paused and smiled wide, "I fucking knew it!"

"Knew what?" Dev asked in confusion.

"I knew where I'd read it before. Vincent is the weasel." She told him excitedly.

"The weasel? Ok I'm not following, you are going to have to dumb it down," he said.

"Have you ever wondered about the origins of nursery rhymes?" she asked him.

"No, can't say I have," he said, allowing her to take him for a ride on her crazy train.

"Fun fact, the nursery rhyme "Pop Goes The Weasel" is actually about poor people selling their jackets for food. The weasel was the name of a jacket at that time. They would sell their jackets to buy food. Do you recall the words to the rhyme?" she prompted.

"Half a pound of tuppenny rice—" he began casually before his eyes grew wide. "Feck!" He said, "The black goo was treacle! What about the skinning though, I get the bullet "pop" where does the skinning fit in?"

"He was skinned… but only the top half; from his neck to his wrists...did they skin off a jacket?" Jen said slowly, not quite certain about her explanation.

"You clever bugger!" Dev grinned at her, leaping to his feet, and giving her an excited kiss on the forehead. Jen blushed at his unexpected outburst and then laughed out loud as he dragged her by the hands, onto her feet and swung her around in a child-like dance, while singing the rhyme.

"Half a pound of tuppenny rice,
Half a bag of treacle.
That's the way the money goes,
Pop! Goes the weasel."

"Ok, the little leprechaun clearly ate his lucky charms this morning," Matt loudly announced to the room, while Wren stood gaping. Jen and Dev stopped their crazy merriment to look at each other and then burst out laughing.

"Believe it or not," Jen started to say between giggles, wiping the tears from her eyes, "there's an explanation for this."

"I'd hope so," Matt replied, chuckling at their antics, "Otherwise I'd want to know why I wasn't invited to the party."

"Come on, Dimples, let's let them join the party," Jen teased, pulling him along playfully by the hand she still clasped before letting him go so they could sit down and recount their discovery.

"So, if I'm to follow on from what you're telling me, what does that make Rosa's murder?" Wren asked, still unconvinced by their "off the wall" explanation.

Ash, who'd been quiet and withdrawn since he'd entered the huddle, spoke up for the first time. "She's 'Roses Are Red'." That's her rhyme. They took that sweet woman and turned her death into a goddamned nursery rhyme for kids, like some kind of sick joke!" He fumed through clenched teeth.

Matt put his hand on Ash's shoulder in a show of support, but Ash shrugged it away and stormed off to the canteen. Matt gave the rest of them a look of apology and took off after him. There was a moment of silence before Jen recited. "Roses are red, Violets are blue, you can't see me, but I can see you… he's right. Her rhyme is 'Roses Are Red.' The flowers in the bath will probably be identified in the report as violets."

"Aye," Dev shook his head with sorrow, "So we know what the message is and that's grand, but does anyone want to take a guess at what it all means?"

They all paused to consider his question but no one spoke. The DCI strode into the room and stopped next to them.

"What do we have? Anything new?" He asked.

"We have 'Pop Goes The Weasel', 'Humpty Dumpty' and 'Roses Are Red' nursery rhyme murders and abso-fucking-lutely no clue why," Wren answered.

Wren explained their theory and he nodded. "Ok so do we have an idea why they would do this? Is this some kind of psychological childhood trauma thing? Do they just like nursery rhymes or is this some kind of game?" He speculated.

"We've only just figured out it was nursery rhymes, Sir, we hadn't got an answer as to why yet," Dev said, "though now you mention it childhood trauma might fit. But at what point did a child come into contact with those three separate individuals and are there any more involved that we need to be worrying about? Any idea what criminal activity they are involved in? It's not human trafficking is it? Might explain it if a victim got free."

"Lord, I hope not," the DCI replied, "as far as I'm aware that isn't something they have been linked to in any previous investigations, however there's nothing to say they didn't branch out or been involved and just not had any attention drawn to it. Whatever it is, this person didn't just wake up and decide it might be fun to murder in nursery rhymes; it means something. We just have to figure out what that is."

"It's hard to believe that Rosa would have been involved in human trafficking though, she also really dislikes Marco's associates, so where does she fit into all this? Do you suppose she knew something she shouldn't? She called me and the message said there were things she needed to say but had been too scared to before. Her death also seemed a little less…tortured than the others. It still wasn't pretty but there was no flaying or amputation. Apart from her eyes being missing she had the rest of her body parts. Hers was different somehow. Like she was given leniency." Dev speculated.

"She also had some interesting reading on her coffee table." The DCI stated.

"What?" Wren asked.

"The preliminary for that isn't in yet, I just saw them at the crime scene while waiting for the SOCO team to arrive, the Super took over and I came here to run the incident room and deal with the press. She had some newspaper articles on there about some old police investigation or other." He divulged, shrugging.

"What case?" Dev asked suddenly, extremely interested.

"I didn't read it, just noticed." The DCI said.

He looked to Wren with a pointed look, and understanding crossed her expression before she asked, "Is that the case do you think? The one bugging you?"

"Seems awfully coincidental if it's not," Dev confirmed his suspicions, "We need to know what that article was about."

"I'll give the SOCO team a ring then," the DCI said, with a solemn nod. "Let's get this bastard."

****

Jack McNamara was still keeping a low profile. He'd been immensely pleased to hear that Rosa would no longer be a problem, so that at least was no longer a concern. He'd also begun to suspect that the rumours were true, and Keir was in fact alive. Considering the people that had been slaughtered had all had a hand in his fate, he was beginning to suspect that he might be responsible. God knows he had good cause to want revenge. Jack couldn't let this stand though; he'd paid for the sins of the father and now he would have to pay for his own. Just as soon as he could find the fucker.

Jilly entered the room and approached him. He smiled and gave her a quick kiss as she cuddled into him.

"I have some news for you, darling," she purred.

"You do? What might that be?" he enquired warily, he was not fond of "news" considering recent events.

"You're going to be a father," she told him happily.

"I am?" he asked in surprise, "When did you find out?"

"This morning, I've known for a while, but I wanted to wait until I could get a scan…It's a boy, Jack," she informed him smugly.

His smile lit up his face. His poor excuse for a wife had never been able to give him the son he required but this woman, she had finally given him what he'd always wanted. An heir. It would seem his wife was now surplus to requirement. He had found her replacement.

****

Keri was surprised by the call she'd received from Mary McNamara, she wasn't exactly mother of the year, so her demand to see Keri had come a bit out of left field. She arrived at the house, Jack had gone to ground to avoid the police and no surprise, it was that bitch Jilly he had taken refuge with. Keri hated her with every breath in her body. She was actually surprised Jack had kept her around this long but where Mary was cold, Jilly was hot. Hot tempered, hot if you liked women and she supposed, most likely hot in the sack. The crazy ones always were apparently.

"Good you're here," Mary said, "We have a problem."

"We do?" Keri asked, confused.

"That bitch, has finally done it, gone and got herself pregnant. With a boy, no less. So, I'd say we have a problem," she spat.

"Strange, seems more like a 'you' problem," Keri considered.

"Girly, you owe me more than you can ever repay, I assure you but even if that were not true, who do you suppose will be taking the keys to the kingdom now your *Daddy* has a baby boy in the wings? What do you want to bet Cameron is soon to be replaced as the golden child?" she sneered, hitting her mark as she usually did.

"Huh! Go figure, it would seem *we* do have a problem." Keri agreed, "How do you even know she is?"

"I have spies of my own, it was confirmed today. I have the scan and her medical records, this is happening. Now the question is, how do we plan to deal with it?" Mary retorted, coldly.

"We should call Cameron, he's usually rather good with these types of situations. He has as much to lose as either of us. Also, I'm sure he can get his father on board, might take some subtle nudging but I doubt he'll be particularly happy with this development. He's been expecting his son to take over after all, his son and Jack's daughter. Probably won't be happy to have the arrangement changed at this late hour," Keri suggested,

"Maybe father needs a helping hand with his retirement plan."

Mary smiled, her sharp eyes shining gleefully. "Connor has always been a very distinguished man. Quite easy on the eyes. He used to have a thing for me, you know? Might be time to trade up."

"Mother!" Keri pulled a face.

"Ok… we have a plan, I knew I could count on you," she said.

Chapter Nineteen

It had taken a while for the SOCO team to get back to the DCI about the clippings. Instead, the whole team were trying to find any connections the McNamara's had that might indicate that they had any links to human trafficking. They came up empty. Next they sifted through old cases that had been supplied by various units. There were some implications of drug trafficking and various other rackets. None of which linked to children as far as we could see. Basically, they had nothing to link the cases to some kind of theory that made sense.

The DCI was called away by the pathologist, which was a good sign; he didn't want to wait for the report so he went to get an update in person hoping it might shed some extra light on something we could use. Dev had tried to ring Alec for an update hoping he might be able to lead us there quicker, but he hadn't found anything new either. Which could mean one of two things; he hadn't found the right one yet, but it was there somewhere, or it wasn't a case from that station. Figuring that Alec would be taking care of the first option they decided to try looking at option B.

Jen scrolled through cases as far back as ten years but even with all of us going through them, they'd found nothing which fit the criteria and involved the McNamara's. They tried a second run at them excluding the mentions of McNamara when they considered they hadn't been connected to it at the time but again they came up empty handed. That was when they got the email from SOCO with the photocopies of the two articles in question.

The first was an article about a murder in a storage warehouse that had been put down to gang crime. Liam Whelan was found with his head missing according to the article, all the way back in February 1990. The article was short on details because it was an update, not a crime report and we couldn't see how this connected to our nursery murders. Jen took the date from the article and began running a search to get the police reports if they were even on the system. It was so long ago that we might not be able to find it. However, they could likely trace back the article to the source and find linking articles in the archives of whatever news outlet had published the one we were looking at now. While Jen focused on getting us any details on that front, Wren and Dev took a look at the second.

This article was dated a month after the first, and was about two boys involved in a hit and run incident. No names were given, all it said was that one had died instantly and another had been left in critical condition. It had occurred quite some distance from here; on the outskirts of a small town called Berkhamsted. Neither article related to the other in any way that they could see, and Wren was going insane. Jen was going to set up a separate search for the article on the two boys, but at least this one had mentioned children. However, Wren couldn't see the nursery rhyme link. Still, they could likely try and find the outlet for that and see what they could find out. She just hoped all this digging would pay dividends and they could get to the bottom of it, hopefully with some fresh suspects to look at…or any suspects would be good.

This was where the DCI made a return. He brought with him the cliff notes of Rosa's preliminary report with the full report to follow. She'd had her eyes sewn closed, this at least matched up to Vinnie and Marco so we were looking at the same perpetrator, which they had already deduced but it was nice to have confirmed. The writing had been identified as blood, though tests were being done to confirm. Her eyes had also been removed, as had her fingers, though they had no idea why and unlike the others it had been done postmortem. The flowers had come back as violets as expected and her throat and wrists had been cut. This they suspected was for an expedient death.

 Whoever had done this was either aware of the fact she was expecting Dev or chose to give her a quick death, which as Dev had pointed out differed from the other two and had a sense of mercy to it. Almost like she'd died more out of necessity, as opposed to wanting to see her suffer like the other murders. Rosa's murder would appear to be the key to solving this case. They just had to figure out the anomalies and maybe they would be able to find out why this was happening. In most crimes what you are looking for are the things that shouldn't be there. The things that don't belong. Rosa didn't belong so if they figured out why she was involved, they could likely find the needle in this haystack.

"We've been at this for hours," Jen whined, "Someone needs to get food or something. I'm getting hangry."

"Fine. I'll go but I'm going to need a hand getting it all back here. Are you coming?" Wren replied then looked to Dev.

Dev nodded and said, "Aye, I could use some air. All this reading is giving me a headache."

****

As they drove from the station Wren took a peek at Dev, who looked tired and weary. She'd seen him become increasingly unfocused as the day had worn on and was concerned. So, she tried to decide on the best way to ask him if he was doing okay without seeming like she was questioning his capabilities. Men were touchy when it came to people thinking they couldn't cope. Like because they were men they shouldn't admit to struggling. It was an unrealistic standard to expect from them; they were people not machines and, as such, should be given the leeway to admit when they weren't at their best. However before she could decide on her approach he spoke.

"Whatever it is you want to say, you should just say it. You'll wear yourself out arguing in your head." He chuckled wryly.

"Are you ok?" she blurted, "you seem like you're tired, is it the nightmares? Are they bothering you?"

"Aye," he admitted, "They are some. It's been so long since I've had them I thought it had passed but this past week it has been relentless."

"Do you want to talk about them?" she asked gently, "Maybe talking about them will help put your mind at rest."

"I would if I had anything to say. I don't remember what they are about. Although for the first-time last night I actually saw faces so maybe that one is a new addition. I never have before, last night though I saw the faces of our victims. I also suspect I've been sleepwalking…" He said, sheepishly.

"Really? Is that dangerous?" Wren questioned, a worried look, creasing her forehead.

Dev shrugged. "I don't know, I don't recall it happening before, but my foster brother told me I used to do it when I was younger."

"Foster brother? If you don't mind me asking…what happened to your family?" Wren pressed, curiously.

"I don't know. In fact, I have no idea where I came from, I woke up in a hospital at the age of eight, no idea who I was, no family, no memory. I'm a blank slate before that age, nobody could ever work it out, me included," he explained.

"That's awful, I'm so sorry. Nobody tried to find you?" she asked, trying to get her head around that.

"As far as I'm aware, I have always been just me," he affirmed.

"And the nightmares? How do they fit into that?" she wondered, thinking aloud.

"I was told I'd been severely injured when they found me, there were signs of previous injuries when I was examined, and they suspected the nightmares came from whatever happened to me before I lost my memory. I've never remembered the time I lost and honestly I don't know that I'd want to. As a police officer, I suspect whatever caused the injuries didn't exactly paint a picture of a happy home, so maybe it's best that I don't remember it," he said nonchalantly, trying to play it off like it didn't matter.

Wren wasn't buying it though. It had to hurt that it was likely, the people who were supposed to love him and protect him, had likely caused him harm, and left him to die. Wren found her heart ached for the young boy Dev had been and when he'd joked about wishing he knew who he was, he'd not been being evasive but genuinely didn't know. She felt a little ashamed of how hard she'd been on him. They pulled up to the cafe and

Wren parked the car. The mood had turned solemn, and she felt the need to try to lighten it. She unfastened her seatbelt and pasted on a devilish smile.

"All this talk has made me hungry. Let's get food. Whoever's last in is buying and before Dev had even registered the words she took off for the cafe, leaving him to lock the car, and stare after her. By the time he finally caught up with her she grinned mischievously and teased, "I hope you bought your wallet, I'm really hungry and I plan on getting a LOT."

"You cheated!" He argued.

"Now Dev. Have you ever heard the tale of the two wolves? There are two wolves inside all of us. One is filled with anger, envy, jealousy, self-pity, guilt, resentment, inferiority etc. The other is filled with joy, peace, love, hope, kindness, generosity etc. which wolf wins?" she asked, innocently.

"The one you feed." Dev relented.

"Na, it's still me. Now feed me, you loser." Wren cackled at her own joke and Dev laughed with surprise and gave her a playful shove.

****

Keri watched them from a distance. She wasn't sure why she was so interested but she found she enjoyed watching them playing and joking around. He looked happy, well happier than he had been when they'd first pulled up and Keri found that she liked that the white-haired girl was able to do that for him.

During the time she spent watching him he'd had an air of sadness about him that had made her feel sad for him, but seeing him here she hoped that he had a chance for more moments like this one. A pang of jealousy hit her, she wished she could have had moments of messing around like that with him but that was never going to be, she was going in a vastly different direction from Keir now and that was just the way of life.

Sometimes people's paths were only meant to cross for a short time before they went on their way. Instead, they were destined to be on opposing sides of a war neither one of them had asked to be involved in, they were just born into it. Fate had spoken and just because you didn't like what the bitch had to say, didn't mean she didn't speak the truth.

She needed to stop watching him, no good would come from this. She needed to remember that feelings had no place in her world. Only power and violence, manipulation and ruthlessness. Anything less and the people would tear you apart like wolves and swallow you whole. Only the strongest could survive it and she had survived it for a long time. So now was not the time to forget the lessons she'd been taught. Now was the time to show her teachers what a good pupil she'd been. It was time for the pupil to surpass the master.

****

They had decided it would be better to order for themselves and have their food inside, then get the others food before they left so their own wouldn't get cold and the rest would stay as hot as it could on their way back to the station. That and neither of them were ready to go back to dredging through old articles while they tried to find the information they were looking for.

It was sometimes better to get away from the situation for a while so that you could look at it with fresh eyes upon your return. Or at least, that was their excuse, and they were sticking to it.

They had finished their food and were having some coffee before they headed out. Dev was drinking his usual black no sugar, Wren had decided to forgo tea in favour of a sugary delight that included cream and syrup. She'd taken a small sip of the drink and Dev laughed at the sight of cream sitting on her top lip like a large white moustache, that paired with her hair colouring looked hilarious. He laughed at it, and she frowned.

"What are you laughing at?" she asked, confused by his mirth.

"You have some cream," he explained, indicating where the cream was situated on her face.

"Well shit," she said wiping at her mouth, "Did I get it?"

"No Angel, you still have some at the corner," he smiled, watching as she patted at her mouth, trying to get it off, before finally taking pity on her, "you're missing it, here let me..."

He leaned forward brushing her hand away and cupped her chin with one hand, while lifting a finger to the corner of her mouth and wiping the cream away. His hand lingered and the mirth fell from his face as he looked at her, his green eyes grew darker and she held her breath, trapped by the intensity she found there. They stayed that way until a crash came from behind them jolting them back to the present, and they looked around to see a flustered waitress, hurriedly picking glass off of the floor, as she blushed with embarrassment under the weight of the onlookers' stares. Dev cleared his throat and muttered about getting the food order in while she finished her coffee and stalked away to the counter.

Ten minutes later they carried away the brown takeaway bag and coffees and got into the car. There was an awkward silence between them, and Wren put on the radio in a bid to fill it without having to address the moment in the restaurant as she was itching to do. They finally arrived back at the station and upon entering the incident room, they were accosted by slightly irritated locusts, pulling at the goods like they hadn't seen food in a year.

"You took your time! Anything you want to tell us?" She asked, scrutinising them suspiciously, making Dev and Wren both shift uncomfortably. Wren made some hurried excuses and went to the bathroom leaving Dev to stand uncomfortably while the team looked at him expectantly for an explanation.

"We decided to eat in and clear our heads..." He said lamely.

"And did you?" Jen asked sweetly in a mocking tone. Dev looked at her blankly. "Clear your head?"

"What? Oh aye, all clear…" Dev muttered looking away, unable to meet her inquisitive gaze.

"Seems like it," she chuckled before attacking her food with gusto.

Wren returned with some tea, and they all polished off the food before getting back to work. After hours of scrolling through various articles, police reports and such, they found little more, and the Super came in and told them to call it a day. They all left feeling as though they had little to show for the day's work, but at least they had some idea what they were looking for now.

Tomorrow they would have the full report on Rosa's death, and they could look further into the articles and with luck they would eventually find something worth all the time they had put into it.

As Dev opened his car and lowered himself into the seat he felt Wren's presence at the opening. He looked at her and she said quietly, "Try to get a good night's sleep and if you have any nightmares or anything and want to talk, you have my number." Then walked off without so much as a backward glance.

Chapter Twenty

January 26th, 1990

"What the fuck happened?" the big man with the scary expression shouted at Marco.

"She jumped, boss," he lied.

"She fucking jumped. How did she get the window open without the two of you stopping her?" he asked with disbelief.

Marco shuffled from one foot to another, before deciding that the truth would be the most believable. "We were smoking so we opened it."

"And she jumped? Why didn't you stop her?" he questioned angrily.

"We were dealing with the kids," he hedged, "We took our eyes off of her and she was just gone."

"Get out of my fucking sight! Useless fucking eejits!" the scary man shouted.

They scuttled from the room cowering, when the man turned to another and asked, "Did they clean it up?"

"Yes, boss. She's ready to dispose of," he replied.

The boy upon hearing this, spoke up defiantly, silent tears running down his cheeks. "I want to see her! I want to see my ma!"

The scary man turned on him, quiet rage on his face and back handed the boy who put his hand to his sore cheek and looked up in terror. Then the man smiled down at him with a ruthless grin, "You want to see her boyo? Lee, the boy would like to see his ma. Why don't you take him and put him in the "back" so they can see each other. He can help you lay her to rest."

"But boss..." Lee went to argue.

"Did that sound like I wanted your opinion? Do what I say!"

The boy was dragged from the room by the man called Lee and outside to a large vehicle where another man stood waiting.

"She's all loaded up," he told Lee.

"Open the boot." Lee ordered.

"What? Why? What's the brat doing here?" he asked as he noticed the boy being dragged along behind.

"Boss' orders." Lee informed him without further explanation.

The second man shrugged and opened it, and the boy was picked up, then deposited into the boot of the car. He tried to fight them and get away, but they closed it down and the boy looked around for a way out and came face to face with the terrifying remains of his mother. He screamed. The boot opened, and Lee shouted for him to shut up. The other man grabbed some duct tape they'd used to package up the boy's mother and stuck some unceremoniously across his mouth before doing the same to his hands. "There, that should keep you from being a pain in the ass, now say your goodbyes to Mummy, because after today you won't be seeing her again."

The boy was closed back into semi-darkness, and stared in fear at the blood-spattered face of his mother staring back. Her red hair, almost black with dried blood. He remembered what she'd told him not even a week ago. "Close your eyes, Keir. And whatever you do, don't open them, not for anything, no matter what you hear, you keep them shut. Do as I say, understand?"

So, he closed his eyes and kept them shut. It wasn't long before the car stopped moving and the boot was opened once more, the boy kept his eyes closed though.

He was lifted from the vehicle and his hands were unbound. He began to fight again but the man shook him and said in a menacing tone, "Best you behave boy or else I'll see your sister punished for your bad behaviour." At his words, the boy stilled. He was set on his feet and a shovel was chucked at his feet.
  "Start digging boyo."

Chapter Twenty-One

7th August 2014

When Dev woke up, he was disorientated and cold. He opened his eyes and was confused to find himself outside. He felt panic rising in his chest and looked around, perplexed at the strange surroundings. Where was he? How did he get here? He took a few deep breaths to calm himself and took a more detached survey of the area. His perusal stopped fast on a shovel a few feet away, sticking up out of the ground. Alarmed, his breath caught, and he patted himself down for his phone. When he found it he let the breath he'd been holding go, and pulling it out he dialled.

"Hello?" Wren answered, sounding as though she'd been pulled from sleep.

"I need you," Dev almost pleaded, in a tone he himself didn't recognise.

"What's wrong?" Wren asked, her tone sharp as she seemed to register the urgency in his own.

"I'm not sure. I don't know where I am. I woke up outside, I don't know how I got here or how long I've been here and there's a shovel in front of me… Angel, I won't lie, I'm freaking out." Dev rambled, his teeth beginning to chatter as he spoke.

"I'm calling Jen, she should be able to locate you by triangulating your phone signal. Stay on the line for me, okay? I'll talk to Jen on my landline, look around and see if you can see anything we could use as a landmark to help us find you. Just hold on, help is coming." Wren reassured him in a soothing tone. Dev nodded, forgetting that she couldn't see him and took another look at his surroundings. He was surrounded by a wooded area, stood in a clearing amongst it, but he couldn't place it and instead found himself staring at the shovel before him. The sight of it incited panic and dread, and he found himself beginning to hyperventilate. He could hear Wren's voice on the phone calling for him and telling him to breathe but he couldn't seem to follow the directive. The world started to spin around him, and his head thumped painfully, as though something inside it was trying to break out. He felt nausea rise and the world careened, and he was falling, the floor meeting him, as the world went dark.

****

Wren was shouting Dev's name into the phone, but he was unresponsive. On the landline she had pressed to her other ear, she could hear the clicking of keys as Jen furiously worked trying to locate him. Please let him be alive, she prayed silently.
"I think I have the area he is located in, I'll call the others so we can get a search together," Jen said.
"Give me the location," Wren demanded. Then she was out of the door and running. She arrived at the area and Jen called to inform her the others were also arriving, and they began their search. They fanned out, so they could cover the area in the shortest time possible, in the hope they could find him that much quicker.
When she finally reached him, she'd found him lying unconscious on the ground. She rushed to him checking his vitals for signs of life, after a few nerve wracking seconds, she found it. He was still with them. Relief flooded her and she heard the sounds of an ambulance siren in the distance. Jen must've called for them to attend. She called Jen briefly to inform her of

her position and not long after the paramedics were on the scene and checking over Dev who was still lying on the ground at her feet. They fired off questions, but she had no answers and Dev finally stirred, regaining consciousness. Thanking God, she turned her attention to where the DCI and Ash were emerging from the trees.

"What the hell happened?" The DCI shouted, demanding an answer as he approached.

"I'm not entirely sure, Sir," Wren answered honestly, as the paramedics loaded a confused Dev onto a stretcher and headed to the ambulance while he protested.

Matt made an appearance behind the DCI and a paramedic asked if anyone would be escorting him to the hospital, if so they would need to come with them to the ambulance.

"Ash, go with Dev, when he is able to, find out what you can and report back to me immediately," the DCI ordered. Wren started to argue but the DCI cut her off with a scathing look. "You will remain here, DI Jones and explain to me why I am out in the ass end of nowhere, with an officer being loaded into an ambulance and staring at a shovel." He finished his tirade and Wren followed his line of sight. For the first time since she'd arrived, she noticed the shovel, perfectly balanced into the ground near where Dev had been laying. Looking back to the DCI she nodded in agreement, she would get this done and check on Dev later. That's what he would want her to do.

****

Sean O'Connell was worried. He'd rung his brothers and arranged for them to meet, they would know what to do. When they finally arrived his eldest brother asked, "What's this all about? Why did you call?"
"The police are there. Where Chastity is buried, they are there. I don't know how they knew where to find her, but they are there, and they're sealing off the area," he told them, his voice betraying his concern. He cast his mind back to the fateful night that he and Marco had been watching her, the night Marco had jokingly held her at the window, at the time he'd found it entertaining, enjoyed watching her fear as she balanced precariously from the ledge. Until he watched as she plunged to the ground, and it hadn't been funny anymore. He furiously searched through his memory of the night, such a long time ago now, he had to strain to recall if there was anything they had done that could tie them to this.
"I don't know why you're so worked up, we cleaned up well. The boy buried her, not us. There should be no way to connect us to it." Lee assured him, disregarding his fear.
"But how did they even know where to look? It's been twenty-four years, and nobody has even tried to find her, why now? I'm telling you, someone knows," he countered, his panic only increasing as he explained his concern to his brother.
"It's not what they think they know, it's what they can prove, ain't it," Paul answered this time, his voice calm, "if they could prove it, they would already be here arresting us, wouldn't they?"
Sean felt the fear abate, he was right. It would've been hard to prove back when it had happened, it would only

be harder to prove now that so much time had passed. "You're right," he said, "they have nothing."

"Too right, I'm right," Paul acknowledged, arrogantly. "Now get yourself together and go home. If you start fretting and get all jittery, people will get suspicious, you'll draw attention to yourself. Stay calm and keep your cool. All of this will have blown over in no time. We need to just go about our lives like nothing has changed and give them no reason to focus their attention on us. It's business as usual."

"Right," Sean agreed," Business as usual, nobody can prove a thing. I'm just paranoid, and letting my mind run away with me."

"Are we done with this bullshit?" Les asked impatiently, speaking for the first time.

Paul looked to his brother in question, "You done?"

Sean nodded. Everything was A-Okay.

****

The SOCO team had been called out once again. The area surrounding the shovel had been isolated and a perimeter once again set up and they had finally arrived, trudging dismally toward the scene—one particularly cranky member asking if this was likely to become a nightly occurrence—now they waited to see if there was anything to be found.

It took them quite a while, as they cautiously attended the area, in a bid to not disturb any evidence they might find should there be victims buried in the dirt beneath them. They had no way of knowing if this was actually the case, but they were erring on the side of caution. As time slowly ticked by, they were beginning to suspect they had it wrong, but they finally got confirmation that human remains had been buried there. Since they'd found evidence of a burial site they would have to arrange for a specialist to attend and ascertain whether or not they had others buried here. Continuing any further activity here could contaminate the scene and be detrimental to any other cases they may have to investigate should more victims be discovered. They had been discussing how to proceed, and the conclusion was to bring in a cadaver dog to see if there were any more sites they would need to isolate and only if it was necessary would they use geophysical methods.

What they had discerned from the discovery, was that this was no recent crime. This victim had been dead for some time. So now Wren had more questions. Was this related to their current investigation or a separate crime? Since it seemed likely it was connected considering the circumstances of its discovery, the next question was, what did this body buried here have to do with the crimes being committed in the here and now? "Well, this gives a whole new meaning to the term 'digging up old skeletons' doesn't it?" Matt joked flippantly, trying to diffuse the tension.

"I'd just started to think we are getting somewhere with this and then shit like this happens and I feel as though we are back to square once again," Wren remarked, choosing to ignore Matt's attempt at a joke.

Wren's mind turned over all the questions she now had. If this is linked to their investigation how did it tie in? Did this person's death mean something to the perpetrator? If it did, are they a relative? Was this the only body or were they going to uncover more? How did it all relate to the articles they'd been looking into?

Was any of it related at all? Her mind went around and around until Matt grabbed her arm, pulling her back to reality.

"What's got you thinking so hard?" he asked.

"I have so many questions and I can't see how they relate at all. Maybe Dev will be able to tell us more, somehow they got the drop on him. It's the only explanation for how he ended up here. Why do you suppose they chose him? Do you think it's because he's new to the area and he wouldn't know where he was, like some kind of game to mess with us? Or has the killer taken a shine to our Irish man? Why do they seem to be communicating with us? Is it all of us or Dev specifically? Is he going to become a target?" Wren speculated, wildly.

"You need to slow your roll, Wren," Matt said, trying to stop her descent into madness. "We do this the same way we always do, we wait for the experts to tell us what we have, and we investigate what we are given, same as always. We have done this the same way a thousand times before, so why are you in such a frenzy this time?"

"I'm worried about Dev, I thought they got him, you know? I thought we wouldn't make it in time, and he'd become just another victim to add to the tally," Wren's eyes became misty, and she blinked back the tears, the stress of the night taking its toll.

"I know, I thought the same thing," Matt told her quietly, giving her shoulder a squeeze, "he's still here though, so let's concentrate on the positives. We have leads, our boy is still alive and kicking and will no doubt be back in the thick of it before we know it and we may have just found our motive. If we figure out why, it might not be that much longer before it leads us to who."

****

Dev was in and out of consciousness for a few hours, he was just so tired that he couldn't seem to keep his eyes open, he heard voices but couldn't seem to understand any of their words, so he just lay and let it all wash over him as the activity went on around him.

He tried to get his mind to focus on anything that might bring him out of his numbed state, but the drowsiness just kept pulling him back under. After some time had passed he felt something wipe at his forehead, it felt nice, and a cool voice spoke to him soothingly.

"It's okay, just rest I've got you," it whispered, "nobody can hurt you, I'm with you now. Don't worry, I'm going to take care of you, just wait and see." What he assumed was a cloth stopped wiping his brow and the voice seemed further away now. "Rest easy, Keir."

The next time he woke up he was more aware than he had been previously, he opened his eyes to see Ash and Jen sitting with worried looks at the end of the hospital bed. Upon seeing his eyes open, they stood and moved closer.

"You had us all worried there for a while, mate," Ash said solemnly.

"Aye, was a little worried myself to tell the truth," Dev croaked his throat dry, "What happened?"

"We were kind of hoping you could tell us," Jen chipped in.

"Is Wren here?" he asked, looking around them.

"No, the DCI wanted her to stay at the scene. He needed someone to give him an update and since he couldn't address the source of this evening's entertainment, because of an unexpected trip to the hospital, she was the next port of call," Ash explained, "they are currently still on scene waiting for a cadaver dog. They found a body."

"Where? Who?" Dev asked abruptly.

"We don't know yet, the body they found has been dead for some time. They discovered it not far away from where the shovel had been," Ash informed him.

At the mention of the shovel Dev felt the room spin and suppressed the urge to vomit. They must've seen the sudden change in his pallor because Jen grasped his arm, as though to steady him and told him to lay back down, they would call for someone and they would wait outside so he could rest some more. Dev did as she bade him, and he was asleep before his head had hit the pillow.

Chapter Twenty-Two

Wren found herself immensely relieved when the cadaver dogs gave no indication that there were any other bodies buried in the area, other than where they had already been digging. They weren't going to uncover a mass grave, at least that was some positive news. With that done, the DCI gave her the go ahead to leave the scene, so she could go to the hospital and check what progress, if any, they had made there. She was thankful for the directive, wanting the chance to see how Dev was fairing. When she'd arrived she found Ash, Jen and Matt lingering in the waiting area and she rushed to join them.

"How is he doing?" Wren asked.

"He's been in and out of consciousness. He was awake for a short time but all he could tell us was what had happened when he woke up there, he couldn't recall how he came to be there at all," Jen replied.

"What's the update on the scene, did the cadaver dogs find others?" Matt questioned.

"No, just the one, did they take blood from him for toxicology so we can find out if he was drugged?" Wren fired back.

"They did but we won't get the results back for a while, with all the work being processed from the various sites, there's a backlog," Ash informed her, joining the discussion.

"Is he awake now? I'd like to see how he is for myself," Wren enquired, looking to the door, itching to check on him.

"He's been in and out for a while, but he might be back with us, you could go in and see," Jen said, "he asked if you were here when he first woke."

Wren's face dropped at this, feeling as though she'd somehow let him down by not being there, then she reminded herself that she hadn't been given a choice in the matter. "I'll look in now, if he's not awake I can call back a bit later," she thought aloud.

"I can come with you, I haven't been there myself yet," Matt offered.

Wren considered this before deciding, "I'll go ahead, if he's awake I'll come and get you, if not there will be less chance of disturbing him if I go alone."

"Yeah, that's probably best," Matt agreed.

She opened the door carefully, trying not to make much noise and closed it behind her with a hushed click. Wren turned to approach but as she did she went stiff, her eyes widening at what she saw.

Dev was struggling and thrashing in the hospital bed, as though he was fighting for his life. Sweat poured off of him, as quiet tears slid down his cheeks and fell from his face.

"Ma! Wake up ma…Mama please! You can't leave us, we need you." He begged, his voice child-like and terrified. His whole body shook with tremors, as if Jack Frost himself had a hold of him. "Mammy please, you have to be okay, who will look after Kelly, I can't do it on my own. Please, please wake up," His body was wracked with sobs now, though he never woke. He went still for a brief moment before he started up again. "No, no, no, no! I'll be good, I promise, please don't make me… I can't…please don't…I'm sorry mama. I'm so sorry!"

Wren couldn't stand it anymore, tears of her own were falling at the broken, begging man before her. She went to him, pulled him close and stroked his hair, trying to stop the sound of the heartbreaking pleas coming from him.

"It's okay baby, mummy's fine, everything is fine..." she cooed, swallowing the lump forming in her throat. He finally seemed to lose the rigidity and tension he'd been holding himself with and settled murmuring, "I love you mama," before slipping into a sound sleep.

Wren held him for a while longer, wanting to be sure it was over before she slid away from him and left the room with the same stealth she'd used while entering. When she got to the other side of the door she took a few steadying breaths before turning to face the others.

"Wren? What's wrong? Is he okay?" Jen asked, rapidly firing questions, taken aback by her friend's obvious distress.

Wren shook her head and looked away, indicating that she couldn't speak, emotion was thick in her throat at the display she had been witness to. When she felt she had herself under control enough to speak, she said, "He was sleeping, he's well…he was having some kind of nightmare…" she trailed off not really knowing how to put into words what she'd seen in the room. It was so hard to put into words, she found herself going quiet.

The others looked at her unsure what to do. Matt finally cleared his throat and muttered something about getting coffee, nudging Ash as he passed him. Ash followed, glad to be leaving the awkwardness of the moment in favour of having something to do and left the silence behind him. There was a pause while they watched the men leave before Jen turned to her friend.

"Aww Wrenny," she said playfully, hugging her with fervour, "tell your Auntie Jen everything."

"It was just…bad. I was caught off guard, no wonder he has trouble sleeping. I didn't know, when he told me I didn't think. I didn't know…" Wren rambled, incoherently.

"It's okay, love, I'm sure he's fine, well he's definitely fine but I'm sure he's okay too." She joked light-heartedly, and Wren smacked her, then pulled away, finally getting a hold of herself.

"See! There she is! That's my girl." Jen smiled, happy to see her friend snap out of it.

"What the hell happened to him, Jen?" Wren asked, sadly.

"I don't know," Jen replied simply.

A doctor emerged from the room behind them, hands on her hips, obvious anger radiating from her. Wren looked at her confused, not able to recall her entering.

"What did you do to my patient?" She asked in a cold, hard tone, "He is a mess! Did you upset him? He's in the hospital!"

"I...I didn't!" Wren stammered, "He...he was having a nightmare... I tried to help..."

The doctor gave her a stern, assessing look before asking, "Does he usually suffer with nightmares? I'll have to warn the staff attending him if that is the case."

"He says he hasn't had them frequently since he was eleven, only on the odd occasion if he's stressed, recently though he has been getting them regularly," Wren answered, "they seem disturbing though, I've never seen anything like it."

The doctor's countenance softened, "Nightmares can be like that sometimes, leave him to rest a while. I'll see him right as rain," she said. The men returned carting coffee in disposable cups and the doctor went on her way.

"Everything okay?" Matt queried, looking in the direction the doctor had moved in.

"Yes, she was just checking him over," Jen replied.

"So…What's next?" Ash asked.

"I'll hang here until Dev wakes up, see if he has rested enough to remember more. Matt can stay with me, you and Jen should head back to the incident room, see if we can make any further progress on the articles. Also check and see if we have any further updates from SOCO, maybe they have news on our new addition," Wren suggested.

"Sounds like a plan to me," Matt replied, sipping on his coffee.

****

When Dev woke again, he felt better. The remnants of the headache that had been hanging over him since he'd first woken up in the clearing had passed, the rest had obviously done him some good.

"Sleeping on the job. What would the Don say?" Matt joked. He looked up and saw Wren and Matt waiting expectantly.

"Aye, laugh it up, ya eejit," Dev retorted, flipping him off.

"How are you feeling?" Wren enquired, her usual snarkiness nowhere to be seen, instead replaced with tenderness and worry. It made him slightly uncomfortable, which is why he purposely misinterpreted her question.

"They say you are as young as the person you feel…"

Wren's nose screwed up and she rolled her eyes with disdain. There now, Dev thought, that was more like it. Smiling at her, he gave her a cheeky wink.

"Well, you appear to be in better shape," Matt chuckled, "Can you tell us any more about what happened?"

"No, not really. I woke up there, I was cold. I saw what I saw, and I called Ang… Wren. I woke up when the paramedics came and then nothing until Jen and Ash. That's all I have. Did they learn anything from the scene?" he asked.

"They found some human remains, old ones," Wren answered,

"We aren't sure how it all connects yet. Jen and Ash have gone back to continue working on the article leads, we're waiting on SOCO for an update on what they've found, otherwise not much more to add."

"So, when can we blow this popsicle stand?" Dev said.

****

Jen had got a hit on one of the articles. The case in question had been concerning the death of Liam Whelan. They had already known he'd been beheaded and found in a storage warehouse and it was suggested that gang crime was responsible, but there were a few details left out of the article. On the police report it was stated he was discovered on a carousel that happened to be in storage and as well as the decapitation, his heart had also been removed. The other strange thing of note from the case was that none of his family were ever found.

They had been unable to inform his family, as they hadn't been seen for weeks before his death was discovered. They had looked into this in the beginning, as often times the person responsible for the murder is someone they are close to, however during the course of the investigation a few of Liam's close friend had informed them that Chastity Whelan, his wife, had left him and taken the kids, after she had discovered he'd had an affair. Would you look at that! Marco Salvador was his friend... now, wasn't that interesting. Jen wondered if his wife was still in town or if they had gone into hiding as originally planned before Rosa's death. She'd have to send Ash to check it out. Maybe she knew what had become of the Whelans.

****

  Ash arrived at Marco's house, pressed the doorbell, and waited. No sound came from the inside. He waited a little longer. A sound came from inside, the voice of a young boy. He pressed the bell again, more persistently, now that he knew there was someone inside.
"Who is it? I have a gun pointed at the door. I swear to God I will shoot!" The scared voice of Geena Salvador came from the other side.
"Mrs Salvador, I'm DC Ash Carter. Do you remember me from the hospital? I called Rosa and escorted her in when your son was missing, could you please let me in?" He asked.
"I don't need any more trouble. I've lost my husband, my baby's Abuela and his Tía all in the space of a week. Will you not be satisfied until we join them?" She accused, her voice shaking as she spoke, "We are leaving tonight. Leaving all this evil behind us."
"Please Mrs Salvador, the only way for anyone to be truly safe is if we find who is doing this and stop it. Do you want to be looking over your shoulder for the rest of your life, wondering if this will be the day your son

is taken and not returned?" Ash pressed. There was silence from the other side, then the door opened.

"I'll give you fifteen minutes and then I'm done, do you hear? I will leave here and never return. I plan to go back home to Spain. Our flight leaves in a few hours," she warned.

"I will escort you myself, just answer my questions and I'll see you safely on that plane, so you and your son can be free of all this," Ash promised her.

"I'll take that deal," she said, looking less agitated, then she stepped aside and let him in.

Once inside, she showed him into a dining area where Alexis sat playing on the floor, suitcases lined up nearby. "Ask your questions," she said.

"We found an old article amongst Rosa's things. One is about two boys involved in a hit and run. The other was about the death of a man named Liam Whelan. Can you tell me anything about these articles? Your husband was named in a police report during the investigation into Liam's death and we were hoping you could help us," Ash asked.

"I don't know much, I wasn't with Marco then. There was only one occasion where this subject came up, during an argument between Marco and his sister. It was the only time he allowed her to address it. She asked what had happened to the family, she knew the mother hadn't left, she had seen her with her own eyes. She wanted to know where they had gone. Marco said the mother had jumped from a window after she'd been assaulted by a bad man. She asked again what had happened to the children, he said the daughter had been taken by the gang who had killed her father, sold to human traffickers and the son had been killed in a hit and run with another young boy, whilst hiding after the death of his parents. Rosa cried and they never spoke again, not until my Alexis was born. That is all I know." She answered.

"Do you know what the living child's name was?" Ash asked, not really sure why it mattered but if childhood trauma were a motive, he figured the father being murdered by gang members, their mother jumping out of a window and a brother dying in a hit and run, would make the cut.

"Kelly. Kelly Whelan." She replied.

"Thank you, Geena." Ash said with sincerity.

"Don't thank me, get me the hell out of this place and on a plane, I can't stay here. I need to save my son." she implored.

"Which airport?" he queried and then helped her load her suitcases.

A few hours later he used his police privileges to escort her onto the plane and watched just to be sure she left the country safe. It was the least he could do.

Chapter Twenty-Three
February 2nd, 1990

It had been nearly a week since the mother had met her unfortunate fate and the two children had been forlorn and lived in constant fear of what would happen with her gone. He'd heard voices discussing updates on their father's whereabouts and whether or not he would be returning soon with the money he owed.

Two men had been told to watch over them and over time the children had heard them referring to each other as Paul and Les. They seemed to be annoyed that they'd been charged with the care of the two children and felt they would have been of more use in tracking down their father. As they discussed this quietly in hushed, angry voices, the boy spoke for the first time since he'd been dragged forcefully from the room a week ago.

"You are all stupid if you think he's coming back," he said, "It's been too long, if he'd been coming back he would have come by now."

"Who're you calling stupid, boy?" the one named Les shouted, angrily, rising up to grab at the boy. "You would've thought that watching what became of your dear sweet Mammy, you might've learned to keep your mouth closed. Perhaps you need to be reminded further," he threatened.

"Whatever you plan to do with me, you should just do it already," the boy retorted his face void of all emotion, as though he was completely spent and had no more to give. He seemed to have accepted his fate, the constant anticipation and fear finally becoming too much for him, wiping out the emotions entirely.

"Are you feeling brave, little boy?" Paul called from where he was positioned, "Take his clothes off," he said to Les. The man looked at him in question, watching as Paul removed his belt and cracked it into his other hand, supplying an answer. Les nodded and did as he had instructed, the boy fighting him furiously until he was eventually subdued and succumbed to the man pulling his clothes from his little body.

"In my day, boy. If a child didn't respect his elders, he'd get a leathering," Paul told him, his voice a quiet calm that felt unnatural in the situation they found themselves in. He looked at the young girl, she looked as though she may try to defend her brother, so he addressed her. "Stay out of this little girl, it was your poor choice to take a bite out of Marco that led to your mother taking a nosedive out of the window, wouldn't want you to be the cause of your brother's death too, would we?" The little girl flinched with the weight of his words, and cowered once more.

He returned his attention to the boy and stepped toward him. The boy fought against the grasp the other man held him down with. There was a whoosh as the belt was released in a strike and a crack as it connected with flesh. Over and over the sound repeated; the whoosh and the crack perfectly in chorus with the unholy noises that spilled from the boy's mouth each time a blow landed. The girl covered her ears, unable to stand the sound and closed her eyes, as she rocked back and forth in crazed movements trying desperately to block it out. She never heard when the man named Paul finally stepped away again, and commanded the other in a cool, unperturbed manner to "clean him up, he's making a mess of the place," before returning to his previous perch and ignoring the *rocking of the girl left in his care, while the boy was removed from the room.*

Chapter Twenty-Four

August 8th, 2014

When Ash had called Jen with the information he'd gotten from Geena, she had understood how the two articles they had found fit together. It was a terrible tragedy. She wondered then if that meant the body uncovered in the clearing, where Dev had been found, belonged to Chastity Whelan. If that was the case, with the father being brutally murdered and the boy killed in a hit and run, which of itself was pretty suspicious, the only surviving member of the Whelan family, according to the statement, was Kelly Whelan. Assuming that she had survived human trafficking, if she had, could she be their suspect?

Looking at their victims, Jen wasn't sure. Would a woman have the strength to subdue, carry and dispose of the corpses of the two male victims? It seemed unlikely, unless she had some kind of specialist training. For it to be plausible she would have to be something that would make it feasible, such as military personnel or a weightlifter. Something that would make her able to comfortably lift that kind of weight. While she would most certainly fit the profile as far as motive went, the only way Jen could suitably see that working—unless she fit the few exceptions she had considered—was if she'd had help.

Although if the woman had survived her father's murder, her mother's abuse and suicide, the death of her brother to a hit and run incident, and a trafficking ring, living to tell the tale; there was a small chance she would have the mettle it would take, as well as more than enough motive to see it done and achieve the unlikely. There were whole books dedicated to stories of people surviving or accomplishing great feats when the circumstances called for it, so Jen settled on it being possible.

With all that, it was still an avenue for her to explore, which was more than they'd up to this point. She needed to update the team so they could begin to unravel this pandora's box they had unwittingly opened. Ash would likely be a few hours at the airport, and she felt a small sense of relief knowing that Geena and her small child, Alexis, would be safe while they looked into it further.

****

Dev was given the all clear to leave the hospital, however the DCI had ordered him not to return to work for the next few days while he "recovered." It was Dev's opinion that if the hospital deemed him suitable for release then he was already recovered; unfortunately, he was alone in this assessment. Having not yet had it confirmed if he'd been drugged, the DCI wasn't prepared to take the chance that he may suffer from lingering side effects, that may put himself or one of his colleagues, at risk whilst on duty.

Wren had dropped him at home, she and Matt clucking over him like a couple of demented mother hens, only increasing his irritation and heightening his sour mood. Despite being left out of the investigation for the immediate future, Wren had promised to give him regular updates in a bid to brighten his spirits. It hadn't really achieved this goal, but he could admit, it was better than nothing. Dev gave them both a short nod of acknowledgement when they had said their goodbyes, needing to get back to Jen and the incident room for the updates she'd told them they needed to discuss.

He'd checked his phone and found various messages from Alec asking him to call and update him, several calls with messages demanding he call back and let him know how he was. Dev wasn't in the right frame of mind to deal with him right now though. Instead, he looked around his new home and felt lost. The only people he had met since he'd arrived, had been officers from the station where he was working, and now that he was on strict orders to stay home, he wasn't entirely sure what to do with himself when he wasn't there. He needed to get a life, maybe he could arrange for that drink he'd promised Stephen when he had spoken on the phone with him. Or he thought, when he unenthusiastically dismissed the idea, he could set up a murder board of his own, he had nothing but time after all. He'd need supplies though.

****

Wren and the others were in the incident room going over the intel they had to date. There had been a substantial amount of data to go through for the short amount of time they'd been working on the case, and they needed to get it straight. That way they could better focus their attention on where it was needed, in order for them to resolve this case and catch the perpetrator or perpetrators, which Jen had implied it could be.

They began with the initial incidents of 1990. They weren't entirely sure of the timeline of these crimes, therefore they began with the murder that was on record first, the one with evidence that suggested it was murder; they began with Liam Whelan's death.

They started on a fresh white board, on the opposite side to the one that held the information they had previously collected, so they might better organise the information as they processed it. Liam Whelan's death had, as far as they could ascertain, been the result of a run-in with a "gang," at this time they had no further details on this crime and it was put on a list of things to look into further. This event had been a catalyst subsequently leading to his family being targeted. From his name they wrote the three family members onto the board, Chastity, Kelly, and his son. They would need to identify the boy but at this time he remained unnamed. Jen wrote a note to also look for photographs for these key people, which considering that the age of social media hadn't yet taken off, would be harder to find, so for now we would go with what we had.

They focused next on Chastity. Based on the statement Geena had given, that she had been attacked by a "bad man" they had tenuously linked this to Vincent. It would explain why he had been targeted and given that they were pursuing him before his death in connection to a series of sexual assaults, it seemed like a reasonable assumption. The DCI had taken a moment here to ring and see if there had been any progress on the tests taken, he wanted to confirm his DNA was a match for that taken from the victims of the assaults. What he had been told was; that while the tests were still being processed and it couldn't be conclusively proven that he was the perpetrator until this was completed, initial assessments indicated that it was likely he had been the offender.

That meant they would likely be able to close that case and inform the victims that their attacker was no longer alive. From this we followed to the part of Geena's testimony that had addressed Chastity Whelan, that spoke of her death by suicide. The team had opposing opinions on the truth of this statement. Matt had argued that from a standpoint of a family man, his wife would not leave her children defenceless and at the mercy of gang violence, to jump from a window. Ash countered that while his wife might be "the rule" not all women were as morally upstanding, and they should consider that she might have been "the exception." Jen entered the fray by pointing out that since we had nothing to discern the truth of either statement, it might be wise instead to focus on what we did have, drawing our attention to the fact that we should consider if the human remains they had recovered from the clearing, might in fact be the remains of Chastity Whelan. This had brought silence to the room as everyone took in what she had suggested.

Wren pondered over that. If that was true, who had disposed of the body? Why had they not reported it at the time but instead chose to cover it up? If there was nothing suspicious about her death, what purpose did it serve to bury her? With that in mind she decided it was more likely Matt's assessment of her death would be most plausible, unless her death might have had police digging where they hadn't wanted them to dig.

The DCI reached for his phone once again, this time to speak to the team who had extracted the body. He divulged our suspicions and asked if they could use this information to corroborate our theory, also to ask if we could have a preliminary report on the death to confirm the cause of death, so we might tally up the two and see if we had recovered Chastity Whelan. They agreed that this was possible and also indicated that they may be able to do a forensic facial reconstruction from the skeletal remains. This process used a combination of anthropology, osteology, and anatomy in combination with an artist's skills to reconstruct markers on the face of the skeleton to reproduce a picture of the victim for identity purposes. The DCI continued on the phone while the whiteboard was updated.

The next line of inquiry fell on the two children. From their intel, the article found in Rosa's apartment and Geena's recollection of the argument, leading to the two siblings not speaking for several years, the boy had died in a hit and run incident on the outskirts of a small town. Jen had scanned through the system to see if she could find the identity of the detective who had investigated the incident at the time, unfortunately he appeared to have died a few years previous of heart failure. Disheartened but not discouraged, she noted down several ways she might be able to find out more information, promising to look into hospital admissions, death certificates and social services. She also considered there may be long serving officers from around that time, who may be able to recall the case, that she could call upon to try and fill in the blanks.

This brought us to the other child, Kelly Whelan. Trying to trace victims of a human trafficking network in the here and now was hard graft, though not impossible. However, the thought of trying to trace one from twenty-four years in the past, had them all tearing their hair out. They could likely spend hour upon hour on this trail and the likelihood of finding the girl, after they scoured for an untold amount of time, would probably be for naught. It, nonetheless, was written on the list of leads to investigate, despite the fact it would be like going down a rabbit hole into wonderland. This left them with one link still left to explore. The gang who were responsible for the demise of Liam Whelan. Who had they been? Had any arrests been made regarding this crime? If so, they were going to need names. They may be considered suspects themselves, maybe a disgruntled member determined to be the detriment of the gang for his own safety? Or they may be intended victims, on an imaginary board that the killer had been removing them from like chess pieces, in a game only they knew they were playing. If they could find them first, they may have a shot of tracing Kelly Whelan, assuming she had survived the traffickers.

Wren studied the whiteboard, now completely covered in lines looking a little like a spiderweb. It showed progress, slow progress but it was more than they'd had before. The DCI thanked them for the work they had put in and told them to keep up the good work. He then left to go and deal with the mounting interest we'd been receiving from the press. With all that had happened over the course of the week, it was not a surprise that they had been doggedly pursuing leads of their own, harassing staff as they entered the station, anxious for any information they could dredge up in order to use it to their own advantage. Having suspicions, though no confirmation had yet been given, that a serial killer was in their midst, they had been outlandishly dubbing the murderer as "Jacques" or "Brother John," a reference to the "Frère Jacques" nursery rhyme. The headline of our own local newspaper screaming from the front page, had read

"Fear a Jacques," wilfully inciting unrest throughout the area. The words to the rhyme, taking on a more macabre connotation in conjunction with the words they printed within the pages.

It was curious that they had linked the murders as they had to their nursery rhyme counterparts and whilst Wren worried that it might have been leaked, she chose instead to believe that these ferrets had managed to see the signs as they had, without the aid of inside help. She truly hoped this was the case, she didn't like to think they had cause to suspect one of their own officers as the source.

****

Jack McNamara was getting twitchy. He had received news that the body of Chastity Whelan had been found and he was more convinced than ever that the boy was responsible for the attack of his employees and long serving associates. He decided it might be time to make a few moves of his own but that couldn't be done while he was laying low. It was time to take action. He had things to get in order, shipments he would need to deal with, a wife to dispose of and an old loose end to tie up. He needed to locate the boy and he needed to do it fast. It was time to call in the Executioner. It felt fitting that since the Executioner had been the one to eradicate the father, it should fall to him to also dispose of the son. A fitting end for the boy, considering all the trouble he had caused him.

He picked up his phone and dialled. That was the end of that then. It was going to take longer than he had hoped though, the man had other things he was currently working on, but he had assured him that he would be able to meet him within the next two weeks. After all, a work of art took time. Jack frowned at that, he wasn't sure what made the man's mind work, he seemed to have some eccentric belief that murder was an artform. Jack didn't agree with this assessment; it was a necessity needed to ensure order and instil fear into those that challenged you, nothing more. That being said, as long as the results were the same, who cares how you viewed it. The boy's days were numbered, that was all that mattered. Smiling in satisfaction at this prospect, he whistled as he went about his day.

Chapter Twenty-Five

Wren had called him and given him updates on all they had discussed in the incident room. Which was nice of her but who knew what she'd left out in her cliff notes version? It wasn't the same as hearing the information as it came up and picking up the parts you might find important, that perhaps they had not considered. Unfortunately, given the circumstances he would have to work with what he could get. He organised the pieces of coloured card filled with notes he had taken while she spoke, he'd filled them with information and coordinated them, so each colour represented a specific person of interest, he attached them to the wall—in the places he felt were most appropriate—with blu-tac. They were then linked together with string attached to ordinary everyday gold topped pins that held them into position on the wall.

Further along the wall he had a large map of the local area as well as any other maps that pertained to the case as points of interest. On them he had pins with coloured tops that correlated to the person of interest it matched. All the pins on the maps corresponded to locations in connection to the case. Vincent's colour was green for a snake, and all information pertaining to him was written on green card, all pins on the map that linked to him were also green and so it went, until his wall was covered in card of all colours and pins with matching colours dotted the maps.

He'd scoured the internet for the articles they'd been looking into, plus any additional ones he felt connected to the ones they'd had. They too had been attached to the wall with coloured pins. He had also chosen to use the plain white card for a separate assignment, where he wrote any lines of inquiry he thought were worth pursuing. Overall, he had a wall that rivalled one he'd once seen during an arrest of a suspect whilst investigating a stalking incident.

Feeling suddenly uncomfortable with just how much effort he'd put into his "crazy wall", he studied it. After a long pause, he realised he was thirsty and left the seat he'd been in to go in search of caffeine. His compulsive need to arrange the case in a display he could follow, without having to keep referring to his notebook and flicking through the pages to try and find what he was looking for, had tired him out.

Cup in hand, he sat taking a large mouthful, before resting it on a nearby table. He resumed his position and stared at the wall once again, his mind following each thread meticulously, as he searched for something he could see that wasn't already being addressed, he did this until he couldn't keep his eyes open any longer.

****

Paul had finally closed the doors to the Rose and Crown not twenty minutes ago. His brother, Les was in the cellar attaching new beer kegs and replacing the empty ones so that it would be ready to go for the next day. His other brothers were due to arrive for their regular after-hours poker game that they always held on a Friday night once the bar closed. He heard the knock and went to answer it to let whichever brother had arrived early inside. When he opened it, his surprise at the person before him had him freezing in place and, before he could do anything to stop it, he felt the prick of a hypodermic needle puncturing his skin.

As he sank to his knees his mind clouded over, and as he went, he suspected that what would follow was going to be very unpleasant and he wasn't entirely sure that he didn't deserve it. His last thought as he fell victim to the liquid his body had taken, was that he hoped his brother Les would fare better than he had.

Les was bending down, just about to place the last fresh keg on the floor when he heard his brother Paul approaching. "I'm almost done, I just have to attach this last one and I'll be right there," he said as he placed the heavy keg down. He felt a sharp sting at his neck and swatted the area, sometimes gnats would congregate here where it was cool, damp and the occasional spillage occurred—this was a particularly regular occurrence during the summer—and once again he had fallen victim to a bite from one of these flying, tiny parasites.

Rubbing the sore spot, he turned, and the room span around him, his sight becoming fuzzy. He saw his brother's silhouette at the entrance of the cellar and reached out for him to assist him. But, no assistance came.

Tommy knocked on the door, but got no answer, shrugging to himself, he fished in his pocket for his keys and let himself in. As he walked through and called out for his brothers, he found it was strangely quiet and usually dark. He went over to where the light switch was located and felt a flash of pain, as his skin was stabbed with no care to be gentle, then he was pushed roughly against the wall. Caught off guard his head connected with it hard, and he immediately lost consciousness.

Sean had been running late. He'd tried not to let the fact that Chastity had been found get to him, nevertheless he'd found himself to be a little on the jumpy side. He figured that his brother's had likely already begun without him and let himself in, finally able to relax knowing that his brothers were here, and they would put his anxious mind at ease. He walked through to the bar and saw his brothers sitting around a table, they must have been really into the game because none of them spoke or seemed to hear him enter. As he approached he called out to get their attention when he realised something wasn't right with the picture. Just as he'd noticed the brother nearest to him had one arm attached to the side of the chair, he felt it; the twinge of a needle entering. He began to struggle but was held fast, the mixture working quickly and attacking his senses making him too disorientated to put up much of a fight. He heard the sound of a sinister chuckle and the words, "look at that, I have a full house" were whispered in his ears just as he lost the battle and finally collapsed where he stood.

August 9th, 2014

During the course of the morning, they had been hard at work in the incident room, following up on the leads they'd identified the day before. Jen had spent hours glued to her screen, her eyes flickering over page upon page of words.

Wren and Matt had diligently read through pages of printouts that Jen had handed them to peruse. If she felt the information might be of interest or could be related in any way to their investigation it came their way, allowing them to assess the information and decide what they deemed to be relevant.

Ash had been assigned the task of placing calls to various departments in the area, following up on any names that cropped up during this process and adding any information they needed to address to the whiteboard.

The DCI checked in on any progress made in between meeting with the Don, checking in with progress on other cases within the department and dealing with the press. All in all, it was a busy morning. The morning rush of activity only increased further when the Super entered the incident room at around 10.30am.

"There's another scene. Everybody get your asses in gear!" she ordered and left as abruptly as she'd entered, waiting in the corridor for the DCI to join her. There was almost a stampede as everyone sprang into action in synchronised movement, the DCI appeared as they all began to make for the door.

"We're heading to the Rose and Crown. Go hell to the leather!" He commanded and led the procession as they hurried to do as they were bidden.

When they arrived on scene, the rush continued as people followed the directives that were being bandied about by the Super and DCI, who were coordinating their commands in a perfectly choreographed routine. Parameters were put in place, the building sealed off from the public and an hysterical woman was being led away by a couple of PC's as she wailed in anguish.

Once they had control of the scene, the Super and DCI got suited and booted before entering the premises, careful not to disturb the scene any more than was required in order to process the scene and decide if they needed to call the coroner's office to report the crime. When they re-emerged, they were both equally pale and stone faced. Wren interpreted this to mean that whatever had lain in wait behind those doors, was not for the faint of heart.

The coroner's office had been informed and they had assigned the required people to attend the scene. Due to all the work that had been thrown in their direction, the SOCO team were going to take a while to attend but had assured them they'd be on their way as soon as they could get to them. After an hour, the group assigned from the coroner's office arrived. Heading up the procession was the divisional surgeon who had attended the first scene. Katarina was closely followed by Jodie hot on her heels. Taking a look around at the heavy police presence, Kat remarked, "Where's the fire?"

"Hold your tongue, girl!" the Super directed sharply, "Get in there! MOVE!"

Kat snapped to attention and hastened to obey the order, a surprised look on her face, not entirely sure how she had spoken out of turn. She disappeared into the building, and they waited for her to return. When she came back outside to report in, she began to speak, her discomfort obvious, "I am so sorry, I didn't know." At the Super's icy nod she proceeded, "I can confirm all four victims are deceased," she said hurriedly and then scurried away seeking refuge from the Super's glacial glare.

"All *four* victims..? Wren repeated hesitantly, almost too afraid to ask, while the Super's frosty countenance radiated off of her in waves. The Super nodded briskly but didn't speak at first, she instead fixed her gaze upon the photographer and when he met her look said, "You're up," and followed behind him into the building.

There was a collective release of air, as all those who had been in the Super's vicinity, released the breaths they'd been holding. Despite her usual laidback manner, when the Don was on a scene the aura was intense, her attitude went from family friend to in command so quickly you didn't have a chance to blink, or you'd miss it. There was not a single officer looking for her attention to be on them if they made a mistake on a crime scene that she was attending. It was both intimidating and motivating, all rolled together in a tidy little bundle of something that wasn't exactly joy.

"Does anybody know what happened inside?" Matt whispered, as though scared he may summon the Super back if he spoke too loudly.

"Not that I've heard, I could go and ask Katrina." Wren answered, undecided on whether she should do so without being directed to. She certainly wasn't looking to incur the Don's wrath, however curiosity got the better of and she went to speak with Kat.

She tentatively left her post to approach the shaken divisional surgeon, who looked around her to make sure she was alone, and the Super hadn't followed behind. She visibly relaxed when she saw that she wasn't there. "I didn't mean it, I couldn't have known, it's an expression!" she said all in one quickly expelled sentence.

"What couldn't you have known?" Wren asked gently.

"I didn't know they would have been all burnt up like that," she replied, explaining quickly, justifying her behaviour defensively.

"How are they burnt? The building is untouched. Nobody reported a fire?" Wren enquired, puzzlement clear on her face.

"I'm not entirely sure without a proper assessment, if I were to guess I would say they had isolated or contained the fire to specifically burn each individual, also some were...fresher than others, which if I were again guessing, would indicate that they were burned in turn. Though in order to replace the clothes on their bodies, without them melting into the surface, they would first have had to allow them to...cool." she speculated, while Wren's understanding of the situation was still not completely assured.

"Let me see if I am getting this straight. We have four victims. Each burnt with no fire damage to the property, they were carefully burnt to a crisp ensuring that the fire was isolated to only the bodies, am I getting this right so far?" At the surgeon's nod, she continued, "Some were fresher as they were burned more recently than the others, which means...they were watching as the victim before them was set on fire. Now this is the part where I am lost. The clothes were *returned* to the body of the four victims, postmortem, is that what I am to understand?" Wren waited again for confirmation, and again she received it, "and this was likely done after the perpetrator waited for them to cool or assisted the cooling process, is that correct?"

"Yes, redressed them and posed them in a circle with their arms crossed. That covers it, oh, that and they are very certainly deceased." Kat concluded, finishing with a matter-of-fact tone.

"That certainly covers an awful lot of things," Wren said, bemused and slightly horrified at the level of depravity that had occurred within the building. Comprehending the reactions her superiors had left with, on their departure from the scene inside. Remembering how the conversation had started she addressed Kat's fear when she realised why the Super had been angry with her. "I'm sure the Superintendent was angry at the crime, not the remark. I think it was just delivered at an ill-timed moment. She will have already forgotten about it," Wren tried to assure her, though she wasn't entirely sure if that was the truth. At the very least it would offer comfort, even if it were to be of the temporary variety.

"I had better return to my post, the Super will likely be back soon, and I don't want to upset her further," Wren said, excusing herself and making her way back to Matt.

"So?" he asked, waiting for her to divulge her findings, Wren recounted her conversation with Kat, and Matt's face lost its colour, she could tell he wished he hadn't asked.

"What's going on?" Ash asked, "Why does Matt look like he's coming down with something? Did he go inside? What's happening?"

"Trust me, son. Don't ask." Matt replied, as the DCI came outside, a string of curses were muttered under his breath. He paused and looked to the sky, in what Wren thought looked like a silent prayer, before addressing them. "It is obviously too early to be sure, but I think we have ourselves 'A Ring, A Ring Of Roses.'" He stated flatly.

"What makes you say that sir?" Ash asked.

"I just saw the pathologist bag up tissues that contained flowers and there are roses scattered around the scene where the bodies were staged to lie in a ring but as I said it is likely speculation," he said, sarcastically and a hush fell over them as they processed that.

Chapter Twenty-Six

February 5th, 1990

The little girl was freaking the men out. She'd done nothing but rock back and forth for days since the boy had been beaten. The men complained about this so extensively, they'd eventually decided that it might be better to try and occupy her with some toys and see if that pulled her out of the trance she seemed to be in.

They'd brought in some dolls and some miniature buildings; consisting of a doll's house, a play shop, a school building, and a miniature church, which had made a play village, hoping this might be just the thing to bring her around. Her eyes had strayed to the toys, and she'd hesitated at first, however as time passed she eventually moved closer to them, before she couldn't resist the temptation any longer and began to play. She'd been playing with them all day yesterday and had even slept now her mind had a new focus.

Today the boy was returned to the room and the girl had brightened further. She'd been so pleased to see him that she rushed to hug him. The boy, still sore, flinched but allowed it when her face dropped. Out in the hallway, the sound of raised voices could be heard, and the two children froze.

"I'm sick of waiting for him, he says he needs more time. I told him that he has two days after that he will lose a child. Should he wait a further two days the second one will follow. After that I will hunt him down to the ends of the earth and make his torture so spectacularly painful, he will be happy to die."

Two days later the girl was forcibly removed from the embrace of the boy, kicking, and screaming the entire way. The boy had fought to hold onto her but eventually he couldn't stop it. The scary man, Jack, had laughed as he'd watched. The boy never saw the girl again.

Chapter Twenty-Seven
August 9th, 2014

Dev was bored. He'd spent all morning going over the board and following some leads he'd wanted to chase up. It turned out that they hadn't been leads after all, just more dead ends. That was when he'd looked at the article about the boys. It was true the boy who had been the son of the Whelan family had died, he was curious however what had become of the second boy. Maybe if he could locate him, the boy may have something he could use to help locate the girl.

That was when he'd decided to take a leisurely jaunt down to the small town of Berkhamsted. The worst that could come of it was that he'd had a drive for a few hours and came back no worse off than he'd left. Best case scenario, he might find another thread to pull. He knew that the officer who'd investigated the case had long since passed. There was a small chance though, that a long serving officer who had worked with him may have some details he could impart.

It took him a while to get there but since he hadn't been in a hurry, he just enjoyed the peace and quiet of the drive down. It had actually been quite soothing. He'd turned left at the small crossroads, before he finally made it down to the small high-street station, and parked up in a small car park situated behind the local library.

He walked down the road and turned the corner to enter the police station. Once inside he strode confidently over to the station desk, where he found a young female officer manning it. He suddenly thought to himself that he probably should've called ahead but it was a little too late for that. He explained to her why he'd come, and she announced that she knew just who to ask. When she returned she was followed by an older male officer. He held out his hand and introduced himself and Dev began, "DI Doyle, did your officer explain why I came?"

"Yeah. You're in luck I recall it, those two boys," he shook his head sadly.

"In the article I read, the boy's names were left out. Do you happen to recall what they were?" Dev enquired.

"The boy who died, his name was Keir Whelan, he was originally from your neck of the woods, found his birth certificate in his pocket." He began, and Dev's ears pricked up at the name jotting it down as the officer continued, "I'm afraid we were unable to identify the other boy, after the accident he was so badly injured he couldn't recall his name, no family claimed him, he was just…nobody. We suspected he may have been a traveller, he was Irish you see. The other boy was too; we believed perhaps that's how they knew each other. Don't know what became of him though, he was likely dealt with by social services," the officer finished.

"Don't suppose you found out why the boy who died was so far from home, did you?" Dev asked.

"We looked into it. His father had found some trouble down your way, with a gang, we figured the boy had scarpered to avoid getting caught up in the fallout. Maybe took off with his traveller friend and ended up here. For a boy of eight with no home and no money, it's not strange. Berkhamsted has some wealthy residents after all. Maybe they were hoping to fleece some folks and move on again. Also, he probably thought no one would look for him here. It's a small town after all. A boy that age, on his own, I'd be more interested to know how he'd made it this far. Must've been quite resourceful, shame he ended up the way he did." He replied.

"And the boy who survived, don't suppose you know where I could start if I wanted to locate him, do you?" Dev asked, "I was hoping perhaps he might have some recollection of where he first came across Keir Whelan, maybe he had shared some of his story with him."

"I'm sorry, that is where I have no more to give. See, it was Bill who dealt with that end of things, I moved onto another case once he'd woken up in the hospital. Bill arranged his placement. There might be a record of it with Social Services though, of course it has been a long time..." the officer answered, trailing off when he wasn't sure what else to say.

"Well thanks for your time anyway, I'll have a think and see if I can't find another way to track him down." Dev said and then made his excuses and left.

After leaving, he decided he was feeling a little peckish and figured there must be somewhere along here where he could grab a bite to eat so he took a casual stroll up the high-street and found a pub a short distance from the local Tesco. He entered the King's Arms and placed an order, sitting at a table near the bar. A few of what Dev presumed to be, "the regulars" were gossiping not far away. Dev listened to them without really paying much attention and after he finished his food, went to the bar to get a bottle of water. One of them looked at him and pulled a face before addressing him, "You look a little familiar, you aren't from around here though, are you. I know all the locals."

"No sorry, just passing through..." he began, then he paused and figured if he knew the locals that well, maybe he knew other things and said, "I just popped down to ask some questions about a hit and run of two boys back in 1990." Dev waited to see if the fish were biting.

"I remember that!" the man said excitedly, "Shame about those two boys though, the traveller boy was squatting in an old rundown industrial building up Bridgewater way somewhere. The other boy was around town for a few days, though I could've sworn when I read the article that the boy who survived was the one named Keir, guess I hadn't been paying as much attention as I'd thought." He laughed like his mind had been playing tricks on him.

"Really? You think it was the Keir boy who lived?" Dev asked, the thought making his mind race.

"Like I said, I was probably mistaken," the guy said and shrugged.

"Aye, it's possible," Dev said, as he thought, but what if he wasn't. Dev was even more determined to figure out where the boy had gone.

****

They had finally been excused from the scene and had headed back to the incident room to try and figure out how the new murders fit into their investigation. As they sat deliberating, they made an educated guess that the four O'Connell brothers were likely the victims, though by all accounts it would involve looking at their dental records to identify them now. The names had then been added to the whiteboard and they began adding the details they had managed to garner from the scene that they would be able to update further when the preliminaries came back.

"So, if the nursery rhyme that correlates to the scene is "Ring Around The Rosie," Matt began, "How does the burning fit in?"

Jen paused to consider and began tapping keys, presumably to find out. "Well, that explains it," she muttered, then addressed the room as she read. "That particular rhyme is based on the bubonic plague. The 'roses' or 'rosie's' are the red marks that appeared on the skin of the victims. 'Posies' were used by doctors to mask the smell. Apparently mass death doesn't smell so good, go figure. The ashes represent the cremated bodies, although in our case we have *actual* cremated bodies, 'a-tishoo' is self-explanatory, we have actual tissues though. And 'we all fall down'? Well, that's obvious too, they died."

"Yep...Ok...I think that covers my question," Matt rambled, "I might not be a fan of the results, but I can't argue that the symbolism is sound. Burn the rats...kill the plague. Check."

"Do you ever think before you speak? Or do you just let it all spill out and see what you get afterwards?" Wren asked, "Curious minds would like to know."

"Sometimes I think about it, then I just say it anyway for funsies," Matt replied grinning.

"Funsies?" Ash scoffed, laughing, "Are you a ten-year-old girl?"

"Why?" Matt returned without missing a beat, "Do you wanna be my Daddy?" He pulled a cutesy face and fluttered his eyelashes at Ash, who looked horrified and shuddered.

"Too far man," he said, shaking his head in disgust.

"You know I sensed that was the case, then I was like fuck it and said it anyway," Matt admitted, chuckling.

"Hey! Laurel and Hardy! It's not comedy night and this ain't happy hour," Jen scolded, "Wren is about two minutes away from adding your names as victims to the murder board." She indicated where an unamused Wren stood, scowling in their direction.

"Sorry," they murmured in unison.

"This feels like it's going to be a two coffee kind of day," Wren sighed, "I think I'll get coffee and go update Dev, I need a time out from the Chuckle Brothers." Then she left before another word could be spoken.

Wren pressed the phone to her ear and waited for Dev to answer her call. He didn't. She made herself a coffee and sat down in the canteen and dialled again. When she still didn't get an answer she waited for the beep of the answer phone and left him a recorded message giving him a brief update, short enough to fit the time before the message clicked off but with enough information that he would understand what had occurred. Sitting alone in the silence of the canteen she continued to drink her coffee as she contemplated the case and tried to fill in the missing pieces of the puzzle.

She ran through the list of players on the board, all persons of interest tied to their case at this point and turned them over on repeat until her mind stopped on Liam Whelan's murder. They had tried to trace the gang who were supposedly responsible for his death but oddly, they'd never been identified. She also found it peculiar that the case would be closed based on hearsay from witnesses without corroborating them as facts. What did Rosa, Vinnie, the four O'Connell brothers, Chastity and Liam Whelan, and Marco Salvador have in…

Wren's mind raced as a thought crossed her mind and she raced back to the incident room, heads turning at her entry as she called to get Jen's attention. Jen had her eyes glued to the monitor in front of her, but they left it at Wren's tone.

"Jen! Can you search any links you can find that connect Liam Whelan to Jack McNamara?" she said, excitedly.

"Sure I can, but why?" Jen enquired, curiously trying to see where Wren was leading her so she might better apply the theory to the searches she'd asked for.

"What if the information we have has been spun? Almost all of the information; the gang who killed Liam, Geena's statement, Rosa's articles, they all have one thing in common." Wren waited for Jen to catch up with her, before adding, "The source." Wren explained, when she didn't follow quick enough.

"Marco Salvador!" Jen exclaimed.

"And who did Marco Salvador work for?" Wren said, spoon feeding her the information.

"Jack McNamara!" Jen replied, her smile broadening, "You think that Jack McNamara fed the police the information to cover up his own involvement in Liam Whelan's death?"

"I do," Wren confirmed, "Now prove me right."

"On it like a car bonnet!" Jen replied, swiftly turning to her monitor, stretching out her arms and interlacing her fingers, turning them over and stretching her fingers out until they clicked, before reaching for her keyboard and letting her fingers fly across it, while Wren prayed she was right.

****

   Keri McNamara slipped into her parent's house unnoticed. With her father not in residence it was no longer guarded by his minions, as it would have been on a regular day. She wanted to gather information while he wasn't here so she might better implement their plans. She heard a noise from upstairs and froze. Nobody was supposed to be here right now, her mother had told her that she would be meeting with Connor tonight. She crept upstairs with deft, nimble steps, finding the door to her mother's room ajar. She peered cautiously through the opening to a sight she wished she could unsee.

   Before her, her mother was naked, her head thrown back as she sat astride a well-built, muscular man, riding him with a passion that Keri had never seen from her coldblooded, viper of a mother in the entire time she had known her. Maybe she had been meeting Connor after all. As she had just decided to vacate the premises she heard a deep voice, murmuring a moan and it said, "That's it baby, ride me! You always do that so good."

   Was that..? No...it couldn't be! Holy fuck! It bloody well was! Keri backed away faster and hastened to make her exit. It wouldn't do to have the attention of "the Executioner" upon herself. What was her mother up to? Whatever it was, it wasn't good, that was certain.

She knew her mother well and she needed to figure out what was going on, and get ahead of this clusterfuck before something happened that she couldn't prevent.

****

Dev had finally returned home and when he had heard the message Wren had left him, he'd quickly returned her call. Goddammit no answer! He tried again. Swearing under his breath he waited and left a message of his own.

"Wren, I got your message, I just wanted to let you know that I don't think that Keir Whelan is dead. I was in Berkhamsted today and I heard something. I think there was a mix-up, somehow the identity of the boy who died and Keir Whelan were confused. I think he's alive. I just need to try and trace his movements, see if I can figure out where he ended up and maybe we'll find our killer," he looked at the time and continued, "It won't be possible today, the offices will be closed but first thing in the morning, I'm going to find that boy."

Hanging up, he looked to his murder board and got to work updating it. When he finished he sat in his chair exhausted and fell asleep.

Chapter Twenty-Eight

Jack McNamara had been sleeping cuddled up to Jilly after he'd "thanked her" for giving him what he had always wanted. He'd woken to the feel of something being injected into his neck and his eyes widened as he realised that he'd been so distracted by the thought of his unborn son, that he had forgotten his other priorities, and that had been a fatal error. He didn't even get a chance to wake properly before he was once again out cold. Jilly screamed from beside him and the intruder sighed before punching her with all the force they could muster, quite sure her tooth had lodged in their fist and proceeded to inject her so she wouldn't be able to cause any more trouble.

****

Wren sat impatiently, waiting to see if Jen could find what she was looking for. Unfortunately, it took time to find something that was twenty-four years or longer in the past. Eventually they had decided to call it a day and pick it back up in the morning. When she had finally started to head to her car she noticed that Dev had called and, upon hearing his message, changed course and headed for his home. When she got there he didn't answer. She rang his phone again and heard it peel out from within the building. She knocked louder this time and waited, it was late, perhaps he'd fallen asleep.

Finally, he answered her call, his tone gravelly with sleep and not long after the door opened. As it did she got an eyeful of a mass of muscle, his bare chest on full display as his dark hair fell in a mess over his face, and when she met his gaze he was grinning mischievously, as he said, "You done eyeing me up, Angel or do you need a minute?"

Wren blushed furiously and snapped, "Most people don't come to the door half-dressed, I wasn't 'eyeing you up' I was trying to figure out if you usually wandered around half naked." Then she brushed past him and let herself in, uninvited.

"Come in, why don't you," He chuckled behind her. As she entered the living room her eyes widened at the pandemonium gracing the wall there. Taking in the sight of the makeshift murder board, it looked like a mass explosion that rivalled the one in the incident room.

"Holy shit Dev! You need to get a hobby," she commented.

"Are you offering, Angel?" he taunted, his voice dropping to a husky tone, and she shifted uncomfortably, shaking herself when she realised she'd been considering his question.

"Dev... That's not why I'm here—"she began but before she could finish her sentence he had her pressed to the wall and leaned down into her, taking her mouth with his own. Surprised, she found herself responding and the air around them became hot and electric as his mouth devoured her own. She had almost completely forgotten why she'd come, so lost in this moment that had her hot and clawing at his messy dark hair, that she yelped in surprise when a coloured top pin dug painfully into her flesh. At the jolt of pain, she remembered and pushed at Dev who, at her insistence, eased away panting as he took air into his lungs, his dark green eyes studied hers intensely as they assessed her expectantly.

"Angel… I…" but he didn't finish the sentence.

"It's okay, I was there with you, but the pin and… we have things to discuss, and this isn't the time to get into," she flicked her hand back and forth before continuing, "whatever this is."

He nodded and brushed the hair from her face, then rubbed at his neck awkwardly and took a few steps back, allowing her to right herself and regain her composure. "Tea?" he offered, walking towards the kitchen.

"Please," she murmured absent-mindedly, and studied the wall in front of her now that he wasn't in her space anymore. When he returned he'd put on a shirt, and she found herself thanking the Lord for that. She focused on the two steaming cups he carried with him and waited for him to speak. When he didn't, she took the cup he offered silently and sipped at it, wondering how to start.

"I think we might have to fix that part of my board," he joked, indicating the skew-whiff section where they'd been pressed not moments ago, and suddenly they were laughing like it was the funniest thing that had ever been said. When they finished he straightened it up and she finally found her words again.

"So, you think Keir is alive? Why?" She asked, her mind firmly back on the reason she'd come.

After Dev explained his trip and what he'd learned Wren looked at him cynically, "That's a bit of a leap though, isn't it?" she said.

"Aye, I hear you, it does seem a little far-fetched, but look at it like this; Liam is killed. The mother dies; accident, suicide or murdered, take your pick. That leaves the boy and girl, if the girl went to traffickers based solely on the intel, what are the odds of her survival? Not much considering the age she would likely have been.

"Also factor in the likelihood of her accomplishing the murders, women for the most part aren't suitably built to lift a dead man's weight. A man however, with a severe grudge and fit enough, could do it a hell of a lot easier." Dev argued his point and Wren seemed to waver from cynical into speculative.

"Could it be possible that they're working together?" she asked, adding her own thoughts to the mix.

"I don't know, realistically they could both be dead. If that is the case then we are pissing in the wind with nowhere to turn," he replied, honestly, "however the chance of finding a trafficking victim from over twenty-four years ago, is a lot less likely than finding a boy who was involved in a hit and run, found by police, and entered into the Social Services' system. Chances are we would find him, if he is in fact Keir, long before we saw either hide or hair of Kelly."

"You're right," Wren admitted begrudgingly, "We can look into the boy, and let Jen see what she can dig up on Kelly after she has checked into Jack and Liam's possible connection. We'll follow all the leads and see which pays dividends first."

They looked over the board some more, going over it for anything else they could use to try and identify the killer. Wren took notes of things he thought might be worth checking into and added some cards to it that he hadn't been able to without details from the O'Connell murders. As they finished up the tea and then came to the end of their brainstorming session, Wren paused and said teasingly, "Have you considered becoming a detective?"

"Aye," Dev said grinning, "the thought has crossed my mind."

With that she got back into her car and drove into the night leaving Dev with a lot to think about and the taste of her still on his lips.

****

Keri McNamara watched as the woman with albinism had left the house and watched as Dev stared after her. She was in a quandary. She'd learned a lot this evening. After she had found her mother literally in bed with "the enemy" she'd decided she would instead look into Jilly. She headed back into work, after her lunch break trip to her mother had spoiled her appetite, and she had nosed through Jilly's records and found something remarkably interesting indeed.

Jilly wasn't pregnant, well she had been technically she supposed, but Keri now knew why she hadn't announced said pregnancy in the extra way that was normally her natural inclination. She'd had an ectopic pregnancy. She'd also had it privately removed on the down low. She wasn't pregnant at all. She had however, decided to lie, perhaps hoping she could get pregnant again after she'd talked Jack into disposing of her mother, or faked a miscarriage.

It didn't really matter which route she had decided to go in, Jack would've killed her himself if he had done what she wanted and not produced an heir at the end of it all. Hell, maybe she'd planned to buy or steal one, this wouldn't surprise her, Jilly was a first-class bitch after all.

All of the trouble that woman had started with her lies, had already started rolling down a hill like a snowball and it was now too late to slow or stop the fallout, all that was left was damage control. A battle between two titans had begun all because one dumb little bitch had had a brain fart without considering the repercussions.

Now here was her quandary, did she try to slow the roll and end up joining the snowball as it rolled down the hill, or did she let her mother continue on this path of madness and see which titan won? She looked once again at Keir's home and thought about the man inside. Either way, Keir was in the spotlight and heading straight for the collision, nothing she could do would stop that. She could at least ensure he survived the wreckage. She hoped anyway.

****

Jack McNamara woke up and took in his current situation, realising he hadn't acted fast enough. As the figure approached and he saw who had him at their mercy, his eyes widened, and his face paled.

"Do you know where the origin of the rhyme Jack and Jill is thought to come from?" A voice asked with menacing glee. Jack remained quiet.

"No? Let me tell you. It is thought to be about King Louis XVI of France and his beloved Marie Antoinette. It tells the story of their reign of terror during the French revolution. Going up the hill is said to represent the steps leading up to the guillotine," Jack flinched at that, and the voice continued, "Ah, I see you understand. I'm glad. I'd hate for you to not appreciate the symbolism. What with your upcoming execution."

With that, they left him and an unconscious Jill, as they went to prepare.

****

Mary McNamara had been thinking about the past a lot lately, wondering what she could've done differently to put a stop to the fateful events so long ago. She had always been a keeper of secrets, like a Priest but without the fake morals and good intentions. She wondered if all her planning would be enough or if her time would end like her sisters had twenty-four years prior.

Her sister's children had survived though, thanks mostly to her. True she'd done so because it had benefited her own interests at the time, but that didn't change the fact that they had survived because she had seen to it.

If her plan paid off they would survive still. They might not like how they survived but if her husband had had his way, they would have both been dead a long time ago. She had taken up her sister's role, becoming somewhat of a surrogate mother, not that they were aware of this.

She certainly wasn't the cuddly, warm parent her sister had been, but then her sister had nearly allowed them to be killed because she'd fallen in love with the village idiot. She wasn't the surrogate they would've chosen but she had been the one who'd kept them alive. The question was would she live to tell the tale when all was said and done. Family was such a pain in the ass, she didn't know why everyone seemed to want one.

Chapter Twenty-Nine
February 7th, 1990

The little girl was still kicking and screaming as she was dragged down the corridor and Mary McNamara had raced from the far end to catch them up. She followed into the room where her husband was waiting. The girl before him had silenced, as he set his menacing gaze over her, and the men left the room.

"Where is she going?" Mary demanded.

"I have arranged a new home for her. She is a little young, but some men prefer it that way," he answered callously.

"I have a better idea," she replied quickly, her mind whirling as she thought fast.

"Is that so?" he said slowly, giving her an assessing look.

"It is," she said firmly, squaring her shoulders, lifting her cunning face, allowing a smile to curl up on her thin lips.

"Do tell, wife," he invited, curiously.

"We keep her. She bears a resemblance to me. After all, I am her Aunt. We dye her hair, I will not have anything further to do with the men who've been here from now on. We hire new men who can safeguard our home, but they will know nothing of what has transpired here. The men who have had any dealings in this business, will in future only work with you from your business location, having no more interactions with her until enough time has passed that they will have moved on and forgotten her existence and assume, as we say, that she is in fact my child.

"We bring her up as our own, a fitting punishment, keeping your enemy's child and bringing them up to

call you Daddy. "*Your fool men have already taken my sister from me, without your or my approval, I might add. You allowed her to be abused by that foul man Vinnie and that pair of clowns failed to watch her, instead they watched as she plummeted to her death. You have had your retribution. Kill Liam and let the children live. Make his death so spectacular, nobody will ever cross you again. I'll call in the Executioner,*" *she finished.*

"*You know him?*" *Jack's eyes widened and lit with excitement. He had—without success—tried to employ him and he really liked to get his own way. If she could get this man on his payroll, he would give her whatever she wished for in return.*

"*I do,*" *Mary smirked, her eyes also a little crazed with excitement of her own. She knew she had him, and continued,* "*I promise you, he will see to Liam and if your men know he is on your payroll, it is unlikely they would ever want to step out of line. He has somewhat of a reputation, no?*"

Jack pulled his wife to him and kissed her adoringly. This was why he'd made her his wife, the woman was like a piranha. Then he paused and asked, "*Why not keep the boy? Why the girl?*"

"*For several reasons, he's older, not as likely to forget like his sister, who is much younger, she looks like me while he has a look of his father about him. We would never be able to pass him off as our own. He also has a fighting spirit, he would be a lot of trouble to try and contain. Let him go and let fate decide if he should live or die.*"

"*Since I am so very fond of you, wife, I believe I shall let you have your way in this, you can repay the favour later,*" *he winked suggestively and leered at her.*

She chuckled and replied," You know I will, husband."

"Thinking of it, Connor's son isn't much older than the girl. Connor has been restless lately. I think he may be considering getting out. He has been working with our foreign associates so long that I'm not sure if he plans on returning to the country at all. Maybe we could use this girl to sweeten the pot, so to speak. A token perhaps? When they are older we could arrange for them to be married, maybe that would appease him and give our partnership a more solid foundation. He would be more interested if the business were to be a legacy for his own son," he mused, "Yes, the girl may prove especially useful indeed. Take her now and start making the arrangements, we will have the men believe she went where I planned to send her. That way we can still use the story of her punishment as a cautionary tale to any man who thinks to betray me. With that and the Executioner keeping them in line, they will walk the line, no questions asked."

And just like that the little girl had a new family and not long after, a new name: Keri McNamara.

Chapter Thirty

August 10th, 2014

Jen had a lot to do, Ash was currently on the phone trying to track the boy who'd survived, the one Dev suspected was Keir Whelan. He was on hold while a Social Services lady tried to assist them, but with it being so long ago it wasn't an easy ask.

Jen was running through any and all connections she could find that pertained to human trafficking, scouring for any mention of Kelly Whelan but thus far had come up empty. She had taken a break from this particular rabbit hole and instead decided to look further into Wren's suspicion from the day before and continued to search for a connection between Liam Whelan and Jack McNamara. The problem she was having was that the whole mess had happened so long ago, that it was proving difficult to find good threads. It was beyond frustrating.

Ash put his hand over the mouthpiece of the phone and asked, "Any joy from your end?"

"It's like I'm doing research for a historical piece, hard to find the information and a lot of supposition or trying to find my way out of a labyrinth. Oh, look, it's a dead end... Yep another dead end again," she growled with irritation.

Ash nodded in understanding, then removed his hand from the mouthpiece and addressed it, "Yes, I'm still here...Oh. When will she be back? Right, is there someone else I can talk to who might know? What about records I might be able to see and look through, maybe I can find the information I need? How long do you think that might take? Can it be done any quicker? I know it's a lot to ask but we really are on a time crunch. I appreciate that…Ok. At the soonest possible availability, we really would be grateful. Thank you for your time."

Ash hung up the phone and sat down deflated. "It's going to take a while, the caseworker who was in charge of that particular placement is on leave and they're snowed under. She thinks it might take a couple of days, bare minimum," he said, sounding disappointed.

"At least it might be possible. I, on the other hand, have spent the entire morning on a wild goose chase," Jen replied, equally despondent.

Wren and Matt came in, carrying the cups they'd made in the canteen. "Anything?" Wren asked, setting down Jen's cup on her desk.

"Not yet," Jen replied, sulkily.

"Well, that blows," Matt said.

"Unfortunately, Kelly Whelan seems to have vanished into thin air, I can't get a single hit on the trail at all. She has either never come to police attention or more likely the traffickers responsible for her have managed to evade detection. I don't hold out a lot of hope of her still being alive if I'm honest," Jen stated, shaking her head sadly, "I've gone back on trying to find a link between Jack and Liam. Here's hoping it might show more promise."

"What about Social Services?" Wren directed this question at Ash.

"Not quite as dire as Jen's search, however we're not likely to have any information quickly," he said, explaining.

"Ooh, double blow," Matt said, needlessly.

"It's like flogging a dead horse." Ash agreed.

They all sat quietly, each deep in their own thoughts. Wren wondered what Dev was doing. As frustrated as they all were, he was stuck at home twiddling his thumbs. She bet that had to sting.

****

Dev had spent his morning trawling through marriage certificates trying to see if he could find the one that belonged to Liam and Chastity. He'd been wondering if he might find some family he could possibly get some answers from. It was a long shot but with the team taking the leads from the official end, he'd had nothing to occupy himself with. Since social media hadn't been up and running in the nineties, he'd been unable to find any photographs he could use or friends on various sites he could pursue. This was a last-ditch attempt to find someone who hadn't already died or been murdered that might have ties to the case.

As he scrolled through an endless cycle of useless information, he finally landed on the one he'd been looking for. Chastity Scott. That was Chastity Whelan's maiden name. Dev smiled to himself, and hope blossomed in his chest. Maybe it was a tiny chance, but it was better than nothing. He braced himself, adding the information to his wall and opened up a new search and began again from the top. A few hours later he had found what he was looking for. Mary Scott. He had a new name and his eyes widened as he began his research. As it turned out, Mary Scott had a husband of her own.

****

The team had continued to slog and chip away at various tasks when the DCI entered. They all stopped what they were doing and waited to see if he were here to receive an update or deliver one.

"The preliminary is in," he said, "As suspected, the flowers inside the tissues found on the bodies were identified as posies. The four bodies have also been confirmed as the O'Connell brothers using dental records. As discussed, the information provided by the divisional surgeon appears to be sound, however there are a few things of note to add. There appears to be pieces missing."

"Pieces?" Ash asked.

"Body parts," the DCI confirmed.

"The eyes?" Wren queried, there had been quite a few eyes missing thus far.

"Strangely enough, the killer has deviated from eyes, to broaden their horizon. We now have missing fingers and toes. A smorgasbord of missing pieces," the DCI said, grimacing.

Matt groaned, "Well aren't they just a delight."

Ignoring Matt's comment the DCI continued, "I will have the board updated with the details, have you found anything in your searches?"

"Not yet, we have Social Services getting back to us with information on the boy who survived the hit and run, but we've come up short on the trafficking and are now focusing on links connecting Liam and Jack," Wren recounted.

"Keep looking, find them," he ordered, as though by ordering it, they would magically be able to produce leads from thin air.

Wren's phone rang and she stepped outside to answer, "Dev?"

"Aye Angel, the one and only," he teased down the line, his Irish lilt thick.

"This had better be important, I know you aren't busy but here we have shit to do," she scolded.

"You wound me Angel, who says I haven't been busy... I rang because I have a present for you—" he began but Wren cut him off.

"I swear by all that is good and holy, if the present is your dick, I will cut it off!" She snapped.

"Ouch!" Dev replied, quietly, "Not what I was going to say, not sure I would ever say it now either. Anyone tell you, you're a bit of a buzzkill?"

"Dev!" Wren growled, hissing his name with impatience, through her clenched teeth.

"Bejesus Christ!" Dev grumbled, "Try to do the girl a solid, and that's the thanks you get... Chastity Whelan's maiden name is Scott, she has a sister. Her name was Mary Scott, want to take a guess at her married name?" he asked, waiting for her response.

"Spit it out already, Dev. My tolerance level for bullshit is running low today." She prompted, impatiently.

"Mary Scott is our very own Mary McNamara, TA-DA!" he said, his tone suggesting he was pleased with himself. Wren couldn't argue with that since she too was pretty happy to hear this information.

"Dev, honey, I think I want to kiss you!" She announced with excitement.

"Angel, you are giving me whiplash," he replied laughing.

"I've got to go and get Jen on this. And Dev?" she said.

"Angel?" he countered.

"Thank you," she acknowledged quietly.

"My pleasure as always, to be sure," he answered before ringing off.

She raced back into the incident room and said quickly, "Mary McNamara was Chastity's sister, Jen follow that and see what you can find. Ash, see if you can find the officers who investigated Liam's murder and if you can, pick their brains, it was a long time ago but maybe there is something there we can use. Matt. You're with me, we're going to pay Mary a visit."

Wren and Matt pulled up to the house and Wren noted that perhaps if they were lucky, Jack McNamara might also be on hand to answer some questions. She pressed the buzzer on the gate and as before a disinterested voice answered.

"Hello? Who is it?" The recognisable cold, monotone of Mary replied.

"Good afternoon Mrs McNamara, It's DI Jones, you might recall I visited not too long ago?" Wren stated.

"Yes, I believe I remember. What can I do for you this time?" she asked, though her tone suggested that whatever it was, she wasn't entirely inclined to help with it.

"We need to ask a few more questions, if you could spare the time?" Wren pressed.

"I suppose so, I'll let you in. Can you find your own way to the front entrance?" she enquired.

"I'm sure we'll manage," Wren replied, wryly.

"Very well, come in." The gate groaned and opened to allow them entry.

When they arrived at the door, Mary was there to greet them, if you could call the sour look on her face a greeting. She led them into a sitting room and sat down demurely, no drinks were offered, though Wren would not let anything this she-devil produced pass her lips, so she supposed it wasn't really a concern.

"Begin," Mary ordered with a wave and Wren couldn't seem to stop her eyes rolling with disdain. Self-important wasn't a strong enough description for what this woman was.

"We actually have two reasons for being here, Mrs McNamara. We do have questions, but we also have come to inform you that we have found your sister, Chastity," Wren stated, solemnly.

"My sister? Why were you trying to find her? She ran off years ago. That imbecile of a husband got himself tangled up with some local riff-raff I believe, his death did not come as a surprise," she answered with a sniff of disapproval.

"Unfortunately, we believe we have recovered your sister's body ma'am," Wren said and watched closely, gauging her reaction to try and get a read on her, but she gave nothing away. "Sorry for your loss." Wren finished.

"So," she drawled, slowly, "they got her too, did they? What became of the children? Did you find them also?"

"No, just your sister," Wren supplied.

"Such a waste of life," Mary remarked, "My sister was a truly lovely lady, Detective. It's a shame that she was too blinded by love to see what that husband of her's was, before it was too late."

"Indeed," Wren agreed, "It would seem though, that we have a different account of what transpired back then. You see, we have it on good authority that your sister's departure was entirely different to the account you suggest. We were told that she was assaulted and jumped from a window. In fact, we were also told that her children also fared badly, Kelly sold to traffickers by "gang" members and Keir killed in a hit and run, not at all like the account you are giving us," Wren divulged, coldly.

Mary's surprise appeared to be genuine to Wren, though she couldn't be sure if she were surprised by this account or at her knowing it.

"If that is true, then it saddens me immensely. My poor sister. I suppose you haven't caught those responsible?" she enquired, her tone implying she thought they were incompetent, without actually saying so.

"Not yet, but we hope to," Wren answered honestly, giving her a pointed look, also making implications. "We were hoping that perhaps you might tell us about Liam's relationship with your husband?" Wren pushed.

"Relationship?" she snorted at this, "they didn't have a relationship. They knew each other, that much is obvious, but I wouldn't call what they had a relationship. It was an association that was pleasant but not close. He occasionally gave Liam work because Liam had a bit of a problem holding onto money and since his wife was my sister, he felt obliged to give him a helping hand from time to time."

"Right..." Wren said, cynically.

"The facts are the facts, my dear, they do not change just because you will it to be so," Mary remarked in a belittling tone. "Thank you for taking the time to inform me of my sister's passing. I'll be sure to give her a proper burial," Mary began, "Now I do believe I have answered your questions, have I not?"

"Yes, Ma'am, I do believe you have," Wren responded with an equally snitty tone.

"Then good day to you," Mary said, dismissively.

"One more thing, before we go," Wren added, "When do you suppose we might be able to speak to your husband?"

"He's tied up with work at the moment, for an undetermined amount of time. He occasionally skips town for business, I'm afraid he doesn't always see fit to call me with an update, I will pass along the message though. That's the problem with businessmen, my dear, entirely too focused on the unimportant things and forgetting their familial responsibilities," she tittered out a joyless laugh.

"I'm sure." Wren acknowledged," we'll see ourselves out, Thanks for your time."

Chapter Thirty-One

20th May 1981

Mary had coolly entered the Rose and Crown to meet with her newly married sister, Chastity Scott, now Chastity Whelan. Once she arrived, her warm, loving sister had squealed and bounced over to greet her. The two sisters were similar to look at, if you discounted the hair colour. Her sister's hair remained its natural strawberry blonde colouring, while Mary's was dyed platinum blonde. However, they couldn't have been more different in character.

Mary allowed herself to be pulled along by the arm towards a table where her new brother-in-law sat. Another man chatted with him casually. Mary watched, curiously studying the man. He was nothing like her sister's chancer husband. This man had an aura that a powerful, influential man might have. She found herself less irritated by the fact her sister had forcibly coerced her into this "meet up," now, rather interested in finding out who this new man was and how he figured into the picture.

As they approached the table the man looked up, his confident swagger clear for anybody with eyes to see. Their eyes locked and the man's intense, ruthless gaze met her cool, icy one. His lips widened into a grin, and he said arrogantly, "Hello, wife."

She bristled at his words and retorted in a sharp waspish tone, "That's a little bit presumptuous, don't you think?"

"No... I'm just a man that knows what he wants and will do whatever it takes to get it," he replied with a wink.

Mary tilted her head to the side, considering him and his words before replying with dry sarcasm, "So it would seem...husband."

His smile widened at her response, "See I knew you'd see it my way."

"That remains to be seen," Mary remarked cavalierly, "It really rather depends on how convincing your argument is. So, convince me."

"Challenge accepted, Wife," he said, his eyes flashing with delight.

Chapter Thirty-Two

Wren and Matt had returned to the incident room. Matt was drinking a mug of coffee and munching on a snack while Wren stood pacing the room.

"I can't put my finger on it, but I can feel it in my bones, that woman is not on the level. Nothing I can prove but there's something," she bitched.

"I think I found something. Jack and Liam were arrested together in Ireland but were released due to lack of evidence. Liam moved to England later that year and married Chastity not a year after that. The following year Jack followed suit and he met Mary. Liam also had quite a lot of debt, so she was telling the truth about that at least, which was paid off in large lump sums not long before his death. Doesn't that feel too much like a coincidence, do you suppose the money came from a nefarious source? Maybe without consent? Perhaps he skimmed a little off the top?" Jen said, throwing around conjecture.

"There was certainly no love lost between Mary and Liam, she made that very clear," Wren replied, "it's definitely possible, but how do we prove it, there wouldn't be anything on paper proving he was taking money from an alleged criminal network twenty odd years ago. Do you suppose crime networks keep books and would be willing to let us take a look-see?"

"Maybe there's someone who worked there at the time who might be willing to share their thoughts?" Matt offered.

"That's pretty unlikely, specifically since half of them are bloody dead! Our killer has been picking them off, not sure they would want to wave an arm in the air and shout, pick me, pick me, I want that serial killer to take me next," Wren continued, "that's without the fact that Jack would likely be ahead of him in the queue…" Another thought occurred to Wren then. "Shit!" she exclaimed.

"What?" Ash asked, startled by her shout.

"If that is true, I think I know who the next victim will be. We need to find Jack McNamara, NOW!" Wren announced.

****

Keri McNamara had a bad feeling about this. When she'd finished her shift she had been unable to locate her mother, instead she had tried to find her father at Jilly's place but there'd been no answer. She had hoped to let her mother know that Jilly was a lying whore and that perhaps she could be dealt with, and they could call a ceasefire, but it would appear that ship had already sailed.

Instead, she was back on Keir watch. She was a little bit confused though, he appeared to be outside, wandering around but without any particular destination in mind. She had watched him wander aimlessly with a long-handled tool in hand and then she'd figured it out. He was in a wooded area with a shovel in his hand, crying. She approached him slowly, not wanting to wake him and led him back to the car she had followed him in, sitting him in the passenger seat. She took a minute to think that if he woke up at this point then she would likely have some 'splainin' to do but she just couldn't bring herself to leave him there.

She'd managed to get him back to his home and waved a hand in front of his glassy eyes hoping he wouldn't know she'd been here, before hopping out, opening his door, and leading him through his open front door. She settled him into a chair, and leaned down, kissing him on the forehead and whispered, "Sleep soundly, brother." Before beating a hasty retreat. She needed to stop this, she told herself, one of these times he was going to see her and start asking questions.

****

   They got to him too late. By the time they had hurriedly tracked his movements and figured out where to find him, he'd already been dead. Jack and his lover, who's existence had only just come to their attention, had been found, their decapitated bodies at the foot of a makeshift guillotine. It had not taken much, given their names, to figure out which nursery rhyme had been assigned to them during their execution. They now stood within a sealed crime scene awaiting the SOCO team, staring at the "Jack and Jill" crime scene.
   Wren was standing just outside the doorway of the scene and was staring in horror at the "Vive le révolution" banner gracing the room, above a tea party set up with masses and masses of cake. On the table, with teacups before them, lay the heads of the lovers. Jack's decapitated head adorned with a costume crown, Jilly's sporting a wig that barely stayed on given that she had no shoulders to support it. Bunting with the French flag lined the walls and Wren would have laughed if the scene weren't so disturbing.

"You have to give them points for creativity," Matt whispered, and Wren scowled. She wasn't sure she would be drinking tea for some time after this.

"You have *got* to be fucking kidding me!" Wren heard the DCI exclaim from behind her, "Please tell me my eyes are deceiving me and I am not seeing two bodies dressed in costumes with no heads. Is that a white gown? It's hard to tell with all the blood. Has someone alerted the coroner's office?"

"Yes Sir," Matt replied, "I wonder how fresh that tea is... I could use a—" Wren smacked him, none too gently around the back of the head. "OWW! That's assault you know, you call yourself an officer," then he flinched again as she looked to let another one fly.

"How many victims does this make now? I'm losing count," the DCI sighed.

"Hmm," Matt considered, "there was Vinnie, then Marco, Rosa, the O'Connell brothers. Plus, these two...are we counting Mrs Salvador? Because if we are, then that's ten."

"Jesus.." the DCI said, shaking his head.

"Of course, if you included Liam and Chastity..." Matt went to continue, but Wren threw him another warning look and he closed his mouth, miming a locking motion and throwing away a key.

"Woah!" Jodie Malone's voice came from behind them, "Nobody told me we were having a party!"

"Not you too!" Wren groaned.

"Oooh cake! You shouldn't have!" Kat added and the two of them giggled. Matt couldn't contain himself and joined in.

"I work with clowns." Wren muttered, shaking her head, and walking away, letting them go about their work.

****

Dev woke up in his chair and knew something wasn't right. He looked down at his feet. They were covered in dirt and felt a little sore. That couldn't be good. He examined them but there didn't appear to be any damage, but it troubled him that he couldn't remember how they had got that way.

He went to the bathroom and put the shower on to warm up, while he got undressed he paused to look at his phone checking to see if anyone had called but he appeared to have no messages, so he set it down and stepped under the water.

About forty-five minutes later, all cleaned up and dressed, he took another look at his wall, seeing if there was anything new to see on it, though of course there wasn't because he'd added to it before he'd fallen asleep. His mouth felt dry, and he had a bit of a headache so he decided to make himself a drink and his stomach growled so he figured food might also be on the cards. As he prepared it, he wondered what the team was doing. About an hour later, he checked his phone again and then decided he might as well give Wren a call. When she didn't answer he considered what to do next and played with the idea of getting a drink from the bar Wren had taken him to. He grabbed his coat and headed to the door. One couldn't hurt.

****

Keri McNamara had gone from Dev's and returned to Jilly's house, at least she'd tried to. The place was swarming with police, and she had a feeling they weren't stopping by for tea. She called her mother's number, and it rang but she didn't answer so she waited and left a message.

"Mother, I just stopped by Jilly's, literally stopped, before I ran into the police. It would appear that Jack has been found, I can only assume that he is likely dead by the amount of police guarding the house. I thought perhaps this might be of interest to you, though, since you aren't answering your phone, perhaps not…"

She hung up and made a noise of frustration, well she supposed that answered that question. Did that mean Keir was now safe? She hoped so but something in her gut told her this wasn't over just yet.

****

The SOCO team were now on scene and CID were here to man the perimeter, so Wren and the team who were here had now been given leave to go. Wren and Matt needed to go back and check in with Jen who remained behind, to see if she had anything new. Before they had the fun task of visiting Mary McNamara for a third time and informing her of her husband's death before the media beat them to it. They were currently swarming the perimeter, trying to find their next headline. This week had truly been an absolute ball ache from start to finish. She wasn't entirely sure she had seen the like in her entire career. Hopefully though, with some luck, they would catch the fucker, they were bound to slip up eventually.

****

Dev had arrived back at his home, to find an envelope had been posted through his letterbox. He'd eyed it warily and put on gloves as he cautiously opened it, not entirely sure what to expect.

I KNOW WHO YOU ARE, DO YOU REMEMBER YET? IF NOT THE ANSWERS LIE AT THE MCNAMARA RESIDENCE. WANNA KNOW A SECRET?

A chill ran through Dev's body, and he reached for his phone. Dammit Wren! Where are you? he thought. He rang the station next, but the line was busy. He read and re-read the words and tried to make sense of them. Who had written it? Was this the killer? Was it someone who was trying to help him figure out who had done it? If he went, was he the next victim? If so, how did he fit into all of this? Had Liam's murder been the cold case he thought he had a vague recollection of? The questions raced through his mind, and not having someone to bounce them off of was making it harder to focus on the answers.

He paced back and forth, his brain thumping in his head. Like a song you can't get out of your head, the thought that he should know the answer nagged at him and drove him to the brink of losing his mind. What was he missing? When they said "I know who you are" what did that mean? They knew he was a detective. Was it connected to the case up in London? Had they found him? If so, how did that link with the McNamara's? Had they in some way been involved in the incident that had led to him ending up here? So many questions.

The walls of the room suddenly felt as though they were closing in on him and he felt claustrophobic within them. "Wanna know a secret." What was the secret? Also did he want to know it? Do you remember yet...If they were referring to the case that had been nagging at him, then how did they know? Were some of his colleagues feeding this person information?

Suddenly, Dev no longer knew who to trust. If he called and reported this, would he lose an opportunity to figure it out? The questions finally became too much for him and the small space around him could no longer contain him. He swept his keys off of the side table and headed out into the night. He needed some answers and he'd been told where he'd find them.

When Dev arrived at the McNamara estate, something was off. The gate was open, and he couldn't see anybody around. He looked at it warily and hoped that he wasn't being led around by the balls by a killer. He approached with caution, entered the property grounds and headed to the front entrance. He hadn't been here when Wren had come so he wasn't really acquainted with it, not like Wren would've been. He cursed again at the fact she hadn't picked up but hopefully when she got his message she wouldn't be far behind him.

When he found the door at the front also open he withdrew his firearm and called out, wondering if he was entering a crime scene and would find himself once again looking at the body of the killer's next victim. As he came into a sitting room area he saw a table and went to study it. On it lay an old cassette, it looked like a VHS tape. Weird. He didn't think they still did those, curious he picked it up and wondered what was on it. Then he wondered if they would have a

VCR at the station or if Jen would somehow be able to convert it to something playable.

That was when he turned to find Mary McNamara looking at him initially with fascination then her face changed, her mouth opened wide, and her expression distorted into…fear? She screamed. She screamed as though she were being attacked. Dev looked at her in confusion, why was she screaming? He was a detective and her door had been wide open.

"Ma'am, I'm sorry. The door was open, I was worried a crime was being committed. I did call out, I should introduce myself. I'm DI Devlin Doyle," he railed off quickly, hoping to quell her fear, he held his hands up as though surrendering and continued, "I received a letter, and came here to investigate it."

The screaming didn't stop if anything it only increased in volume. Before he knew what was happening he heard another voice at the entryway.

"Put your hands on your head, nice and slow and get on the ground!" Wren's voice called from behind him. He turned to face her and did as she said complying with the order, so she didn't do anything stupid like shoot him.

"Wren, it's me," he told her.

"Dev?" Matt asked, puzzled, he must have been with her, "Why are you here and why is she screaming?"

"I don't know. The door was open. I came in and she just started screaming, I tried to explain but she just screamed louder—"

"Don't play innocent with me, boy" Mary snapped, cutting him off, "I know who you are! You're a murdering son of a bitch!"

"What?" Dev asked, wondering if she was high. Her brain was definitely addled, "I know you know who I am, I told you not two minutes ago when you were screaming at me..."

"Oh, you're trying to be clever now? Is that it? I know who you *really* are, Keir!" she spat.

"What the feck are you talking about?" Dev retorted, clearly the crazy bitch was on something.

"Don't play dumb, boy, you are the spit of your father. You killed my husband and all the others! Now, you're here to finish me off, well you've been caught red handed!" she accused.

"I haven't a single clue what you are talking about, you daft beggar!" Dev slung back.

"Dev?" Wren asked, doubt in her voice.

"If you don't believe me, girl, look at the mantelpiece. There's a photograph there. Look for yourself, you'll see the truth of things!" Mary instructed and Wren hesitated before stepping towards it as though afraid to look. When she looked at it, she gasped. Matt looked at her in question. Her expression went from shock and betrayal, to hurt and anger and she stomped toward him.

"It's true. Dev is Keir Whelan," she said in a monotone voice, devoid of all emotion.

"NO!" Dev denied emphatically, "She's crazy! It's not true!"

Wren thrust the photo under his nose, as he lay there, and he lifted his head to see what she presented. He looked at it and dread filled him.

"I... I don't understand... That isn't me." Dev stammered, the photo was too old to be him, and Mary was much younger in it.

"Boy, stop playing the fool, it's your Da!" Mary shouted, "Liam Whelan, your mother's there too, me and Jack. You remember him don't you? You should do, you murdered him?" She finished ranting and a sob broke from her throat.

"Jack's dead?" Dev said in surprise.

Matt nodded and Wren looked at him warily.

"I didn't do this, Angel, I swear. It wasn't me!" Dev begged her to believe him, "This is news to me too, I've been searching for Keir for days, I've been searching for *myself,* why would I do that, Wren? Why?"

"I don't know... I can't think..." Wren answered with uncertainty.

"If I didn't know. What's my motive? Answer me that?" he said, trying to make her see reason.

"The motives in your hand, boy! That 'I remember nothing' bullshit doesn't wash with me," Mary chipped in with outrage.

"What?" Dev asked, confusion making him slow to understand her meaning before he looked down and realised that he had the VHS tape still in his hand.

"You're a good actor, your thieving father was too." Mary's face distorted with rage, "I found that in Jack's office. I watched it on the old VCR in our loft. I didn't know what was on it, I thought it might be our old wedding video... I saw what they did to you," she continued her face softening some, "I can't believe all this time, I didn't know I was married to a monster, if you weren't here to torture and kill me, I might even feel sorry for you!"

"Give me the tape, Dev," Matt said quietly.

"What? Why are you saying it like I'm trying to stop you having it? Take the bloody thing! I just picked it up because it was lying around out in the open, I was thinking that I didn't know they still had those..." Dev tried explaining, even to himself he sounded like he was trying to talk his way out of something, so he closed his mouth. He stood up and handed the cassette to Matt.

"Devlin Doyle. Wait... Keir Whelan, I am placing you under arrest. You do not have to say anything," Wren began.

"Wren," Dev said cupping her face, "look at me! I didn't do this!"

Wren flinched away from his touch and countered angrily,
"Would you even remember if you had? You sleepwalk, you have nightmares, you woke up next to your own mother's grave with a shovel and didn't know how you got there… You do not have to say anything, but it may harm your defence if you do not mention when questioned, something you may later rely on in court."

Dev let his head drop and hung it in defeat as he allowed Matt to cuff him in a daze. Could Wren be right? Could he have done this? He no longer knew what to believe. He didn't even know his damn name! If it had been her though, he would've at least given her the benefit of the doubt until he knew for sure. He just let the questions repeat over and over. Did I do this? Was it me? Either way he knew what he had to do now. He remained silent. Silent as they led him away, silent as they put him in the police vehicle and silent when they processed and booked him.

Chapter Thirty-Three

Wren had to leave the building. She just wasn't ready to see the team yet. She felt as though she'd been smacked square in the solar plexus, her mind was reeling, and she couldn't recall a time when she'd felt so epically wrecked.

Her head hurt, her heart hurt and so did her pride. She had allowed him to lead her on a wild goose chase and if that wasn't bad enough, it had been that snake, Mary, who had smacked her square in the face with his betrayal, no doubt taking great pleasure in doing so. She got into her car and drove aimlessly. Surprised, she found herself outside her parents' house, a short time later. She sat and stared at it, making no effort to move. Her phone rang out and she looked down at it in slow motion and saw her mother's name flashing on the screen. She answered it but couldn't seem to find her voice, so she remained silent.

"Serenity? Are you just going to sit out there or are you coming in? I don't want to rush you. But I won't lie, you are making me a touch uncomfortable…" her mother said.

"I'm coming," Wren whispered quietly in a barely audible tone.

She walked to the door and found her mother waiting, concern creasing her brow. "What is it, baby?" she asked.

Wren let loose the sob she had been holding back and her mother rushed to wrap her up in her arms.

"Now, now, my little Rennie, you are giving your mother heartburn," her mother joked light-heartedly, "It can't be as bad as all that?"

Wren sobbed harder and her mother squeezed her, stroking her hair, "Come inside and tell your Mama what has you in such a tizzy..." So, Wren did.

An hour or so later, drained, and depleted, Wren finally pulled back into the station. She walked into the incident room and searched it for Matt, but he was nowhere to be seen. Jen turned and saw her and began to speak.

"Wren! I've found something! I found a picture of Liam Whelan and you won't believe it, but he looks just like—" Wren cut her off.

"Dev. I know. Has nobody told you?" she asked, confused.

"Told me what?" she enquired, worry appearing on her face at Wren's tone, "I haven't seen you or Matt since you left. The DCI rushed to holding and Ash said that he and Matt are holed up in the interview room. What the fuck is going on?"

"It's Dev, he's Keir Whelan." Wren informed her stone faced.

"Shut the front door! It can't be! What are you saying?" Jen exclaimed, shock filling her expression as she shook her head in denial.

"He's who we have in the interview room." Wren confirmed.

"Dev? Our Dev? No...you have it wrong—" Jen began.

"We don't have it wrong," Wren spat through clenched teeth, cutting her off once more.

"What proof is there?" Jen argued, her stance becoming one of a defiant child, stubbornly refusing to believe what Wren was telling her.

Wren opened her mouth to reply, then paused as she remembered.

"Where is the videotape?" she asked.

"What videotape?" Jen said, giving her a questioning look now as she tried to keep up with Wren's jumbled thoughts as she spewed them aloud.

"The one Dev had when we found him," she explained, "Do we have a VCR?" she queried in a rushed tone.

"Maybe. I'll go and find out," Jen got up, giving her a look that said she thought Wren had lost her mind. And maybe she had.

****

After some time had passed, they had all reconvened in the incident room. Jen had sourced a VCR and had begun to set it up, connecting it to a TV on wheels that Ash and Matt had pushed in. They all worked silently to assemble the parts so they could see for themselves what was on the cassette. Other officers assembled with them, curiosity at their strange behaviour drew them in and everyone now waited for answers to the questions they had. Finally, they pushed in the cassette and played the recording.

****

Alec had received an anonymous tip from an unlikely source, a woman called Kelly had told him Dev had been arrested for a murder spree. Alec didn't know what was going on, but he knew Dev. He was not guilty of this, he wasn't sure what the staff there thought they had, but whatever it was, they were wrong. He walked into Superintendent Andy

Panderman's office, and the Super looked at him with surprise.

"Something I can do for you, Morgan?" he asked, carefully assessing him with a long, suspicious look.

"Yes Sir, I'd like to request a transfer." He stated without hesitation.

"Am I likely able to guess which station you would like this transfer to?" He replied, knowingly.

"Yes Sir, I think you would." Alec answered and the two of them seemed to come to an understanding.

"I believe I will allow this," Andy Pandy said, nodding before adding quietly, "Go and help our boy."

"Oh, I intend to." Alec said, his resolve firm and his path determined. Whoever had set Dev up was going to wish they hadn't. He stepped outside and took out his phone and dialled.

"Hello, Stephen?" he asked.

"Who is this?" Stephen enquired, suspicion coming through the phone as clear as day.

"I don't know if you remember me, it's been a few years since we went out for drinks. I'm Dev's friend. You gave me this number when we had a suspect in custody who I thought might be innocent…?" he prompted, hoping his memory was as good as he hoped it was.

"Yeah, I remember," he replied, his tone less severe, "How might I help you, Detective Morgan? Does Dev know you're calling?"

"Actually... he's the reason why I'm calling." Alec answered and waited as the line went quiet.

"Tell me," Stephen demanded, short and to the point.

"He needs our help..." Alec began.

****

DCI Richard Head entered the interview room for the second time. Matt was quiet beside him. The team were pretty distraught at this blow and Matt, though also feeling it, seemed to be less emotional than the others.

He took in the sight before him, not much had changed with Dev since he'd last come. The first time they'd entered, Richard had been in an entirely different frame of mind, sure that Dev had not only committed these crimes wilfully but intentionally, as such he had gone at him hard. Dev had remained silent though, his eyes following him warily and his whole body tense. He'd had dark circles under his eyes, which hadn't surprised Richard since they had all been working the case around the clock. Despite Dev being home, Richard knew he hadn't stopped working either. This in itself might have made him doubt Dev's guilt, but he'd been far too enraged to see that then.

He studied Dev closer now. He appeared to be sweating, his fists were clenched, his complexion had a pale, clammy look about it. His eyes were open but instead of the wary, watchful eyes from before, they had taken on a glassy, empty state. Richard thought he didn't look well at all. He considered his stance on the situation for a moment, with the new information he had, he decided to try a different approach.

"Dev?" he began, "Son? Are you there? I understand. I've watched the tape… Have you seen it before?" He waited but no answer came. "I suppose you likely haven't, though since you were in it, I suspect you might be aware of what it contains." he waited again but no response came. "Listen to me, I can see why you thought that these people needed to die. I myself joined the force to stop people like them, people who did things to others no person should have to live through, so believe me when I say that I can see why you would've done this, but this isn't how this works," Richard paused again. He looked at Matt silently asking him if he had any ideas how to reach Dev. Matt sat with an anger, which Richard hadn't seen from him in a long time, it was clearly on display in his posture. Matt nodded in assent, he would give him a try.

"Dev mate? We can't help you if you don't talk to us, yeah? We've watched the tape, all of us. Honestly, I'm with you, they deserved what they got but murder is never the answer. You're one of us, so I know that you know that. You should've reported it, and we could've hit them hard, together we could've taken them down the right way. Not this, never this," Matt swallowed the lump in his throat. He directed a look at the DCI and addressed him, "I don't think that he's with us, Sir," he said hesitantly.

"No, he doesn't appear to be, does he? I'm also not entirely sure I like where I think he might be either," Richard replied. He was no longer entirely positive that Dev knew that he'd done this. Looking at him, at this moment he wasn't sure he was seeing "Dev" at all. This person, the quiet, sickly, frozen person before him, was likely Keir Whelan. It would seem as though he'd re-emerged from whatever place deep inside of Dev he had been hiding in. What remained to be seen however, was whether or not Keir and Dev were one and the same or separate personalities entirely.

"I think we might need to consult with a psychologist." Richard stated.

****

Wren and the others were running through the information they now had. Piecing together events and the evidence to tie it into the murders. It came together and fit a little too well. As each piece of the puzzle slid into place, her resolve cracked a little more. She didn't have the feeling of satisfaction for a job well done, that she usually got when a case came together, and she had the perpetrator bang to rights. What she had instead was nausea. She was barely managing to keep it at bay. A matching sickness was eating at her from the inside, at each part that became clear and at how wrong it felt when it did.

She could tell by the demotivated way the team followed her lead, sombre and quiet, that she wasn't the only one feeling this way. They weren't "saving the world" from bad people and they weren't protecting the innocent from harm. What they were doing was proving that what had once been an innocent child, had done the job they should've done but failed to do and he'd taken some really bad people off of the streets.

The method was beyond unacceptable. There was no question of that, however nobody in this room felt that these people who had died, hadn't had it coming. Wren didn't feel like the "good guy" in this. In fact, the lines were so muddied and blurry, she found herself feeling more like the bad guy. As an institution of justice, they had failed the young boy and that stung. It stung a lot.

The more time she spent putting it together, the dirtier she felt. Like she herself had had a hand in the injustice that had befallen Keir Whelan. Her skin crawled with it, and she wasn't sure any number of showers she took would wash the stain away.

"It's getting late." Jen spoke, her voice barely a whisper, "Can we pick this up in the morning? I'm tired and I don't think I can look at this anymore tonight."

"I'll speak to the Super," Wren replied, feeling her words deeply, as they echoed her own thoughts.

When Wren returned from the Super with permission to leave, the others were all sat looking shell shocked. The door opened and they all swung around as the DCI entered.

"Has he said anything?" Wren asked the DCI, without preamble.

"No," he answered, "He appears to be in some kind of fugue state, he just sits and stares."

"Did you watch the tape?" The DCI asked, after the silence had gone on too long.

"Yeah," Wren said quietly, a lump in her throat, "We all did, it was bad, Sir, really bad."

The DCI nodded. He'd thought the same when he'd seen it.

Wren thought back to two hours ago. They had all watched as the days had played out on the screen. They watched as the mother was assaulted with Dev held at knife point, his eyes firmly closed, tears falling down his face at her screams, they watched as they hung his mother from the window, they watched as Jack McNamara had ordered them to take him with the body, they watched him bury his mother.

Jack had been a sick fuck filming it all, if the actions themselves hadn't been bad enough, he must have gotten some sick kind of pleasure having it available to watch on replay. They watched him get stripped and beaten until he was bloody, they watched as his sister was dragged from the room and as he was told she was being sold to traffickers with glee, while he'd desperately fought to keep her, and they watched as they drugged him and the man in the balaclava had carried him off to "see his father." Lord only knew what that had meant.

By the time the recording had ended, Jen was sobbing uncontrollably, unable to look at the screen, Wren herself had been wiping the steady stream of tears from her face, the male officers had cleared their throats, with every act of cruelty that had crossed the screen, swallowing each feeling as she did she suspected, ashamed that they had arrested this boy for crimes that felt like justice. The wrong kind of justice, that was true, but that didn't make them feel better about it anyway.

"What now?" Wren asked quietly.

"Now we call in a psychologist and hope he talks," The DCI replied gravely.

"Excuse me, could I ask if you are DCI Head?" A clipped voice asked from behind them.

"Who wants to know?" the DCI returned, sharply.

"I am Stephen Doyle, Defence attorney. I believe you are the one investigating my client?" He informed them.

The officers looked at him stunned. Before the DCI stuttered, "Dev? He hasn't requested a lawyer, in fact he hasn't said anything at all..."

"He doesn't need to request me. He's family." Stephen responded, in an "I take no prisoners" tone, before adding, "Will you lead the way?"

Chapter Thirty-Four

Keri had watched in dismay as she had seen them lead Dev from her mother's house, Mary watching them go with a smug, satisfied smile that the officers couldn't see as they proceeded to deliver him to the vehicle. She'd felt in her gut that this hadn't been over, but she couldn't have begun to guess the extent of her mother's cunning. She didn't know how her mother had managed to manipulate the situation so thoroughly to her will, but it was clear she had seen to it that it was dealt with sufficiently, as she liked to do with everything she set her mind to.

She stayed where she was and ran over what she knew in her head, trying to see her next move. She had thought herself so clever, but she had forgotten the source of her training. Mary had given her the talent for persuasion and manipulation and while she had been a quick study, Mary had her beat with experience and motivation to get what she wanted. Her self-importance and entitlement ensured she expected it to go her way by whatever means necessary. Keri suspected the woman was descended from Niccolò Machiavelli himself, if she had any hope to try and fix this she was going to need help. She was going to need to fight fire with fire. She pulled up a number in her phone, when she had been over-seeing her brother on one of his "daydreams" she'd had a sneaky peek at his phone. She had seen the number in his recent calls list and with others that were stored, she'd added them to her own, just in case they should be useful later. She'd dialled and Alec had answered. When she had finished she had begun making a new plan.

****

Dev had sat in the room and as he sat something had happened. He had been somewhere else.

It was dark and he couldn't move, he seemed to be stuck in someone's grip. He tried to get free, but he was drowsy and couldn't seem to make his limbs cooperate. He'd stayed like this for a while and gradually the feeling had returned to his body, and he'd managed to twist around to a sight that made him reel.

He stumbled back and took in the sight of his father without a head, his neck tattoo staring him in the face and in the space above it where his head should have been... as he pushed back even further he noticed the chasm in his father's chest, and he bit his fist to contain the sob. What if the person that did this was still here? He fell to the side of a carousel and staggered away as fast as his disorientated body could carry him.

He left the building quietly, fearful, and paranoid as he made his getaway in the dark. He kept to the shadows and headed for his home, hoping nobody would be looking for him and he might just get away. He snuck in through the back entrance and without caring searched it, looking for money or supplies, and packed up a backpack as he went. He found a small amount of money in a cookie jar squirrelled away in the back of a cupboard and pocketed it, slinging some clothes into the bag as well and then he found his birth certificate. He packed that too.

Then worried he had lingered too long, he headed out into the night. As he did, he caught sight of a familiar face. Marco, the man responsible for his mother's death, loomed not too far from the house. Keir ducked down out of sight and waited, unable to breathe.

Not too far away he saw an open car door and a man appeared to be packing things into it and then headed back into the house it was in front of. Keir crawled along silently and crept into the back of it. He immersed himself under all the luggage back there and lay still, hoping he would make it away without being discovered. The man returned to the car, threw in some final bags, and got in.

He drove off and Keir breathed for the first time since he'd seen Marco studying his home.

Days ran through his head at a fast pace, spinning almost nonsensically, a little town, being chased away by the man in the car, meeting another young boy, stealing food, finding a place to sleep and then a car heading straight for them and pain...lots of pain.

Dev came back to the room and took a long deep suck of air as though he'd been holding his breath; he was sweating, tears silently running down his face and he noticed Stephen sitting patiently, waiting for his attention. He looked at him in confusion and Stephen smiled grimly and spoke.

"Welcome back, Brother."

****

The plan had been to go home, Wren had specifically gone to her office to request that very thing, but with the arrival of Dev's brother, nobody had wanted to go. They all sat waiting for news, wondering if maybe he might be able to crack Dev's shell and they might be able to finally get to the bottom of this mess. Wren, unlike some of her team, did not hold out hope that he would be innocent in all this, however she couldn't quite bring herself to hope that in some way this might work out. It was ridiculous and pretty unlikely, but she clung to it anyway.

It seemed like hours before Mr Doyle had re-emerged from the room. He had asked for privacy with his "client" and added that they should've treated him better sooner, he was innocent until proven guilty after all. He had said that he was aware they could hold him for a certain amount of time, and he would accept the need for a psychologists assessment but if they did not charge him within the allocated amount of time, he would expect his client to be allowed to leave. With that he had swept from the building without so much as a backward glance. Wren assessed the board and wondered for the first time if they had any physical evidence tying Dev to the case. They had motive by the bucket loads, but she wasn't actually sure they had any concrete evidence to that effect. If they didn't find some it was entirely likely that Dev would be leaving the station. They had ninety hours to charge him with a crime and find the corresponding evidence or Dev would go free.

****

Before Alec had left London he had done some digging and he had to admit it didn't look good for Dev. He and Stephen had spoken extensively and together had looked at the flaws in the case. There didn't appear to be any physical evidence to date and the only tie linking him to this crime was that he fit a profile and had a motive. That being said, there were other people who also fit the profile that made his own personal persons of interest, and he felt their case, while compelling, was not "game, set and match" just yet.

   He had packed up and set out almost immediately after he'd made the arrangements and set his sights on his destination. It wasn't over until all the participants had been wiped from the board and he planned on throwing his own hat into the ring. He paused, he wasn't sure that was the correct use for that metaphor, but it would have to do. He had things to do, people to see and a case to crack.

****

   Jen had been the only one who had chosen to leave the incident room. She didn't believe that Dev had done this. She still recalled his mirth when she'd given him the Weasel link and he had pulled her into his stupid dance. No, that man didn't have that in him, and she was going to prove it. She had a particular set of skills, and she was going to use them but how she was going to use them would require illicit means that would not be looked on in a positive way should she be discovered doing it at work. From here however, here she could bend the rules a touch and use fewer savoury methods to get to the root of it all. She could figure out later how she could use what she discovered, in a more acceptable way. For now, though, Jen was going dark. With determination, she set up her system, the screens around her nearly filling the room with their magnitude. She set a pack of caffeinated drinks beside her and settled in for the long haul. This was going to be brutal.

****

Stephen had called in reinforcements. He set his phone down and thought about what needed to happen next. He had managed to get hold of their "family" and they were heading for them in force. Dev may never have really felt that he had belonged with them or seen them as the family they'd been, but Dev underestimated his pull. His quiet kindness had been what had kept them together, often settling the many feuds and tantrums that one might expect from the lost and the aimless. Some of them had similar pasts to Dev's own, each misfit with their own story of woe. Dev might not see how he fit but they did, and they would do whatever it took to save their own. Help was coming whether Dev liked it or not.

He began to write down an outline of what he was going to need to do, to get Dev out of this mess he had found himself in. With that he got to work, while he awaited the arrival of their ragtag group of miscreants.

****

Chief superintendent Andy Panderman was looking at the case Dev had worked on before his enforced transfer. He had studied the case he had been working on and something about the whole thing had his nerves on edge. What were the chances that Dev had been thrown back into this world he had obviously left behind, knowingly, or unknowingly. The timing of it all seemed far too much like it had been deliberate.

The more he looked at it, the more suspicious he became. He didn't like coincidences, and more often than not, they turned out to not be so coincidental at all.

When he had gone to bat for his detective, he hadn't understood their insistence on his transfer, he had also been in doubt of his chosen destination. If it had been so important to ensure his safety, why then move him only an hour down the road? Why not out in the sticks, in the ass end of nowhere, where he could hide more sufficiently? Why also had he been allowed to work on this high-profile murder case if their intention had been to keep him hidden from threats? No…Andrew smelled a rat, and he didn't like the smell.

He set aside the case and considered it in silence before deciding that he should take some time to look further into this, he needed to get to the bottom of it, before it came back and bit him in the ass. But it would need a subtle approach and he would have to do it as quietly as possible if he was going to be able to get what he needed without drawing unwanted attention to his prying. If the wrong person were to find out, the information he required would likely go up in a puff of smoke. Discretion would be key.

****

Mary McNamara smiled wickedly from her "special place", looking through the spyhole at the room, reminiscing. This home had been hers long before Jack McNamara had made his journey to England from his own home in Ireland. She knew all the nooks and crannies he'd never taken the time to discover. Mary had always known that knowledge was power. As such, she ensured she had as much knowledge as she could acquire. She had watched from this very spot, arriving too late to prevent it, as her sister and her children had been brought here. She had not been able to spare her from Jack's wrath, her regrettable choice of husband had been her undoing. She had tried. She had raced to the house and tried to intervene but her husband would not hear of it and so she had come here, and she had watched, she had even filmed it with the VCR system she had set up, she'd considered it possible that she might have a use for it later, blackmail or the like.

She had watched her sister read to the children from the very same book of nursery rhymes they had read together as children. Her sister had jokingly dubbed her "Bloody Mary" in reference to the queen, who had been the origin of most of the Mary references in the nursery rhyme book. They had even shared a name, she'd said, Mary Scott, it had always amused her how she'd mixed the two queens up.

She had then watched as the events unfolded, right here in her hidey hole. She'd made a note of all the wrongs done to her sister and her children. She had also learned of her husband's infidelity in this very room too. She had learned it all and pledged to right the wrongs done here, the wrongs that the filth here had committed before her eyes. She had even watched from afar as they had made the son bury his mother—her beloved sister—in an act of cruelty; the likes of which she hadn't seen before, as the boy had begged and pleaded.

She may have not been able to save her sister, but she had managed to see to it that her children had at least lived. She hadn't been too fond of the boy, he'd had a look of his father about him, and she was reminded of Liam's idiocy that had brought her sister to ruin, every time she looked at the boy, however she had felt a great deal of pity for him, like one might a starving dog. She had seen Liam punished accordingly, therefore she had decided to spare the boy. When she'd caught wind of her husband's plan to kill the boy, after he'd had a change of heart and decided he should die, she had called her lover. The Executioner, known to her and only her, as Cain. Together they had intervened. The hit and run had been arranged so that the traveller boy would die in his place, Keir's birth certificate planted in the dead boy's pocket. Keir would then be free to move on with his life. She'd kept a close watch on him over the years, deciding that he may prove useful further down the line.

It had been unfortunate but convenient that he'd suffered from amnesia. It meant she hadn't had to worry about the boy wandering around poking his nose in places he shouldn't and upsetting the apple cart.

However, things had changed when she'd discovered Jilly's pregnancy. A maid within the household where she lived, paid for with their money of course, had informed her that she had found the test in the trash. That was when she realised what her own fate would be. So she'd arranged for Keir to find himself in a situation where he would need to be relocated, her contacts within the force had taken the money offered and arranged for his transfer as she had demanded. Then she had made her plans; in which he would play a crucial part.

Everyone had always underestimated her and if she was honest, she preferred it that way, it made it so much easier to manipulate them into doing her bidding and lead them down the path she laid out for them. With help from Cain, who made killing an art form, she orchestrated a coup, killed off her husband and his pregnant lover and fulfilled the vow she had made to her sister, all wrapped into one neat, tidy package. She was now free to be what she was always meant to be, Queen of the Underworld. She supposed her sister had been right after all. In the nursery rhyme world she had created with murder, she had indeed become Bloody Mary. It was unfortunate that the boy had been such a perfect fall guy, but at least she had allowed him to live; her husband wouldn't have been so kind. He would get out, eventually, and was bound to get an insanity plea so he probably wouldn't do long inside, likely in an asylum somewhere. Perhaps once he'd been disgraced she could bring him over and have him join the family business, he wasn't entirely stupid, he could prove pretty useful with the right hand to guide him. She'd think about it, see if she could find the right motivation to pull him into the fold. She chuckled and congratulated herself on her performance. She had delivered it to perfection.

"The King is dead, long live the Queen," she whispered, gleefully, then left the house behind and went off into the night to meet Cain. They had a celebration planned and she intended to enjoy every minute of it.

****

Keri McNamara, or Kelly Whelan she supposed, knew what her "mother" had done. This would not do at all. Her brother had suffered for the sins of their father long enough, it was time for him to finally be free. Actually free this time. She had laid in wait, watching the home; patiently waiting for her mother to leave. Her mother was meeting with the lover that she had incorrectly assumed Keri was unaware of. She was wrong. She made her way through the trees and then quietly slipped inside, moving through her mother's home, looking for something she could use to aid in her mission. It was during this time, after hours of fruitless searching, that she had discovered the room, entirely by accident. It would seem fate had finally aligned in her favour. Her eyes lit up, and joy filled her as she let them rest on what she'd found there she knew what to do. She worked quickly, gathering everything she would need and then slipped back out silently. Moving with as much speed as she could muster while carrying her precious load—careful not to be caught in the act of leaving with her stolen goods—her father, Liam, would be proud. She got into her getaway vehicle and drove off. She had a package to send.

****

Wren had remained in the incident room, her mind still running over the unexpected turn the case on the board had taken. She was kicking herself for not seeing it. How had she not seen what Dev had been capable of? The psychologist they'd brought in to consult, had explained that in all likelihood, if they were to honestly believe he had no memory of his previous life, as his medical history suggested? Then he may have suffered what they called a mental break, when he had been confronted with his past. This is what they would call a trigger. She explained that there were several possibilities that could explain it. The first could be that he did in fact remember and he was an incredibly talented performer, the second could be that he was suffering with a severe case of PTSD, and finally he could have a condition known as DID or dissociative identity disorder.

If the last option were true, it would be likely his original identity Keir would assume the role of "protector" and protect his new identity "Devlin" from the trauma of his past. However, until he had been rigorously evaluated she couldn't determine which was the most feasible.

Matt walked over to her with a package clasped in his hands, his demeanour likened to that of a kicked puppy. She understood, none of the team were happy about the turn this had taken. It didn't feel right at all. He was one of their own. Unfortunately, the facts don't lie, and it was their job to uphold the law, whether they thought that it was fair or not.

Matt placed the box down on the desk and said quietly, "This has your name on it, it was just delivered," before handing her a card and putting the box on the desk. She haphazardly threw the card onto the table and studied the parcel. It was marked fragile. She opened it carefully, looking inside she frowned in confusion, and lifted a model church from within. On the front a card had been attached and it read

HERE'S THE CHURCH, HERE'S THE STEEPLE, OPEN THE DOORS….

Wren reached into her pocket in alarm and pulled on some gloves. Cautiously she opened the door of the little church and gasped. From within, eyeballs, fingers and various body parts oozed out and she muttered, in a horrified whisper, "See all the people." Time froze as everyone in the incident room stared at the dastardly sight on the desk. That was when Wren remembered the card.

"WHERE IS THE CARD!" she shouted urgently at Matt.

"What?" he replied, still too shocked to comprehend what this meant.

"THE CARD! CAN YOU SEE IT?" She continued searching the desk.

Matt nodded, remembering himself and pulled the card from under the corner of the box. Wren ripped it open and read.

WRONG ANSWER...GUESS AGAIN.

Wren stared at it in horror, realisation dawning on her. They were wrong. Dev was not their killer, or if he was, he hadn't been alone. She wasn't sure anymore. What she was sure about though, was there was another perpetrator who was still on the loose.

THE END
To be continued in…

Book 2: Snakes and Daggers
Book 2 in The Haunted Past Series

SNAKES AND DAGGERS

DI Devlin Doyle's past has finally come back to haunt him. With his real identity revealed and under suspicion of crimes he didn't commit, he is forced to use whatever resources he can to prove the real killer's identity and clear his name.

Keri McNamara is a double agent in both camps, determined to reveal her mother's true colours and save her long lost brother from an undeserved fate. Can she keep her true intentions hidden and defeat the viper in her own nest?

DI Wren Jones made a grave error. She arrested her would-be lover and left the real killer free to roam the city. With spies in her camp and her colleagues vanishing, can she swallow her pride and ask for assistance from the very detective she betrayed?

Together, can they weed out the snakes and end Bloody Mary's reign of terror, once and for all?

ABOUT THE AUTHOR

My name is Sharon Jackson, mother to a delightful daughter and related to an amazing family. I live in Milton Keynes but originate from Berkhamsted. I work as a pastry chef in a Hospice, and am an avid reader of many genres, with an insatiable thirst for knowledge. I'm also a well-travelled, adrenaline junkie that derives pleasure from finding fantastical adventures to experience; from murder mystery events, to underwater sea trekking and other eccentric yet entertaining activities. I have been reading tarot cards since the age of thirteen after being given a set that had been charmed by an Aborigine in Australia. I like curiosities, mysteries, and challenges.

Thank you for reading My Cradle, Your Grave and I hope you stick around for the next instalment.

If you appreciate the book cover you can contact the artist on: www.creativeparamita.com

Printed in Great Britain
by Amazon